# Readers and Their Fictions
# in the Novels and Novellas
# of Gottfried Keller

**University of North Carolina**
**Studies in the Germanic Languages**
**and Literatures**

*Initiated by* RICHARD JENTE (1949–1952), *established by* F. E. COENEN (1952–1968),
*continued by* SIEGFRIED MEWS (1968–1980) *and* RICHARD H. LAWSON (1980–1985)

PAUL T. ROBERGE, Editor

*Publication Committee: Department of Germanic Languages*

90 KARL EUGENE WEBB. *Rainer Maria Rilke and "Jugendstil": Affinities, Influences, Adaptations.* 1978. Pp. x, 137.

91 LELAND R. PHELPS AND A. TILO ALT, EDS. *Creative Encounter. Festschrift for Herman Salinger.* 1978. Pp. xxii, 181.

92 PETER BAULAND. *Gerhart Hauptmann's "Before Daybreak."* Translation and Introduction. 1978. Pp. xxiv, 87.

93 MEREDITH LEE. *Studies in Goethe's Lyric Cycles.* 1978. Pp. xii, 191.

94 JOHN M. ELLIS. *Heinrich von Kleist. Studies in the Character and Meaning of His Writings.* 1979. Pp. xx, 194.

95 GORDON BIRRELL. *The Boundless Present. Space and Time in the Literary Fairy Tales of Novalis and Tieck.* 1979. Pp. x, 163.

96 G. RONALD MURPHY. *Brecht and the Bible. A Study of Religious Nihilism and Human Weakness in Brecht's Drama of Mortality and the City.* 1980. Pp. xi, 107.

97 ERHARD FRIEDRICHSMEYER. *Die satirische Kurzprosa Heinrich Bölls.* 1981. Pp. xiv, 223.

98 MARILYN JOHNS BLACKWELL, ED. *Structures of Influence: A Comparative Approach to August Strindberg.* 1981. Pp. xiv, 309.

99 JOHN M. SPALEK AND ROBERT F. BELL, EDS. *Exile: The Writer's Experience.* 1982. Pp. xxiv, 370.

100 ROBERT P. NEWTON. *Your Diamond Dreams Cut Open My Arteries. Poems by Else Lasker-Schüler.* Translated and with an Introduction. 1982. Pp. x, 317.

101 WILLIAM SMALL. *Rilke - Kommentar zu den "Aufzeichnungen des Malte Laurids Brigge."* 1983. Pp. x, 175.

102 CHRISTA WOLF CROSS. *Magister ludens: Der Erzähler in Heinrich Wittenweilers "Ring."* 1984. Pp. xii, 112.

103 JAMES C. O'FLAHERTY, TIMOTHY F. SELLNER, AND ROBERT M. HELM, EDS. *Studies in Nietzsche and the Judaeo-Christian Tradition.* 1985. Pp. xii, 393.

104 GISELA N. BERNS. *Greek Antiquity in Schiller's "Wallenstein."* 1985. Pp. xi, 154.

105 JOHN W. VAN CLEVE. *The Merchant in German Literature of the Enlightenment.* 1986. Pp. xv, 173.

106 STEPHEN J. KAPLOWITT. *The Ennobling Power of Love in the Medieval German Lyric.* 1986. Pp. vii, 212.

107 Philip Thomson. *The Poetry of Brecht: Seven Studies.* 1989. Pp. xii, 224.

108 Gisela Vitt-Maucher. *E. T. A. Hoffmanns Märchenschaffen: Kaleidoskop der Verfremdung in seinen sieben Märchen.* 1989. Pp. x, 236.

*For other volumes in the "Studies" see pages 141–43.*

**Number One Hundred and Nine**
University of
North Carolina
Studies in the
Germanic Languages
and Literatures

# Readers and Their Fictions in the Novels and Novellas of Gottfried Keller

Gail K. Hart

The University of North Carolina Press
Chapel Hill and London 1989

Library of Congress Cataloging-in-Publication Data

Hart, Gail Kathleen.
  Readers and their fictions in the novels and novellas of Gottfried
Keller / Gail K. Hart.
  p. cm. — (University of North Carolina studies in the
Germanic languages and literatures; no. 109)
  Bibliography: p.
  Includes index.
  ISBN 0-8078-8109-0 (alk. paper)
  1. Keller, Gottfried, 1819–1890—Criticism and interpretation.
2. Books and reading in literature. 3. Authorship in literature.
I. Title. II. Series.
PT2374.Z5H28   1989                                    88-27918
838'.809—dc19                                            CIP

The first part of chapter 1 of this book is a slightly changed
version of "The Functions of Fictions: Imagination and Socialization in Both Versions of Keller's *Der grüne Heinrich*,"
in *The German Quarterly* 59 (1986): 595–610. Some of the material in chapter 2 appeared as "Keller's Fictional Readers,"
in *Seminar* 23 (1987): 115–36.

The paper in this book meets the guidelines for
permanence and durability of the Committee on
Production Guidelines for Book Longevity of the
Council on Library Resources.

Printed in the United States of America

93 92 91 90 89   5 4 3 2 1

For my grandparents, Arthur and Margaret Melville,
who remember the nineteenth century

# Contents

Acknowledgments    xi

Introduction    1

1. Fictions and Feuerbach: Keller's Progress toward
   Intellectual Independence    17

2. Pankraz, der Leser: Sulking and the Didactic Author    41

3. "Romeo und Julia auf dem Dorfe": The Romance of
   Realism?    60

4. *Züricher Novellen*: Didactic Literature and Unreceptive Life    85

5. *Das Sinngedicht*: Beyond the Futility of Utility    100

Notes    117

Bibliography    135

Index    139

# Acknowledgments

I am grateful to Sveta Davé, Thom Heine, Kaspar T. Locher, Jeffrey Sammons, and Walter Sokel for reading various parts and versions of my manuscript and making suggestions for improvement. I have also benefited from the comments of readers for the University of North Carolina Studies in the Germanic Languages and Literatures and for *The German Quarterly* and *Seminar,* where some of this material has appeared. These two journals have kindly granted me permission to include that material in this book. Reed College provided a publication grant, for which I thank them. Also, Susie Schmitt did an excellent job of proofreading the galleys.

I am especially indebted to my husband, Thomas P. Saine, who gave generously of his time and expertise, reading and criticizing my work and helping me prepare the manuscript for publication. Even as I write this acknowledgment, he sits patiently at the computer, coding characters, reforming paragraphs, and compensating for my eccentric use of the space bar.

# Readers and Their Fictions
# in the Novels and Novellas
# of Gottfried Keller

# Introduction

The heroes and heroines of novels and novellas are notorious readers. Indeed, many of the principals of prose fiction in the eighteenth and nineteenth centuries would be inconceivable without their books. Maneuvering within their own stories, they grasp at other stories and practice a kind of "misreading" rarely encountered outside literature—namely, the uncritical reception of literary fictions as life-imperatives or as specific models for self-comprehension. They are literally enthralled by their reading and subsequently they engage in the most bizarre attempts to alter their "reality" and bring their lives into closer correspondence with the fictions that fascinate them. Such an effect—a fictional person's enslavement by another fiction—is but one manifestation of the complicated interplay between fiction and "reality" that is characteristic of the epic genres, especially the novel. In such cases, authors, who seem to be telling us that fiction is not real (by allowing their characters to act upon the opposite assumption), do so within a fictional context whose reference to reality they have, perhaps unintentionally, relativized from within.

The "book within the book" is a long-standing fixture of novelistic literature, and its history, functions, and implications cannot be summarized in a few sentences. It is a literary figure that takes many forms, beginning with the book symbolism and related topoi examined by Ernst Robert Curtius[1]: the book of the world, the book of life, man's face as a book where his thoughts can be read. Here, the book as familiar object is used to illustrate the larger order of things, suggesting that certain mysteries can be contained and deciphered by initiates. Another possibility is the reproduction of specific titles and specific passages, the kind of intertextuality explored by Hermann Meyer's *Das Zitat in der Erzählkunst*. Meyer's contention that literature feeds upon itself is echoed in Klaus Jeziorkowski's study of literary allusion in Gottfried Keller's works—though Jeziorkowski shows a preference for more explicitly organic metaphors: "Literatur wird zum eigenen Dünger, zum eigenen Mistbeet und Treibhaus."[2] Authors quote, paraphrase, and allude to the books of other authors, and books are part of the "life" they seek to reproduce in their fictions. Thus, literature is self-nourishing, as well as incestuous and narcissistic, most eager to regard itself within the hermetic company of its "own kind."

Whereas books usually represent knowledge in Western society—a notion that led medieval and Renaissance scholars to emphasize the distinction between the possession of books and the possession of knowledge—they often appear as duping agents in novels and novellas, reflecting a deep-rooted suspicion of the fictitious, of the "untrue," within literary fictions. It is this particular function of books within books that concerns this study—though the reduction of a vast field of inquiry to a single type of manifestation does not yet make it particularly manageable in general terms. The reader-hero who is led astray by his books is a stock character in the novelistic tradition, and the variety of situations in which we encounter him and the diversity of interpenetrations of fiction and reality represented by these situations may never allow for comprehensive treatment. Ralph-Rainer Wuthenow's introductory remarks to *Im Buch die Bücher oder Der Held als Leser* allude to the difficulties of such a project: "An eine umfassende informierende Übersicht ist . . . gar nicht zu denken, sie würde die Kräfte eines Einzelnen übersteigen; es überrascht freilich, daß dieses fesselnde Phänomen bisher so wenig Beachtung gefunden hat."[3] Wuthenow acknowledges the near-impossibility of a thorough account of the topos in Western literature, but, at the same time, he wonders why so little has been written on books within books as such. It is indeed surprising, considering the potential interest of literature's established practice of reflecting on the reciprocal relations between itself and the "life" it imitates. But Wuthenow answers his own question before he asks it—the field is simply too vast to admit of thorough treatment.

The specific topos "literature influences life" has been a standard requisite of the epic tradition at least since Dante's Paolo and Francesca ("Galeotto fu quel libro e chi lo scrisse"[4]), though it achieves its most famous (and labyrinthine) formulation in Cervantes' *Don Quixote*. It is almost as old as everything else under the sun, and its occurrences are so frequent and its forms so protean that it cannot be characterized either synchronically or diachronically as a whole. The dynamics of imagination and desire, fascination and influence, that underlie the reorientation and redefinition of the (fictional) self according to literary models, are variable functions in an endless series of equations, which defy taxonomy or overarching theory. Each instance has its own internal logic, be it the presentation of a moral lesson, a meditation on fictions and their functions in personal development, or even a parody of the author-reader relationship, and studies of this novelistic archetype and realist stereotype are generally bound to the isolated occurrence.

I do not mean to suggest that these isolated occurrences have nothing significant in common. Of course they do, and their general similarities deserve comment here. The reader-hero, who conspicuously reads and draws conclusions from his reading, is most familiar to us (in his eighteenth- and nineteenth-century manifestations) as an instructive device, the focus of a literary lesson in confronting the world, the moral being that beautiful fictions are deceptive and should not be understood as presenting attainable goals or guidelines for behavior. Such lessons range from extreme implications that fictions pose a danger to the free exercise of will (the creed of book burners everywhere), to less vehement indications that readers should be wary of nonreal forms of "life." The corollaries of this position (whatever the intensity with which it is held) are that reality is preferable to appearance/fiction, active participation in the affairs of the world to the social isolation of reading, and critical distance to naive gullibility. All of these recommendations—a "realistic" attitude, participation in the affairs of the world, and the healthy skepticism associated with critical distance—are easily recognizable as male bourgeois virtues. One could conclude that readers should either be wary or be women, but, assuming that the reader, She, will readily assume the role of the reader, He (or Him), the typical performance of the reader-hero of this era serves to reinforce the dominant bourgeois values. She, whose contribution to society derives ideally from her appearance, isolation, and naiveté, should in any case be informed about what to seek in a protector. As we shall see, this "lesson" of critical distance need not be accomplished in the form of a straightforward didactic message, because it is also contained more subtly in the nature of the phenomenon itself.

One may object that a literary fiction that teaches the folly of orienting oneself according to literary fictions is itself a poor conveyor of this message. Certainly the moral is inescapably compromised by its own context, though I believe that this particular challenge to the text is interesting only where we detect some consciousness of the paradoxical relationship between context and message. The author who tacitly exempts his own work from the general mistrust of fictions that he is trying to evoke, probably fails to consider the paradox at all, and, in the case of a text that *is* conscious of this paradox, naive didactic intent is no longer tenable. J. M. R. Lenz's *Die Soldaten* is an obvious example. Here, the danger of the comedy to a young woman's virtue is (ostensibly) a major thematic issue, and yet the play is subtitled "Eine Komödie."[5] Clearly, Lenz does not intend to convince us that literature, in the form of theatrical comedy, can be ruinous to

young ladies. Rather, he presents his nominal support for the contemporary suspicion of nonserious theatrical spectacles ironically, in
the very form that is, by his definition, untrustworthy. This ironic
application of the topos "literature influences life" creates—and
blissfully ignores—a double bind, which, in contrast to the ends of
straightforward, unreflected presentation, tends to redeem the context at the expense of the "message." This is not a simple reversal of
the didactic message—Lenz is not encouraging readers or spectators
to send their daughters to the comedy—but an impish reflection on
the contradictions inherent in transmitting such a message from the
very pulpit it seeks to obstruct.[6]

The thematic agency of literature's influence on life need not be
bluntly didactic or as heavily laden with irony as in Lenz's piece. It is
part of a familiar pattern, a variation on a larger theme of Western
literature—especially the novel—that follows the deviation of an errant hero from his given circumstances, the consequences of this
error, and the labors involved in overcoming it. George Levine describes the realist novel in terms of this pattern, noting the involvement of books. It is "the story of a hero or heroine who must learn to
recognize and reject youthful fantasies (normally first learned from
books) in order to accept a less than romantic and more tediously
quotidian reality."[7] Within these thematic parameters, literature, a
"mithandelnde, mitbestimmende Figur,"[8] usually plays a negative
role, retarding personal development as in Levine's paradigm or in
some cases blocking it completely—although this lack of response to
social norms may be regarded as a virtue, especially in romantic
writings. The (real) reader of these books about books encounters
something of a mirror image, not of reality, as Uwe Japp points out,
but of himself: "Das Buch wird auf komplexe Weise zum Spiegel,
nicht der Welt, sondern des Lesers selbst."[9] However, the reader
reading about the reader reading generally retains a critical perspective on the object of his efforts, a critical distance that is usually
augmented by a perception of the fictional reader's uncritical, or less
critical, reception of literature.[10] Japp stresses the refracted nature of
this mirror image and

die gut begründete Reflexion darauf, daß die Welt nie so, wie sie
ist, im Buch widergespiegelt werden kann. Das zu glauben war
die Illusion eines naiven Naturalismus. Die Verdoppelung der
Lektüre im Buch ist deshalb als Kritik an diesem Glauben zu
lesen. Die Literatur ist nicht der klare Spiegel der Realität, sondern die perspektivische Brechung, als welche der Leser Realität

im Buch erfährt. Das Buch im Buch, dort, wo es Teil der Hand-
lung ist, bringt genau diese für alle Lektüre grundlegende perspektivische Brechung ins Bewußtsein.[11]

It follows from Japp's observation that the spectacle of fictional
reading has a specific effect on the reading of fiction, that of "distancing" the reader by reinforcing his consciousness of the "untruth"
of fiction—a product of its simultaneous resemblance to and noncorrespondence with "reality." This distancing function of the refracted
mirror image works to neutralize any potentially seductive features of
the fiction itself (by placing it in a category distinct from "real" experience) and should block any attempts at stepping through the looking
glass. The distancing process occurs prior to the apprehension of any
moral lesson that may aim to achieve the same effects—though moralizing on this subject generally aspires not only to stress the fictional
nature of the text or genre under attack, but also to prevent the
reading of such material.

It is highly likely that *literal* seduction by literature is almost exclu-
sively a literary phenomenon—not an imitation of life, but an internal
convention of fiction. This is not a universally held opinion, nor is it
necessarily a crucial issue for this undertaking. The continuing public
debate on the potentially damaging effects of certain fictions—cur-
rently focusing on "objectionable" films and the lyrics of popular
songs—testifies to a certain faith in the power of fictions to influence
the behavior of real readers/auditors/spectators. Indeed, much didactic literature (and much censorship) rests on similar assumptions,[12]
and the question of Keller's attitude toward literature's potential for
influencing the behavior of (real) readers will be discussed in this and
coming chapters. For the present, I bring up the point in order to
emphasize the distinction between real reading and this particular
fictional convention.[13] Norman Holland touches on the question of
(alleged) real-life influence by fictions in *The Dynamics of Literary Response*. In the actual moment of involvement with a fiction—be it
book or theatrical performance—"motor inhibition" is the precondition of "regression into fantasy."[14] Thus we do not act in the physical
world during the immediate experience of a particular fantasy and,
though we may retain ideas and impressions of that fantasy after the
experience has ended, these do not significantly affect character,
which—according to psychoanalysts—is "firmly structured"[15] by the
time we begin to read. Jeffrey Sammons believes that the notion that
literary fictions exert a direct and calculable influence on their recipients "lacks sufficient empirical verification." He writes: "[It] appears

to be simply not known whether literary texts can form and generate behavior patterns in readers—apathy or rebelliousness, affirmative or critical views of the status quo, violence and prejudice—or whether they serve at most as codifiers and reinforcers of value dispositions."[16]

The experience of (real) reading has been illuminated considerably during the last few decades by "Reader-Response" and reception theorists, like Holland, who have studied the mental processes of reading a text, as well as the text's own anticipation of such processes ("readers in texts," as distinct from the reader-heroes or fictional readers who are at issue here) in order to develop a greater understanding of literary language and its strategies of communication. Yet this particular field of inquiry is bound to the mental activity of (hypothetical) real readers and—given this "bias"—has little direct bearing on the fictional representation of reading as literary convention. Though authorial attitudes toward real reading have to some extent affected this representation (as, for example, Jeremias Gotthelf's ideas about how and what farmers read), reading and reception within fictions are less a unified field for systematic study than an aggregate of instances that, as products of various imaginations, informed by tradition and occasion, do not depend on typical mental and physiological processes, which can be posited or assumed in the case of a real reader. This relative (and hypothetical) consistency of response and reaction cannot be posited for fictional readers, although a certain consistency of "desire" (the often indistinct longings of the imagination for fulfillment) does emerge from a cross section of such situations.

The great study of the dynamics of fictional reading is (still) René Girard's *Deceit, Desire, and the Novel* (*Mensonge romantique et vérité romanesque*). Here, Girard identifies a small group of novels that reveal the workings of "metaphysical desire," the impulse at the base of fictional characters' abdication of self in favor of the imitation of literary (as well as other) models.[17] Metaphysical desire, a mental yearning that is both mediated by the subject's imitation of another's desire and detached from its physical object, is not confined to the reader-hero's special relationship to his text(s): it also arises from human interaction within literature and represents, Girard believes, an actual trend in "real" life. Girard sees in the development of civilization a gradual loss of spontaneity as it yields to the human instinct for imitation in matters of desiring. Our desires are, he reasons, not our own insofar as we tend to desire only what others desire, even while we maintain the illusion of a capacity for autonomous or spontaneous desire. Imaginative literature is the most effective vehicle for presenting (not necessarily spreading) metaphysical desire in all of its possible permutations, and Girard distinguishes between "novelistic" literature, which reveals the mechanisms of borrowed desire (in a climate of denial), and "romantic" literature, which depicts desire as originating within the subject without connection to models.

*Deceit, Desire, and the Novel* does not address extraliterary metaphysical desire.[18] Girard confines himself to literary representations of this "cultural sickness" and most of his examples involve books within books—specifically, the fictional character's selection of an unworthy model from fiction, an act that refers us to the "psychology" of that character: "When the 'nature' of the object inspiring the passion is not sufficient to account for desire, one must turn to the impassioned subject."[19] The first of these subjects is Don Quixote, who, enthralled by Amadis of Gaul, surrenders "the individual's fundamental prerogative: he no longer chooses the objects of his own desire—Amadis must choose for him."[20] Amadis, fictional character and model of chivalry, thus becomes the "mediator" of desire for Don Quixote, who will pursue the objects and ends that he believes Amadis himself would pursue. This "desire according to the Other" is the principle behind the reader-hero's attempts to imitate or realize elements of the fictions he reads. It is a "real-life" emotion, which, according to Girard, makes the will behind these endeavors intelligible to us, however implausible the imitation. In the novel, "the itinerary of the hero is a shift from this fascination to a realization that the printed text, the work, is really a human act, a human action among others which may be replaced; in other words, a victory over this fascination."[21] Thus, novelistic literature is also "message" oriented, but in more subtle (and less particular) ways than the naive didactic model mentioned earlier. Its purpose is to expose metaphysical desire as a cultural trend and to uncover the roots of a fascination, which—though we know it intimately—we might otherwise fail to comprehend. In this sense there is a correlation between the reader-hero's emotions and those of the (hypothetical) real reader, but still no confirmation that literary texts exert significant extraliterary influence.

In the case of Gottfried Keller, it will be necessary to impose a rather significant mediator between Keller's particular representations of fictional reading and Girard's more general findings: Ludwig Feuerbach. Girard's account of the subject's relation to the mediator of desire closely resembles Feuerbach's model of man's relation to the deity, which in turn parallels the relation between reader-hero and literature in Keller's fiction, though this parallel weakens with time as Keller broadens his perspective on the functions of fictions. Girard describes the dynamics of mediation as follows: "In the experience which originates the mediation the subject recognizes in himself an extreme weakness. It is this weakness that he wants to escape in the illusory divinity of the Other. The subject is ashamed of his life and his mind. In despair at not being God, he searches for the sacred in everything which threatens his life, in everything which thwarts his mind. Thus he is always oriented toward what will debase and finally destroy the highest and most noble part of his being."[22] And further: "Men who cannot look freedom in the face are exposed to anguish. They look for a banner on which they can fix their eyes. There is no longer God, king, or lord to link them to the universal. To escape the feeling of particularity they imitate *another's* desires; they choose substitute gods because they are not able to give up infinity."[23]

In the context of Keller's intellectual environment, Girard's mediator (substitute god) is Feuerbach's God, an image determined by the subject to which he surrenders the better part of his nature in exchange for the metaphysical comfort of being answerable to a being outside the (degraded) self. This mediator, Other, or "God" is the unified or glorified abstracted self as it takes form in the subject's mind. In Feuerbach's words:

> Es ist gemüthlicher, zu leiden, als zu handeln; gemüthlicher, durch einen Anderen erlöst und befreit zu werden, als sich selbst zu befreien; gemüthlicher, von einer anderen Person, als von der Kraft der Selbstthätigkeit sein Heil abhängig zu machen; gemüthlicher, zu lieben als zu streben; gemüthlicher, sich von Gott geliebt zu wissen, als sich selbst zu lieben mit der einfachen, natürlichen Selbstliebe, die allen Wesen eingeboren; gemüthlicher, sich in den liebestrahlenden Augen eines andern persönlichen Wesens zu bespiegeln, als in den Hohlspiegel des eigenen Selbsts oder in die kalte Tiefe des stillen Oceans der Natur zu schauen; gemüthlicher überhaupt, als sich selbst durch die Vernunft zu bestimmen, sich von seinem eigenen Gemüthe bestimmen zu lassen, als wäre es ein anderes, wennschon im Grunde dasselbige Wesen.[24]

Without leveling the distinctions between Girard's twentieth-century theory of metaphysical desire (based, in large part, on nineteenth-century novels) and Feuerbach's nineteenth-century attack on metaphysics in general, I would like to point out that they rest on the same perception: that of a prevalent cultural tendency to affix the Self to an Other and to live in the shadow of this Other, who is nothing more (or less) than a self-generated fiction. Keller, who began his career as a prose writer under the direct influence of Feuerbach, his friend and teacher, extends this cultural critique to *literary* fictions and their readers. In the first version of *Der grüne Heinrich*, he makes a direct connection between literary fictions (of a certain type) and religion (*Spiritualismus*) as defined by Feuerbach. In the words of the third-person narrator as he criticizes Heinrich for his belief in God:

> Der Spiritualismus ist diejenige Arbeitsscheu, welche aus Mangel an Einsicht und Gleichgewicht der Erfahrungen und Überzeugungen hervorgeht und den Fleiß des wirklichen Lebens durch Wundertätigkeit ersetzen, aus Steinen Brot machen will, anstatt zu ackern, zu säen, das Wachstum der Ähren abzuwarten, zu schneiden, dreschen, mahlen und zu backen. Das Herausspinnen einer fingierten, künstlichen, allegorischen Welt aus der Erfindungskraft, mit Umgehung der guten Natur, ist eben nichts anderes als jene Arbeitsscheu; und wenn Romantiker und Allegoristen aller Art den ganzen Tag schreiben, dichten, malen und operieren, so ist dies alles nur Trägheit gegenüber derjenigen Tätigkeit, welche nichts anderes ist als das notwendige und gesetzliche Wachstum der Dinge.[25]

The fervor of the disciple is especially apparent in this early passage, which is clearly "mediated" by Keller's devotion to Feuerbach—a devotion that brings him dangerously close to denying his own brand of creativity, although "Romantiker und Allegoristen" shoulder the blame in this case. Much of the early work is marked by a struggle with creativity as a value, a struggle that Keller never completely resolves, even though he does "emerge" from it in later years.

It will be the task of this study to follow Keller's development from his early suspicion of literary fictions, seen as mediators and manipulators of desire and behavior, to his later, more playful attitude toward fictions—which he himself manufactures. Metaphysical desire and *Spiritualismus*, or, better, Feuerbach's notion of human selfishness (that excessive concentration on self which causes the subject to abstract interior life from its grounding in the material world and to imagine possibilities beyond the mundane), will figure prominently in this process. Though Keller never attains the full illumination of Girard's novelist-narrator, "a hero cured of metaphysical desire,"[26] and though he ceases to preach actively and conspicuously the materialist doctrine of Feuerbach's "ganzer Mensch," he does achieve his own peculiar (literary) compromise between the desired and the available, the real and the imaginary, and it is the nature of this particular compromise that is of interest here.

I would like to begin with a statement of authorial intention, which I will postpone (briefly) for the sake of some prefatory qualification. When Keller died, he left behind hundreds of letters, several autobiographical essays and a few diaries. Material from these personal documents has been reproduced with such frequency in the critical literature that Keller's remarks on his literary writing—his statements of didactic intention in particular—have become an issue in themselves, in spite of the prevailing tendency to regard such authorial remarks with suspicion. Whether Keller, whose autobiographical fiction deliberately calls attention to the mind that generated it, constitutes a special exception to the rule of excluding an author's experience and opinions from consideration of his work, is unclear to me. The rule is transgressed in other quarters and often to good effect.[27] Yet, to judge by even the most recent scholarly books and articles, Keller, the man, is far more likely to be associated with his texts than are his less blatantly "confessional" contemporaries, such as C. F. Meyer, Theodor Storm, or Paul Heyse. Keller's narrators are commonly referred to as "Keller," and one often gets the impression that *Keller* is the actual object of Keller scholarship. Interestingly, the most discussed works of Keller scholarship of the last decade are Adolf Muschg's (psycho)biography and Gerhard Kaiser's attempt to elucidate the laws according to which the author's imagination works.[28] I do not, in principle, object to the inclusion of biographical material in studies of Keller, and I will allude to the author's life in these pages where I consider it to be relevant. For the present, however, I will focus on one particular statement in order to suggest that such material can be misleading if taken out of context.

Keller made a rather forceful statement of intention in an 1860 letter to Berthold Auerbach, and this apparent declaration of purpose, one of the most frequently reproduced passages from Keller's eminently quotable correspondence, has been taken at face value— that is, as an accurate representation of Keller's goals as a writer, and sometimes as a fair description of his life's work. In answer to Auerbach's praise of the solidity and stability of (democratic) Swiss society, Keller points out that many internal problems persist, noting:

dagegen halte ich es für Pflicht eines Poeten, nicht nur das Vergangene zu verklären, sondern das Gegenwärtige, die Keime der Zukunft so weit zu verstärken und zu verschönern, daß die Leute noch glauben können, ja, so seien sie und so gehe es zu!

Tut man dies mit einiger wohlwollenden Ironie, die dem Zeuge das falsche Pathos nimmt, so glaube ich, daß das Volk das, was es sich gutmütig einbildet zu sein und der innerlichen Anlage nach auch schon ist, zuletzt in der Tat und auch äußerlich wird. Kurz, man muß, wie man schwangeren Frauen etwa schöne Bildwerke vorhält, dem allezeit trächtigen Nationalgrundstock stets etwas Besseres zeigen, als er schon ist; dafür kann man ihn auch um so kecker tadeln, wo er es verdient.[29]

"Etwas Besseres zeigen, als er schon ist"? Could it be that Keller, who in 1860 had already created such "*un*schöne Bildwerke" as the errant (and dead) Heinrich Lee, the sulking Pankraz, the two greedy farmers whose children commit suicide, and the miserly "gerechten Kammacher," thought of his prose as a potential repository of positive models for imitation? If we take "Poet" in the narrower sense as a writer of verse (though the prose piece "Das Fähnlein der sieben Aufrechten" is the subject of this exchange), we do find a great deal of pleasant imagery in Keller's poetry—but most of this refers to nature. People in Keller's poems tend to be melancholy, no longer young, and not infrequently drunk—also not the kind of pretty pictures one would want to display before a pregnant nation. Keller is a master of "keckes Tadeln," the second method he mentions, but hardly the purveyor of "schöne Bildwerke." He does seem to be aware of this discrepancy between the ideals he articulates and the less-than-ideal figures who populate his works: he tells Auerbach that his next collection of novellas will feature "mehr positives Leben" (*GB* 3/2:197) than the previous *Die Leute von Seldwyla*,[30] but he nevertheless gives the strong impression that these are the principles that have ever guided his pen.

Actually, Keller's remarks may be sufficiently compromised by context to render them invalid as sure evidence of consistent intentions. As noted, he is writing to Auerbach, the well-known and established author who, on the basis of his enthusiasm for *Die Leute von Seldwyla*, had solicited a contribution to his *Deutscher Volkskalender* from the relatively obscure Keller, reminding him that "die Zahl derer, die ich zur Mitarbeiterschaft, namentlich zur poetischen, auffordern kann, nur sehr klein ist, und in dieser an den Fingern abzuzählenden sind Sie" (*GB* 3/2:187). Mindful of this rare privilege, Keller may have exaggerated (or embellished) his own poetic aspirations in order to pay lip service to Auerbach's rather rigid notions of didacticism and public edification.[31] Several letters to Hermann Hettner indicate that he was not above such ingratiating insincerity. Keller writes in 1856:

"Auerbach ist ja außerordentlich wohlgesinnt; ich will ihm gewiß dieser Tage schreiben, obgleich ich, unter uns gesagt, ein wenig dabei heucheln muß" (*GB* 1:428–29); and again in 1862: "Zudem kann ich sein [Auerbach's] nutzbringendes und wirtschaftliches Lehr- und Predigtwesen und das in hundert kleine Portiönchen abgeteilte Betrachten nicht billigen, möchte das ihm aber nicht vorrücken, da er auf der Welt ja nichts hat als seine diesfällige Tätigkeit" (*GB* 1:443–44).

Thus Keller's remarks are colored to some degree by context. It is impossible to determine that his words are entirely insincere; but his work, both before and after the Auerbach letter, seems to be less the reflection of the "schöne Bildwerke" recipe for *Volkserziehung* than a confrontation with it and with the ethical and aesthetic problems of creating fictions in a "material" world—of representing this world accurately *and* beautifully and of doing this to some extra-aesthetic purpose. This is a demanding agenda, which is rarely implemented in the manner suggested to Auerbach.

Another passage from the same letter is important to an assessment of Keller's position with regard to literary fictions and their possible effects. After requesting that a character's name be changed in order to prevent the men who were the models for the seven patriots in "Fähnlein" from recognizing themselves in the story, Keller muses on general reader reaction to such recognition: "Allerdings ermutigt mich diese Eigenschaft des Volkes, sich in den poetischen Bildern erkennen zu wollen, ohne sich geschmeichelt zu fühlen, zu obiger Hoffnung, *daß es durch das Bild auch angeregt zur teilweisen Verwirklichung werde* (*GB* 3/2:196, my emphasis). What is already implied in the remarks on "schöne Bildwerke" is stated quite explicitly here: readers do tend to recognize themselves in the beautiful fictions they read, and Keller *hopes* that they will be inspired by this recognition to narrow the gap between their real circumstances and the idealized fictional models presented to them—in other words, that they will *imitate* literary fictions. This vision of (real) reader-response, which neatly addresses Auerbach's "Lehr- und Predigtwesen," may or may not represent a conviction on Keller's part—but it certainly represents the occasional *wish* of any author with a social mission. It is interesting, however, that Keller, who consistently depicts literary fictions as a breed of unworthy Other leading errant readers into the realm of fantasy and distracting them from the business of being, would articulate his views on potential audience reaction in this way.

Whereas much imitation of literature occurs in Keller's novels and novellas, this imitation is invariably presented as folly, evoking in many cases the paradox that Lenz emphasized in *Die Soldaten*. The message is, I will argue, neither *"do* imitate" nor *"don't* imitate," although the first version of *Der grüne Heinrich* does represent literary fictions as dangerous and seductive fantasies (see chapter 1). Rather than enforcing social norms via the encouragement or frustration of the instinct for imitation, these books within books and reading heroes are part of a less literal (and more quixotic) project of defining or identifying the borders between fiction/fantasy and life—borders which the mind crosses freely, giving rise to the main and ubiquitous issue of Keller's fiction, that of imagination and its conflict with social reality: "Unverantwortlichkeit der Einbildungskraft."[32]

Regarding the social-didactic possibilities of the topic, Keller's works conform to a pattern where the good are overtly rewarded and the bad are converted, punished, or ridiculed. On the basis of this pattern, Heinrich Richartz has argued for the existence of two "levels" in a Keller text: a simple moral fable designed to edify the less sophisticated reader, and a level of more subtle intellectual content to hold the interest of educated readers who will get essentially the same message as the first-level readers.[33] But with due respect to Richartz and to the power and lucidity of his arguments, Keller actually wrote only for the lettered and learned and not for the merely literate.[34] His works are no more susceptible to simplification than those of any "difficult" novelist of his time, because his "moral fables" function predominantly as a backdrop, an accepted convention for representing the world order, against which Keller muses on the disjuncture between this order and imaginative activity. Though the Keller of the correspondence seems to have had delusions of broad public efficacy, his writings are, for the most part, well beyond the reach of the average reader of uncomplicated moral fables.

Keller chooses to illustrate the conflict between imagination and social reality most frequently on the example of literature within literature, and most of his heroes betray some exposure to literary fictions. Heinrich Lee reads everything from trashy novels to Goethe and continually modifies his behavior according to his understanding of these works. Wenzel Strapinski plays the *Romanheld* of sentimental fiction for his audience in Goldach, and Züs Bünzlin owes a good number of her bizarre mannerisms to an equally bizarre assortment of books that adorn her shelves. Sali's and Vrenchen's reading of love poems at the village fair has a far greater effect on their notion of absolute love than has yet been acknowledged, and Reinhart of *Das Sinngedicht* allows Lessing and Logau to be his guides to living when he interprets Logau's "Küß eine weiße Galathee" as an imperative that he go search for one. There are also the writers: Heinrich, Viggi Störteler of "Die mißbrauchten Liebesbriefe," Herr Jacques of the *Züricher Novellen,* and the notorious John Kabys and Adam Litumlei of "Der Schmied seines Glückes." In an attempt to establish Kabys as Litumlei's heir, these latter two decide, not to falsify documents, but rather to collaborate on a novel that they believe will validate the filial connection. The novel concerns Litumlei's stormy love affair with a certain Lislein *Federspiel,* from which union Kabys is supposed to have issued. Its authors, who presuppose the kind of reading practiced by so many of Keller's characters, feel that a literary fiction will prove far more convincing to future generations than will official documentation.

Clearly, *Federspiel* plays an important role in Keller's fiction, where literature, product of the creative imagination, stimulates the fictional reader's imagination to endeavor to realize the fantasies it presents. Of the ten Seldwyla stories, no fewer than six feature complications resulting from a character's skewed relationship to literary fictions. The second volume is even prefaced by an account of an ostensible real-life misapprehension of the first volume. Recalling the famous dispute over Homer's birthplace, Keller claims: "Seit die erste Hälfte dieser Erzählungen erschienen, streiten sich etwa sieben Städte im Schweizerlande darum, welche unter ihnen mit Seldwyla gemeint sei; und da nach alter Erfahrung der eitle Mensch lieber für schlimm, glücklich und kurzweilig als für brav, aber unbeholfen und einfältig gelten will, so hat jede dieser Städte dem Verfasser ihr Ehrenbürgerrecht angeboten für den Fall, daß er sich für sie erkläre" (H 2:251). The author would have us believe that seven cities are presently vying for the dubious honor of identification with the good-for-nothing town of Seldwyla. Here, literature seems to have induced mass hysteria, though this hysteria is merely the reverse of the "schöne Bildwerke" formula for public edification. Fourteen years have passed since the Auerbach letter, and, naturally, Keller is joking. But the fact that this mass identification with unsavory models is a joke and a fiction casts doubt on the legitimacy of the assumptions in that letter.

Add to the examples just given four of the *Züricher Novellen, Der grüne Heinrich* (both versions), and *Das Sinngedicht* and we have a statistically large portion of Keller's total prose production in which literature figures prominently as an element of plot and as an occasion for addressing the schism between imagined fulfillment and mundane necessity. Although isolated references to reading heroes and their books are relatively common in the Keller literature, the prominence of literary thematics is rarely addressed, possibly because the topos "literature influences life," or "life imitates art," is such a commonplace in nineteenth-century fiction. Of the few studies that do focus on Keller's reader heroes and the reciprocal relations between literature and life in the prose, Siegfried Mews's brief article "Zur Funktion der Literatur in Kellers *Die Leute von Seldwyla*" (1970) is the first scholarly work to explore fictional literary reception in multiple Keller texts. Mews identifies instances of literary influence in six of the *Seldwyla* novellas, noting: "Literatur spiegelt sich in Literatur und spielt als Faktor im geistigen Leben einiger Kellerscher Charaktere eine nicht unbedeutende Rolle: Sie übt einen bemerkenswerten Einfluß auf die Formung ihrer Vorstellungswelt, ihrer Wünsche und Ambitionen aus."[35] Mews concludes that in treating this influence, Keller attacks neither literature nor reader, but rather exposes "ein falsches Verhältnis zur Literatur . . . ihren Mißbrauch als (oft nicht verstandenes) Verhaltensmodell oder als Ersatzwert für fehlende Substanz."[36]

It is this idea of the "falsches Verhältnis" that inspired Richartz's *Literaturkritik als Gesellschaftskritik: Darstellungsweise und politisch-didaktische Intention in Gottfried Kellers Erzählkunst* (1975).[37] Basing his arguments on Keller's manifest social concerns and the frequent occurrence of characters who order their perception of reality according to literary norms, a phenomenon which he correlates with the tendency of the middle class to devalue its own existence, Richartz posits two related goals for Keller's fiction: "Daraus ergeben sich für Kellers Erzählen zwei miteinander in Verbindung stehende Ziele: einmal am Individuum die Konsequenzen aus der Orientierung an der Literatur konkret zu demonstrieren; daneben das schlechte Gewissen des Bürgertums zu zerstören, das sich aus der Konfrontation einer banalen, aber in dieser Banalität richtigen Existenz mit der Kunst ergibt."[38] Richartz sees the misapprehension of literature within the texts as Keller's representation of a tendency in his audience that he seeks to eliminate, and he examines literary thematics as an attempt to neutralize middle-class awe of art and literature—a type of misplaced yearning that deters social progress. Richartz believes that Keller consciously writes in such a way as to block identification and to focus on the futility and the counterproductive nature of this very process.

Whereas Mews establishes the frequency of "influential" literary texts and impressionable readers in the *Seldwyla* novellas, and Richartz speculates on the "werkexterne Absicht" and intended reception of this combination in *Seldwyla* and elsewhere, this study aims to complement—and occasionally to question—their work by examining the *changing* image of literary fictions as it becomes apparent in a loosely chronological arrangement of Keller's novels and novellas, and to correlate successive modifications with the author's developing tendency to regard imaginative creativity as a positive value—a position he reaches only after coming to terms with his own literature's incapacity for influencing errant readers. My work differs from that of Mews and Richartz in that I find Keller's alleged didacticism to be more problematic than they suggest. I do not, in the final analysis, regard Keller as a consistently didactic author, but rather as a student of mental life, who is primarily interested in presenting its problems—and not their solutions. The organization here is simple. An initial comparison of the two versions of *Der grüne Heinrich* will suggest two very different perspectives on imagination and its potential compatibility with social circumstances. I will then attempt to account for the twenty-five years in between by following imagination as a value in a selection of texts that address the problem of "dangerous" literary fictions and impressionable readers. A final chapter concerns *Das Sinngedicht* and Keller's "artificial" solution to these problems.

# 1. Fictions and Feuerbach: Keller's Progress toward Intellectual Independence

### The Functions of Fictions in *Der grüne Heinrich*

Gottfried Keller's two great novels, both of which bear the title *Der grüne Heinrich*, were written in the years 1850–55 and 1878–80 respectively, the latter being the mature poet's revision of his first published work of fiction. They are two versions of the same extended tale (much of the second version remains identical to the first), and both follow the "education" of autodidact Heinrich Lee, whose active creative imagination conflicts with the material concerns of his social environment—concerns that are inescapably his own. Unlike a stock romantic hero, whose imagination is its own justification, Heinrich carries within him the pragmatic social values that proscribe such loitering in the world of fantasy as his imagination inclines him to practice. The novels that tell his story are similarly self-contradicting: both promote social ideals of familial, professional, and civic responsibility, and, for both, the center of interest (a value in itself) lies in the narcissistic excesses of the imagination that defy these ideals. Strictly speaking, community ethics predominate in *Der grüne Heinrich*, and this heavy social presence overshadows and interprets Heinrich's subjective inclination to fantasy. Nonetheless, imagination persists as a subversive value that never quite accedes to respectability.

*Der grüne Heinrich* is governed to a great extent by the "literature influences life" topos. Labeled an *Entwicklungsroman* (as well as *Erziehungsroman* and *Bildungsroman*),[1] *Der grüne Heinrich* conceives of "development" as a process of exposure to external forces of an educational or experiential nature, which is actuated by internal interpretation of these forces and by receptivity to their formative influences. It is in many ways a socialization of the imagination, which must "develop" beyond initial solipsism—and thus diminish or cancel many of its most pleasurable and interesting functions—toward a sense of collectivity or membership in society. Insofar as an internal decision to be "developed" is involved, failure to restrict imagination in order to accomplish real (= social) ends can be a source of guilt. This

17

development is therefore an ambiguous goal: duty and guilt over past failures impel Heinrich to strive for it, but a sense of self (uniqueness, individuality) continually impedes his striving. Ultimately, the socialized imagination is an oxymoron for Keller. In all his writings, with the exception of the few most blandly didactic pieces, he seems to be working toward a synthesis of imaginative selfhood and productive membership in the social community, which ideally produces the imaginative, creative, socialized, and happy individual —but in general, these two modes of being remain unalterably distinct from one another.

Whereas *Der grüne Heinrich* I, in the best tradition of the *Entwicklungsroman*, *Erziehungsroman*, or *Bildungsroman*, follows the adventures of a hero whose actual *Entwicklung*, *Erziehung*, or *Bildung* is minimal, I will consider it as the starting point for a genuine "development" in Keller himself, who, as time passes, presents this opposition in an increasingly playful manner, softening the edges with humor and irony.[2] The active creative imagination in its opposition to the prosaic reality that contradicts it is the core problem of all such novels that focus on the hero's transition from immaturity to maturity. The problem is rarely solved. It is at best "deproblematized" from the perspective of maturity, as the attraction of imaginative or artistic matters diminishes for the mature hero, who is then no longer inclined to draw sharp and painful distinctions between appearance/ artifice and reality. The first of Keller's green Henrys fails to achieve this maturity and dies—impaled, as it were, on one end of his dichotomy—whereas the second survives and learns to live with two irreconcilable values.

A comparison of the two versions of *Der grüne Heinrich* provides an excellent illustration of both Heinrich's and Keller's development with regard to the central problem of literary fictions, their use and abuse. Where Heinrich Lee in his second incarnation will, unlike his ancestor, learn to read properly (a feat which is more or less equal to socialization in this context), his author also develops away from a suspicion of literary fictions (as purveyors of dangerous illusions) toward a more positive and appreciative depiction of them.

Keller originally conceived the novel in 1842 as "einen traurigen kleinen Roman . . . über den tragischen Abbruch einer jungen Künstlerlaufbahn, an welcher Mutter und Sohn zugrunde gingen" (H 3:842). Though the book did not turn out to be anything resembling a "little novel" (759 pages in the Hanser edition), Keller did make the "tragic" gesture of killing off his hero at the end—a gesture that, as many have argued, does not seem to follow from the plot line.[3] After all, Heinrich had just spent a healing period at the citadel of wish fulfillment, the *Grafenschloß*, and had returned home enlightened by his conversion to atheism and enriched by the sale of his paintings. Keller's highest aspiration during his Berlin years (1850–55) was to write a tragedy, and it is quite possible that his high regard for the tragic as well as his fidelity to his original concept influenced the outcome of the novel. In any case, the ending has found few admirers and many critics, including the author himself, who remedied the situation in the second version. Yet, given the state of the two novels, there is some logic to the death of Heinrich I and the survival of Heinrich II: the differences in their fates can be accounted for by the extent of their respective socialization, which can in turn be gauged by observing their attitudes toward literary fictions. In both cases, Keller appears to regard development as the emergence from an inner world achieved by the suppression of the imagination, which faculty he explores and illuminates by observing its operations on literature. Literature is a major force—though usually a retarding force—in these sagas of development, where a good (or expedient) rapport with reality must be founded on a clear-eyed recognition of the nonreal nature of fictions that seek to imitate this reality and to improve on it. Both Heinrichs err, according to the terms of their terrain, insofar as they attempt to annex and "possess" literary fictions—that is, to regard them as personalized indexes to their own specific circumstances. This naive faith in fictions is the major expression of the "irresponsible imagination," which impedes (I) and complicates (II) the process of socialization in the novels. For my purposes, no significant differences exist between the 1855 and 1880 versions of the *Jugendgeschichte* section of the novel and, except where specific reference is made to the original or the revision, they will be treated as identical stories, differentiated only by their respective frameworks.[4]

The life of Heinrich Lee is marked by regular significant encounters with literary fictions against a background of social norms that are seen as antithetical to fantasy. His imagination, like Keller's, is primarily a literary one (neither succeeded in painting), and from earliest childhood his world is one of "letters," alphabetical characters, which in the course of the novel grow to form words, sentences, pages, and books. It is the meaning of these letters, or, better, the source and constitution of this meaning, that Heinrich must learn in order to mature and enter society—his and the novelist's ostensible goal. To develop in this atmosphere, Heinrich must learn a self-external context for letters (in their various combinations) and renounce his personal claim to them. That is, he must restrain his freely imaginative response to letters (which inevitably adapts them to his personal circumstances) and learn to recognize and accept their externally determined social content.

Heinrich's first day of school—traditionally the painful beginning of a child's socialization—provides a clear and forceful illustration of Keller's model for growth as a struggle with letters. Abruptly thrust into the social setting of the classroom, Heinrich must effect the transition from the preschool child at home, who holds autocratic sway over letters, words, and their meanings, to the schoolboy who is charged with learning the meanings assigned to these letters by others. Previously young Heinrich was free to match letters and words with objects (or objects with words and letters) according to his fancy, and these self-manufactured referential bonds could be severed by him at will.[5] A case in point is his earlier manipulation of the word "God." Hearing that God is not a man, but a spirit, Heinrich, who could not grasp abstracts, chose a succession of concrete images to correspond to the word. First, the word was made weathercock as Heinrich—dimly aware that the church building was somehow associated with the deity—assumed that the weather vane on top of the church tower was God and directed his prayers to the ornament. He later transferred his childish adoration to the picture of a brightly colored tiger, in this way maintaining subjective control of the word: "Es waren ganz innerliche Anschauungen, und nur wenn der Name Gottes genannt wurde, so schwebte mir erst der glänzende Vogel und nachher der schöne Tiger vor" (H 1:67). He eventually returned to the concept of God as a man when he realized that his prayers consisted of words directed to someone capable of understanding them. Having thus concluded the theological investigations of his childhood, he settled into a comfortable and stable relationship with his God: "So lebte ich in einem unschuldig vergnüglichen Verhältnisse mit dem höchsten Wesen, ich kannte keine Bedürfnisse und keine Dankbarkeit, kein Recht und kein Unrecht, und ließ Gott einen herzlich guten Mann sein, wenn meine Aufmerksamkeit von ihm abgezogen wurde" (H 1:67).

Heinrich describes these childish modifications of his "deity" as his dealings with God and not as manipulations of the word, though he was actually availing himself of the linguistic access to the metaphysical that Feuerbach sought to block in *Das Wesen des Christentums*. In his discussion of the biblical *logos*, Feuerbach, who refers to language as "die sich äußernde Einbildungskraft" (F 6:95), expounds on the folly of confusing the word with the thing it is intended to denote:

"Das Wort ist ein abstractes Bild, die imaginäre Sache, oder inwiefern jede Sache immer zuletzt auch ein Gegenstand der Denkkraft ist, der eingebildete Gedanke, daher die Menschen, wenn sie das Wort, den Namen einer Sache kennen, sich einbilden, auch die Sache selbst zu kennen" (F 6:95). This is the "essence" of Heinrich's religion and of his world-view in general: words are used to create fanciful relations without regard for their ego-external functions, and these created relations, a pleasing world of idiosyncratic sense-making, form an effective substitute for the world beyond them. Like the biblical creator, Heinrich generates his own world on a verbal foundation; like the biblical Adam, he is master of all that he names.

The first day of school is mildly traumatic for Heinrich precisely because here, for the first time, he is being prodded to yield his control of letters. As he enters the schoolroom, he is immediately confronted by "riesige Buchstaben" (H 1:67) painted on the wall. His own previous reflections on the character and meaning of individual letters are his only guide when he is charged by the headmaster with identifying one of them by its (self-external) name: "Nun sollte ich plötzlich das große P benennen, welches mir in seinem ganzen Wesen äußerst wunderlich und humoristisch vorkam, und *es ward in meiner Seele klar* und ich sprach mit Entschiedenheit: Dies ist der Pumpernickel! Ich hegte keinen Zweifel, weder an der Welt, noch an mir, noch am Pumpernickel, und war froh in meinem Herzen" (H 1:68, my emphasis). The schoolmaster's sharp reproof and his violent shaking of the impertinent child "daß mir Hören und Sehen verging" (H 1:68) are the first of many indications of the schism between the child's subjective realm of letters and the socially determined content assigned to the same figures.[6] Heinrich's (brief) formal education is fundamentally a process of relinquishing his own personal associations with letters and the words they constitute in order to recognize what Keller's Pankraz calls "eine . . . außer mir liegende Ordnung" (H 2:27).

Child Heinrich eventually acknowledges this external order of words and meanings, but at the same time he annexes it to his own personal realm and uses it as a means to act upon the reality to which it ostensibly refers. When Heinrich is in his seventh year, a visitor to the Lee home discovers him uttering some rather coarse profanities—again, words he has heard whose conventional meanings are unknown to him—and reports this to his mother. By way of explanation, Heinrich spins an outrageous story of abduction by four older boys who allegedly taught him these words and forced him to use them. He spontaneously creates an imaginary scenario with self-external coordinates, which, though it did not occur, ultimately carries the same consequences for the alleged perpetrators as if it had. School authorities are notified, and the boys are rounded up and beaten. Heinrich's fiction is no simple lie invented to deflect punishment; rather, it is a well-developed, detailed, and coherent account, created for the sheer pleasure of adapting external reality to the flow of his imagination. The severe punishment inflicted on his schoolmates by teachers and parents inspires no remorse in their accuser. On the contrary, it gives him a feeling of great power and satisfaction:

> Soviel ich mich dunkel erinnere, war mir das angerichtete Unheil nicht nur gleichgültig, sondern ich fühlte eher noch eine Befriedigung in mir, daß die poetische Gerechtigkeit meine Erfindung so schön und *sichtbarlich* abrundete, daß etwas Auffallendes geschah, gehandelt und gelitten wurde, und das infolge meines schöpferischen Wortes. Ich begriff gar nicht, wie die mißhandelten Jungen so lamentieren und erbost sein konnten gegen mich, da der treffliche Verlauf der Geschichte sich von selbst verstand und ich hieran so wenig etwas ändern konnte als die alten Götter am Fatum.                              (H 1:107–8, my emphasis)

Heinrich's godlike act of creation, his transformation of word into flesh (or into a sequence of events in the material world) represents a clever compromise with the external order. At this stage of his life, he uses letters and words with due regard for their "objective" significance, but he combines them to create a fiction that he controls and that in this case exerts control over the very persons (school authorities) who had initially challenged his control. Whatever personal power he relinquishes, he replenishes "within the system" by causing the teachers to take *his* word for the literal truth. Heinrich is still firmly allied to his uniquely imaginative interpretation of the world and is effectively resisting the communal or social interpretation that the schoolmasters present to him.[7]

This continuing allegiance to imagination is later condemned by the third-person narrator of the first version, who challenges the more positive assessment of imagination and creativity given by Heinrich himself in the *Jugendgeschichte*. According to Keller's narrator: "Es war so artig und bequem für Heinrich, daß er eine so lebendige Erfindungsgabe besaß, aus dem Nichts heraus fort und fort schaffen, zusammensetzen, binden und lösen konnte! Wie schön, lieblich und mühelos war diese Tätigkeit, wie wenig ahnte er, daß nur ein übertünchtes Grab sei, das eine Welt umschloß, welche nie gewesen ist, nicht ist und nicht sein wird!" (H 1:477–78). Creativity, imagination, and the will to retain his mastery over letters are all impediments to the socialization of Heinrich Lee, who in this first version will ultimately fail to establish himself as a social being and will remain hopelessly "green." Interestingly, it is not only the third-person narrator who sees socialization in these terms, but also Heinrich himself. The latter's account of his life is characterized in both versions by a love of free indulgence in a nonworld of beautiful forms, and yet by an implicit (occasionally explicit) denunciation of this tendency in favor of discipline, duty, and civil service. Indulgence leads to guilt, and Heinrich grows to regard his beloved imagination as irresponsible.[8]

As Heinrich matures from child to young adult his interest shifts from letters and words to self-generated fictions, and finally to literary fictions. This transference of interest from personally defined words and symbols to texts that originate in the mind of another suggests a certain degree of socialization and the hoped-for development. But this is at best a sham development, for Heinrich reserves his rights to letters insofar as he regards literary fictions as verbal allegories of his own particular life. Like so many other inhabitants of novels, reader Heinrich plunders literature for a precise subjective meaning, or *Selbstbezug*, thus ignoring broader social and aesthetic considerations and repeatedly reducing these texts to their (imagined) relevance to his immediate concerns. Heinrich wants something from literature—namely, "truth," by which he understands direct detailed reference to personal "reality" as defined by his desires. Reading is a purely solipsistic exercise for Heinrich, and he aims for a continued possession of letters and mastery over them by means of a willful reduction of literary fictions to literal "truth."

Heinrich has regular run-ins with literary fictions throughout his brief adult life, and though he relates these episodes as steps in a vague progression (from dime novels to Goethe), his proprietary posture remains constant. In the beginning, Heinrich himself (narrating the *Jugendgeschichte*) is aware of his tendency to appropriate literature to serve his own purposes. His brief friendship with the *Leserfamilie*, the clan of maniacal readers who expose him to coarse chivalric novels and stories of seduction, is cited as the source of his habit of lying. A predatory devouring of dime novels, which offer crass ego gratification, has destroyed the moral fiber of the *Leserfamilie* and threatens young Heinrich as well: "Die unzweideutige Genugtuung, welche in diesen groben Dichtungen waltete, war meinen angeregten Gefühlen wohltätig und gab ihnen Gestalt und Namen" (H 1:133). Heinrich's response to the novels is an extravagant foray into the manufacture of tall tales designed to give him the aura of the romantic hero. He steals money from his mother in order to display the wealth he claims to possess, but ultimately, after a painful altercation with the son of the house, he withdraws from the circle and renounces lying. The family, however, continues its moral decline:

> In dem lesebeflissenen Hause wurden indessen der Vorrat an schlechten Büchern und die Torheit immer größer. Die Alten sahen mit seltsamer Freude zu, wie die armen Töchter immer tiefer in ein einfältig verbuhltes Wesen hineingerieten, Liebhaber auf Liebhaber wechselten und doch von keinem heimgeführt wurden, so daß sie mitten in der übelriechenden Bibliothek sitzen blieben mit einer Herde kleiner Kinder, welche mit den zerlesenen Büchern spielten und dieselben zerrissen.        (H 1:138)

The son, victim of his own "vielgeübte Phantasie" (H 1:139), embraces all manner of vice as he grows older, shuns honest work, and supports himself by means of "die sonderbarsten Erfindungen, Lügen und Ränke, welche ihm nur eine Art Fortsetzung der früheren Romantik waren" (H 1:139). He eventually dies in prison; and by way of concluding the episode, Heinrich recalls the boy's unwillingness to restrain his desires to the slightest degree, a quality nurtured by bad fiction, which Heinrich then identifies as the root of imperialism, vindictive jealousy, swindling, and thievery.

The didactic message of the episode is far from subtle. Keller is speaking here of a specific type of literary fiction and he is apparently quite sincere: cheap novels ruin minds and ultimately lead to dishonesty, promiscuity, and civil crimes. This is the grossest form of self-interested reading, and Heinrich believes he has escaped it, though in fact he merely adapts the practice to more respectable reading material.

Heinrich's subsequent development is marked by a changing allegiance to a series of three (real) authors, each of whom provides him with part of the "schönere Wirklichkeit" (H 1:139) that he originally sought in cheap novels. These authors do little, however, to broaden his social horizons, because he scrutinizes their work for its direct bearing on his life and develops a literal understanding of it based on his current needs. Thus, Geßner suddenly becomes the aspiring landscape painter's "Prophet" by dint of what Heinrich perceives to be biographical similarities, a common love of nature and the spellbinding force of the word "Genie" used in reference to Geßner by his biographers (H 1:202). Geßner is soon succeeded by Jean Paul, again called "Prophet," but significantly also "father" and "brother" ("Jean

Paul, welcher Vaterstelle an mir vertrat"; "bei ihm liegt man an einem Bruderherzen!" [H 1:263]). The metaphors of kinship indicate a similarity of world-view: Heinrich, who maintains a strict separation between his creative imagination and prosaic reality, could not read far in Jean Paul (no titles are given) without encountering the same division between the artistic and the mundane. His emotional attachment is actually an identification with the colorful world of Jean Paul's fictions: "[alles] schien mir plötzlich tröstend und erfüllend entgegenzutreten, was ich bisher gewollt und gesucht oder unruhig und dunkel empfunden. . . . Diese Herrlichkeit machte mich stutzen, dies schien mir das Wahre und Rechte!" (H 1:262).

Finally, Heinrich "devours" the complete works of Goethe in a thirty-day marathon reading session (extended to the biblical forty in the second version, and begun during a torrential rainstorm in both cases). He views Goethe as a corrective to his "romantic" dalliance with Jean Paul, feeling that he has learned the "right" things from Goethe. Heinrich represents this newfound knowledge as the ability to distinguish that which is "poetic" from that which is not:

Ich hatte mir, ohne zu wissen wann und wie, angewöhnt, alles, was ich im Leben und Kunst als brauchbar, gut und schön befand, poetisch zu nennen, und selbst die Gegenstände meines erwählten Berufes, Farben wie Formen, nannte ich nicht malerisch, sondern immer poetisch, so gut wie alle menschlichen Ereignisse, welche mich anregend berührten. . . . [D]enn es ist das gleiche Gesetz, welches die verschiedenen Dinge poetisch oder der Widerspiegelung ihres Lebens wert macht; aber in bezug auf manches, was ich bisher poetisch nannte, lernte ich nun, daß das Unbegreifliche und Unmögliche, das Abenteuerliche und Überschwengliche nicht poetisch sind.           (H 1:392)

Heinrich expounds at great length (and quite beautifully) on the tonic effects of his reading of Goethe and, organized as it is—as an extended meditation following the tempestuous resolution of his dual love for Judith and Anna ("Ich fühlte mein Wesen in zwei Teile gespalten" [H 1:387])—this appears as a healing interlude, an act of spiritual reorganization.

It would seem that Goethe has taught Heinrich to exercise imagination responsibly, but this is not the case. The experience is beneficial to him only when viewed in the expansive and nonspecific terms with which he describes it in the passage quoted above. When he (inevitably) reduces the experience to specifics, that is, to a specific course of action that he feels should follow from it, he blunders once again. Heinrich, who already desires to study painting in Germany (rather than learn a trade), is able to appropriate Goethe to legitimize this desire—clearly the biggest mistake of his life—by means of the most curious logic:

> Ich hatte es weder mit dem menschlichen Wort noch mit der menschlichen Gestalt zu tun und fühlte mich nur glücklich und zufrieden, daß ich auf das bescheidenste Gebiet mit meinem Fuß setzen konnte, auf den irdischen Grund und Boden, auf dem sich der Mensch bewegt, und so in der poetischen Welt wenigstens einen Teppichbewahrer abgeben durfte. Goethe hatte ja viel und mit Liebe von landschaftlichen Dingen gesprochen, und durch diese Brücke glaubte ich ohne Unbescheidenheit mich ein wenig mit seiner Welt verbinden zu können.          (H 1:392–93)

The complete works of Goethe appear to tell Heinrich to follow precisely his own prior inclinations. He plans to imitate Goethe's creativity, and his understanding of this imitation is quite specifically representative of these inclinations: the painting of landscapes will forge a connection, a bridge with Goethe's imaginary world (where descriptions of landscapes occur), and will gain Heinrich some (modest) possession of the "letters" that attract him. To this end he will travel to Germany and fulfill another long-standing desire inspired in him by German literature. The third-person narrator of the first version explains Germany's attractions for Heinrich:

> Aber alles, was er sich unter Deutschland dachte, war von einem romantischen Dufte umwoben. In seiner Vorstellung lebte das poetische und ideale Deutschland, wie sich letzteres selbst dafür hielt und träumte. Er hatte nur mit Vorliebe und empfänglichem Gemüte das Bild in sich aufgenommen, welches Deutschland durch seine Schriftsteller von sich verfertigen ließ und über die Grenzen sandte . . . das Schillersche Pathos . . . Jean Paulsche Religiosität und Heinesche Eulenspiegelei schillerten durcheinander wie eine Schlangenhaut; . . . er . . . sah darum begeistert das vor ihm liegende Land als einen großen alten Zaubergarten an, in welchem er als ein willkommener Wanderer mit jenen Stichworten köstliche Schätze heben und wieder in seine Berge zurücktragen dürfe.          (H 1:32–33)

The second version is more succinct. Heinrich recalls his heart pounding after crossing the border: "[denn] ich befand mich auf deutschem Boden und hatte von jetzt an das Recht und die Pflicht, die Sprache der Bücher zu reden, aus denen meine Jugend sich herangebildet hatte und meine liebsten Träume gestiegen waren" (H 1:805). Both Heinrichs enter the land of their (literary) dreams with high expectations and are predictably disappointed. This disappointment inevitably reflects on the literary premises of their expectations, but the indictment of fictions is far more severe in the first version, where Heinrich's image of Germany is more conspicuously (and protractedly) tied to literary fictions—which, the passage suggests, lurk like the serpent in the garden, ready to deceive the impressionable reader.

Though Heinrich's *Jugendgeschichte*, his failure in the *Kunststadt*, and his arrival at the *Grafenschloß* vary little from the first version of the novel to the second, Keller—who bought up all available copies of the first version and burned them while writing the second[9]— introduced some major changes into the remainder of his revision. The most striking of these are the removal of the third-person narrator (leaving only Heinrich to express both sides of the question of imagination vs. social responsibility), the much-regretted excision of Judith's bathing scene, the harmless outcome of the duel between Heinrich and Lys, Judith's return, and, of course, Heinrich's survival. Less apparent, but equally important, is the new perspective on literature, which retains its more or less pernicious function—misused and misunderstood as truth—throughout Heinrich's youth (most of these passages being unchanged) but is redeemed and legitimized as fiction at the end. Heinrich II learns to read unselfishly, that is, to relinquish his purely subjective and self-interested hold on letters, and it is this development that constitutes his socialization *in nuce* and makes further life possible.

As regards their reading and their characteristic proprietary attitude toward literature, the real parting of the ways for doomed Heinrich I and developing Heinrich II occurs over the matter of Dortchen Schönfund's oracular bonbon basket. This peculiar episode, a kind of play within a play, is a *mise-en-scène* of Heinrich's habitual reading process in that it provides a factual basis for his assumptions about the self-specific "messages" contained in literary texts. At the same time, however, it parodies these assumptions and, in conjunction with subsequent events, makes a mockery of his attempts at possession. On the eve of Heinrich's departure, Dortchen, who is in the habit of wrapping various "prophetic" little verses around her candies and offering them to guests as a kind of fortune cookie, "rigs" the basket by placing the same poem in each of the oracular candy wrappings:

Hoffnung hintergehet zwar,
Aber nur, was wankelmütig;
Hoffnung zeigt sich immerdar
Treugesinnten Herzen gütig;
Hoffnung senket ihren Grund
In das Herz, nicht in den Mund!                              (H 1:746)

Here, in the *Grafenschloß*, where all his wishes come true (father figure, love interest, money, and an honorable conclusion to his painting career), Heinrich also realizes his assumptions about reading in the *Hoffnungsspruch*, his ideal literary text. The verses, a "Sinngedicht eines alten schlesischen Poeten" (H 1:745), have been appropriated specifically for him, and they contain a message for him alone—hope of attaining Dortchen, and hope of rebuilding his life on the substantial foundation provided by the count. Insofar as Heinrich seeks prophetic content in literature (Geßner and Jean Paul were his "prophets"), he is curiously vindicated because these verses (in this context) contain predictions about his life by someone who has some control over his future happiness. Yet this particular contrivance of Dortchen's, though it represents the realization of Heinrich's assumptions, trivializes his experience by reducing literature to the status of a fortune cookie and the reader to a consumer of sweets,[10] thus "unmasking" the operations that Heinrich has been performing on literature all along. It does not seem thematically likely that the verbal confection in Heinrich's hand will translate into anything resembling hope. If the word is the imaginary thing, as Feuerbach has indicated, then Heinrich departs with imaginary (literary) hope in his hand, leaving his fairy-tale castle for a social and material world where the imaginary is irrevocably opposed to the real. Thus the auspicious departure is actually ominous when viewed in terms of its "literary" premises, and Keller's "sudden" descent into the "tragic" is not as abrupt as has commonly been perceived.

Heinrich I, unaware of Dortchen's deception, attaches an almost mystical significance to the words that he believes chance has given to him. Yet he carries the paper strip back home to encounter circumstances that appear to negate any basis for hope for the future. His mother, his "unmittelbare Lebensquelle" (H 1:763), has died in his absence, possibly as a direct result of his neglect. After half-hearted efforts to revive his recently acquired civil ambitions, Heinrich, whose insistence on dominion over literary texts has determined the course of his undeveloped life, weakens and dies, holding the verses like a talisman: "[Sein] Leib und Leben brach und er starb in wenigen Tagen. Seine Leiche hielt jenes Zettelchen von Dortchen fest in der Hand, worauf das Liedchen von der Hoffnung geschrieben war. Er hatte es in der letzten Zeit nicht einen Augenblick aus der Hand gelassen, und selbst wenn er einen Teller Suppe, seine einzige Speise, gegessen, das Papierchen eifrig mit dem Löffel zusammen in der Hand gehalten oder es unterdessen in die andere Hand gesteckt" (H 1:767).

The image of Heinrich at table, desperately trying to nourish himself on (imaginary) hope and (material) soup at the same time, represents a last pathetic attempt at synthesizing the two facets of life whose opposition has barred his socialization. Imaginative selfhood and social responsibility, subjective interiority and objective engagement, creativity and mundane necessity, *Schein* and *Sein*, paper and soup spoon remain distinct as Heinrich deteriorates, and a life of reading "selfishly" draws to a close. The precise cause of death is not given, but apparently he chose to let go of the soup spoon and thus to dissociate himself from physical sustenance.

Heinrich I's saga of "development" therefore concludes grotesquely, with his corpse clutching the words (presumably tattered and soup-stained) to which the living man had clung as if they meant possession of hope itself. Even in death he does not relax his proprietary grip on letters, and this green Henry expires in an atmosphere of literary hope and "real" despair. Literary fictions have played a villainous role in the novel precisely because they are "untrue," and, as noted earlier, a novel is a rather inappropriate (though not unconventional) vehicle for this message. Obviously, Heinrich's reading habits are flawed, as is his approach to life (in this context), but literature has been implicated in the "tragischen Abbruch einer jungen Künstlerlaufbahn" and, to judge by the appearance of the body, its contribution was significant. Young Keller's distrust of these untruths, which he himself manufactures, is curiously masochistic, but it reflects a characteristic ambivalence toward creativity (inevitable function of the poet's mind), which at this point achieves its expression in a simultaneous act of creation and "denial." This guilt, the self-loathing of the creative artist (who has yet to serve his fifteen years as a state official), is probably the greatest of the many biographical similarities between Keller and his green heroes.

Whereas Heinrich I's self-interested reading habits prove to be self-perpetuating and ultimately deadly, Heinrich II manages to "reform" and survive, experiencing a development *ex machina* (or *ex Juditha*)[11] at the end, where Judith seems to materialize out of a rock ("es sah aus, als ob der Geist des Berges aus dem Gestein herausgetreten wäre" [H 1:1116]) and teaches him to read "unselfishly." Previous to this "miracle," Heinrich II also faces the oracular bonbon basket and "selects" the hope verses, but he does so under radically different circumstances: he *witnesses* the preparation of the candies from a high window and surreptitiously investigates the basket in Dortchen's absence. When he later unwraps the *Hoffnungsspruch*, he is aware that it has been planted there by Dortchen, and that it bears a calculated relevance to his life, a link between text and self that his imagination need not supply in this case. He also retains the paper wrapping, hoping for its fulfillment, but he keeps it at a distance—in his *Schreibtafel*—and not in his hand.

Unlike his predecessor, Heinrich II willingly lets go of the strip of paper. In his moment of deepest despair over the death of his mother and the corruption that permeates his civil office, he decides that the verses are deceptive and abandons them to the wind:

> Auch zog ich Dorotheens grünen Zettel einmal wieder hervor, der noch immer zwischen einer Falte meiner Schreibtafel steckte. "Hoffnung zeigt sich immerdar treugesinnten Herzen gütig!" las ich und wunderte mich, daß ich das falsche Wechselchen noch bei mir trug. Da eben ein schwacher Luftzug dicht über der sommerwarmen Erde hinwallte, ließ ich es fahren, und es flatterte gemächlich über Gras und Heideblumen weg, ohne daß ich ihm weiter nachblickte.
>
> "Am besten wäre es," dachte ich, "du lägest unter dieser sanften Erdbrust und wüßtest von nichts! Still und lieblich wäre es hier zu ruhen!"                                        (H 1:1115)

Then, as if by magic, Judith emerges from the rocks before him. Her sudden appearance in the moment in which he has relinquished his hold on letters (and has decided that they are false) is as contrived as it is timely. She had heard of Heinrich's misfortune and returned from America (!) to comfort him. She has actually been around for two weeks, walking the mountain paths in hopes of encountering him, but her efforts are rewarded only when Heinrich releases his "grünes Liedchen" and turns away from the fictions that have nourished his imagination. Keller has deliberately set this episode up as the exchange of a false guide (misunderstood literature) for a true one: Judith, who (aside from her rock appearance) has hitherto borne the thematic burden of representing the "real," sensual, material side of existence, in contradistinction to the diaphanous and ethereal Anna.

The contrast between the fates of Heinrichs I and II could not be plainer: whereas Heinrich I dies pathetically clutching his poem, a martyr to his faith in the "truth" of letters, Heinrich II lets go of it, denies letters, and gets Judith who (fresh from founding an independent community in America and shepherding it to self-sufficient prosperity) will ease his entrance into the sphere of social efficacy. As Heinrich puts it: "Du hast mich erlöst, Judith, und dir dank ichs, wenn ich wieder munter bin" (H 1:1122). If Keller were to leave it at that—that is, to imply that literary fictions (which represent the imaginative pole of his dichotomy) are false and misleading and that this is a truth to be recognized—then versions I and II would, despite their differences, convey essentially the same message about fictions and imagination.

Yet Heinrich has not merely traded false literature for true Judith. The poem that he has surrendered to the wind returns to him in a potentially seductive form, practically forcing him to a self-bound interpretation. The great test of his new frame of reference—"wie mit der Schönheit doch nicht alles getan wird und der einseitige Dienst derselben eine Heuchelei sei wie jede andere" (H 1:1122)—comes in the form of a stained-glass window in the inn where he and Judith dine. The old window commemorates the original founder's wedding with a picture of the bridal couple, Andreas and Emerentia *Juditha*, and the identical *Hoffnungsspruch* given to Heinrich by Dortchen and recently cast to the winds. Wedding imagery, which illustrates and hence interprets the familiar verses for Heinrich, combines with the coincidence of names and the present situation—"salvation" by a woman he loves—to suggest a specific course of action that Heinrich is already considering: marriage to Judith. Keller seems to go out of his way to tempt Heinrich's imagination with a most blatant and detailed suggestion of the "truth" he has hitherto assumed in literature. Yet, rather than taking this as a sign that he should marry Judith, Heinrich hesitates, sensing the possibility of further deception by literature—especially these verses—which he now regards as untrue: "Mich aber berührte diese Aufdringlichkeit des Zufalls, die aus der ganzen Schilderei leuchtete, eher ängstlich und beklemmend als freudig; denn dieser Machthaber schien sich förmlich zu meinem Führer aufwerfen zu wollen, und der Spruch konnte eine neue Täuschung verkünden" (H 1:1123).

At this (portentous) point, Judith, who has just redeemed Heinrich, also accomplishes the redemption of the literature he loves by affirming its truth content, albeit on a mysterious condition: "Judith las denselben [Hoffnungsspruch], *ohne auf das Bildwerk zu achten*, und sagte lächelnd: 'Welch ein schöner Vers und gewißlich wahr; *man muß ihn nur richtig verstehen'* " (H 1:1123, my emphasis). Although this remark occurs in the context of their decision to preserve their freedom in friendship and not to marry ("und dafür des Glückes umso sicherer bleiben" [H 1:1124]), Judith's assessment of the hope verses has larger implications for the presently shaky status of literature in the novel as a whole. She ignores the illustration with its enticements to a self-specific interpretation and pronounces the poem "wahr" on the condition that it be "properly understood."

As a guide to the significant act of reading literature in this novel, Judith's prescriptive "richtig verstehen" is not a model of unambiguous clarity, but its very indeterminacy reflects the open, unencumbered, "aesthetic" attitude toward literature and life that Heinrich (rather hastily) develops, and that in turn develops Heinrich.[12] The hope verses are both "schön" and "wahr" only when divorced from restrictive assumptions of literal *Selbstbezug*; literature has been dangerous or "villainous" only because (undeveloped) Heinrich misapprehended its nature. Thus beauty and truth do cohabit literary fictions, although these fictions do not refer directly to life. Life and fiction are still distinct categories—but this distinction no longer mandates a unilateral choice.

In this revised version of his autobiographical novel, Keller vindicates literary fictions that have served as an index to imagination. Nevertheless, he does so only by asserting and "verifying" the disjuncture between literature and life in a narrow sense—while implying an indistinct, yet intimate, bond in the larger scheme of things. The actual "truth" of literary fictions remains, appropriately, a literary puzzle: it is something that exists but can be found only by those who do not seek it,[13] a "truth" that is, perhaps, best conveyed by a literary fiction. And it is in this way that Keller's novel asserts its own reference to reality.

Keller does not collapse his dichotomy in *Der grüne Heinrich* II, but it is no longer a mortal danger to his hero, because the author softens the hard distinctions (still operative) between imaginative possibility and mundane necessity, denying neither and affirming both. What was a moral choice for Heinrichs I and II becomes a matter of ironic perspective as the rigid opposition is mediated by Judith's smile.

Plot, character, and the sequence of events do not change significantly from the first *Der grüne Heinrich* to the second, yet Keller tells two very different stories of imagination in its interaction with literary fictions. This reversal of position, which I have called his development—the deproblematizing of the antagonism between imagination and reality—was not as abrupt as the contrast might suggest. Of the roughly twenty-five years that passed between publication dates, Keller, the creative artist, devoted fifteen to full-time civil service (1861–76), working tirelessly to repay his "debt" to family and society—both of which had supported his studies in Munich (1840–42), Heidelberg (1848–50), and Berlin (1850–55). Naturally, such an experience (work) and such a time span would tend to diminish the guilt engendered by years of (economically unproductive) artistic self-development and to promote a more balanced attitude toward creativity. Yet in conclusion, it is interesting to note that the process of development, as it can be identified in Keller's fiction, already begins in 1856 (one year after the completion of *Der grüne Heinrich* I) with "Pankraz, der Schmoller," whose existential adventures will be the subject of the next chapter.

## Feuerbach's Keller and Keller's Feuerbach

Although Heinrich Lee performs a number of personalizing operations on the fictions he reads, his purpose is not so much to act upon these fictions as (perhaps unconsciously) to project his own desires into them that they might act upon him as stimulators and organizers of desire, and as authorities for the choices he wishes to make. In this respect, Heinrich resembles the novelistic heroes examined in Girard's study. Indeed, Keller's fiction does, in general, tend to feature individuals who suffer from "desire according to the Other"—that abdication of spontaneity and self-determination for a slavish imitation of the desires of another, which Girard insists is not a fiction. The novelistic triangle—subject, mediator of desire, and (improbable) object of desire—figures prominently in Keller, and the catalyst for borrowed desire is not always a book as in Heinrich's case. In "Die drei gerechten Kammacher," for example, this desire is inflamed by the combmakers' perception of their own similarity, which results in rivalry and a madly intensified pursuit of their original goals. In their desperate struggle to distinguish themselves, they erase all distinctions and come to resemble "die Winkel eines gleichseitigen Dreieckes" (H 2:182), the very image used by Girard. Each imitates the other, who imitates the other, who imitates him as they join in a fixed cycle of mutual mediation, trying to outdo each other in feats of thrift, righteousness, and patience and eventually all wooing the same (improbable) woman. The combmakers rank among the lowest of Keller's creatures, so narrow-spirited that their obsession is virtually incomprehensible; they themselves are for the most part so dehumanized that the final assignment of just deserts to Jobst, Fridolin, and Dietrich (death, dissipation, and Züs, respectively) seems an uncomfortably serious intrusion into the general amusement. John Ellis's probing essay on the "Kammacher"[14] argues for the serious nature of the story as a study of "aims and aimlessness,"[15] focusing on the combmakers' choice of a goal and their ultimate discovery of its arbitrariness. Ellis concludes that Keller is less a "pleasantly relaxed writer of an optimistic temperament"[16] than a subtle and meticulous recorder of the human condition. It is in this capacity that Keller appears to validate Girard's findings. However, as noted earlier, a look at Keller's reception of Feuerbach (its impact and its limits) may prove to be more relevant to the intellectual/ideological basis of his fiction than a comparison with (Girard's theory of) the great French novels of his time—novels that Keller largely ignored.

In the case of the combmakers, as well as that of those figures who are unduly attracted by (clearly attractive) fictions, Keller appears to scrutinize obsession with the "Other" in order to lament the waste of psychic energy involved in such a transaction. This concern with misdirected psychic energy and the pattern that conveys it constitute, I believe, the real substance of Keller's intellectual kinship with Feuerbach, a relationship that is usually understood in terms of Keller's literal reception of Feuerbach's philosophy (atheism) and not as a common interest in the progressive erosion of the self as the locus of choice and the surrender of personal determination to a fiction or illusion.[17]

By his own account, Keller's attendance at a series of lectures given by Feuerbach in Heidelberg between December 1848 and March 1849, as well as his personal friendship with the philosopher, contributed to a massive restructuring of his world-view—and Keller was not one to acknowledge influence freely or graciously. The goal of the Heidelberg lectures, to transform the audience "aus Gottesfreunden zu Menschenfreunden, aus Gläubigen zu Denkern, . . . aus Candidaten des Jenseits zu Studenten des Diesseits, aus Christen, welche ihrem eigenen Bekenntniss und Geständniss zufolge, 'halb Thier halb Engel' sind, zu Menschen, zu ganzen Menschen" (F 8:360),[18] appears to have been realized in Keller, who permanently renounced God and immortality for the sake of a heightened appreciation of *this* life and the natural world in which it is grounded. As Keller wrote to his friend Wilhelm Baumgartner, during the course of the lectures: "Für mich ist die Hauptfrage die: Wird die Welt, wird das Leben prosaischer und gemeiner nach Feuerbach? Bis jetzt muß ich des bestimmtesten antworten: Nein! im Gegenteil, es wird alles klarer, strenger, aber auch glühender und sinnlicher.—Das Weitere muß ich der Zukunft überlassen, denn ich werde nie ein Fanatiker sein und die geheimnisvolle schöne Welt zu allem Möglichen fähig halten, wenn es mir irgend plausibel wird" (*GB* 1:275).[19]

Thus Feuerbach can be credited with Keller's personal conversion to atheism (Feuerbach's new "faith" in man and materialism) and (indirectly) with the effects of this conversion on the author's subsequent work, which includes all of the prose fiction that was published during his lifetime. But we have grown accustomed to hearing of a partnership between poet and philosopher, and there is a strong tendency in the scholarship to read Keller's work to some degree as a series of poetic restatements of Feuerbach's philosophy.[20] Insofar as Keller never bothered to develop a systematic philosophy—much less a theology—of his own, the substitution of that of Feuerbach forces an indistinct heterodoxy into more easily recognizable philosophical categories. Peter Goldammer has objected to this reduction of Keller's thought to orthodox Feuerbachian materialism, and Kaspar T. Locher has written extensively on Keller as an asystemic thinker.[21] Even Emil Ermatinger, who maintains that Feuerbach's philosophy "in klaren systematischen Zusammenhang ordnete, was seit langem in dem Dichter als dumpfes Chaos gärte,"[22] acknowledges that "[Keller] sie sich nie in alle Folgerungen hinein zu eigen machte —er ist nie Feuerbachischer Atheist gewesen."[23]

What was Keller's continuing relationship to Feuerbach and to the latter's version of *Diesseitigkeit* after the end of the lecture series? On the practical side, the friendship appears to have dissolved when Keller left Heidelberg for Berlin the following year. No correspondence exists, and the two were never to meet again. Furthermore, a glance at Keller's letters and essays reveals only a very narrow interest in Feuerbach's philosophy. This is not to suggest that Keller was incapable of comprehending the body of his supposed mentor's work (Feuerbach is not known for subtlety), but rather that he found the basic idea sufficient for his purposes and neglected the theoretical background and subsequent development. In the same letter to Baumgartner, Keller complained of the philosopher's "mühseligen schlechten Vortrag" (*GB* 1:274), and he may well have found the published works to be equally tedious. In any case, one of the world's most famous literary disciples of Feuerbach does not appear to have read much Feuerbach. Keller's library was said to have contained only one volume of the complete works,[24] and the correspondence, which mentions few titles, consistently refers to Feuerbach as the proponent of *one* idea, citing the "tiefe und grandiose Monotonie,

mit welcher Feuerbach seine *eine* Frage ein halbes Leben lang abge-
handelt und erschöpft" (*GB* 1:374). Thus we can say with certainty
that the paths of Keller and Feuerbach crossed in 1848–49 and that
Keller radically revised his thinking on the very significant issues of
God and immortality as a result of this encounter.[25] However, as far
as Keller's active interest in Feuerbach's work is concerned, the exchange appears to have ended in Heidelberg, and the philosopher's
influence on the poet is best discussed with a regard for the distinction between immediate and long-range effects. Feuerbach's philosophy, and Feuerbach himself, had a sudden and powerful effect on
Keller in Heidelberg, but the idea of a lasting partnership between
*Dichter* and *Denker* is a literary-historical convenience that obscures
Keller's (admittedly undeclared) intellectual independence.

Although Keller's appropriation of the new materialist philosophy
may have been selective and narrow in the long run, Feuerbach's
drastic influence on the first version of his magnum opus, *Der grüne
Heinrich*, is, as noted, undeniable. The book was conceived in 1842,
but after the Heidelberg encounter Keller revised his concept and
rewrote his manuscript in order to bring the novel directly into line
with Feuerbach's teachings. This was a deliberate incorporation of
Feuerbach and something of an advertisement for *Diesseitigkeit*: the
hero undergoes a conversion similar to Keller's (though this comes
too late to do him any good), Feuerbach is mentioned by name, and
among the various characters we have textbook examples of the right
way to follow Feuerbach (Dortchen Schönfund) and the wrong way
to follow Feuerbach (the young philosophical schoolmaster). Yet beyond these surface particulars, there are more subtle ideological and
methodological correspondences between the novel and Feuerbach's
philosophical writings, which suggest that while writing the first version of his *Grüner Heinrich* Keller had accepted and internalized the
patterns of Feuerbach's thought, building on a basic affinity and ap-
plying these patterns to his own concerns. Keller and Feuerbach are
at this point united by two factors: (1) a common suspicion of that
which is untrue, the conviction that adherence to fictions, illusions
and fantasies constitutes a hindrance to social development, which is
the unquestioned goal of human life;[26] and (2) the shared assumption
that the "unmasking" of these illusions can perhaps eliminate them
and lead to a more productive dialogue with the world and the society at hand. Feuerbach never ceases to proclaim the truths he has
uncovered. But in Keller's case, the optimism of the didactic author
soon begins to deteriorate. Keller sustains this optimism as well as
the Feuerbachian view of the untrue, throughout *Der grüne Heinrich* I,

but his later work, beginning with "Pankraz," indicates an amendment of this view: a loss of confidence in the direct efficacy of unmasking fictions within fiction, and a growing appreciation of these fictions and their inevitability in human discourse.

Reduced to its essence, the form in which it was probably most useful to Keller, Feuerbach's "a-theology" is a long, sustained argument against a fiction: that of the Christian deity who incorporates all that is "good" in mankind and thereby alienates humanity from its own virtues and strengths, insofar as these qualities are understood as deriving from this deity—a misconception that obscures their true origin in man. Feuerbach sought to expose the Christian versions of God and immortality as imaginary constructs arising from human "selfishness." The tendency to give priority to the individual self, to abstract interior life from material nature, is, Feuerbach contends, the source of the fictions of God and immortality. The self, thus freed from its grounding in community and nature, imagines another reality beyond experience, a better world ruled by a deity where the uprooted self can dwell—and does dwell, to the extent that it lives in anticipation of the afterlife. The projection of all that is valued in human nature onto an imaginary deity is the self-alienation of consciousness effected by religion in general, and it saps the "essence" of humanity: "Die Religion zieht die Kräfte, Eigenschaften, Wesensbestimmungen des Menschen vom Menschen ab und vergöttert sie als selbstständige Wesen—gleichgiltig ob sie nun, wie im Polytheismus, jede einzeln für sich zu einem Wesen macht, oder, wie im Monotheismus, alle in ein Wesen zusammenfasst" (F 6:5).[27]

*Das Wesen des Christentums* (1841) is an account of the origins of this fiction, of "praktischen Egoismus," the human tendency to generate such myths, and of the purposes they are intended to serve—one of which is the reassignment of personal responsibility and control to a (non)being outside the self. Quite simply, the book that gained Feuerbach notoriety is an explication of the dangers involved in subscribing to the Christian fiction and the joys of having abandoned it. The consciousness of one's own transitoriness reveals life as a limited and therefore precious opportunity to participate in the affairs of humanity. Individual existence thus acquires real meaning only when it is negated as such, that is, when the individual transcends the boundaries of self (and self-generated fictions) and merges with the community by forming bonds of "unselfish" love. One's essence is then fully involved in the world and not squandered on an imaginary deity. In the absence of a beyond, or *Jenseits*, Feuerbach rushed to fill the gap left by the removal of God and immortality by celebrating

*Diesseits* in exactly the same tones formerly reserved for *Jenseits*,[28] importing all the imagined glory of God and the afterlife to a new appreciation of man and the "only" life—that is, substituting another fiction, the "godlike" potential of mankind, for the one he attacked. This replacement maneuver, exposing and eliminating the deity and reassigning its power to the species, was perfectly in tune with the spirit of the bourgeois century. Feuerbach did not neglect the obvious political implications of such a scheme, and his frequently invoked analogy between Christianity and absolutist forms of government was more than merely illustrative.[29]

Just as the theologian, Feuerbach, scrutinized his own discipline and developed a philosophy intended to subvert theology, Keller, author of literary fictions, attacked the product of his own métier (in the early stages of his career), extending Feuerbach's critique of religion to imaginative literature in the first version of his novel.[30] *Der grüne Heinrich I* is a novel written *against* literary fictions, which, in the course of reader Heinrich's life, dazzle, deceive, and ultimately fade and wither to the tattered strip of paper in the dead man's hand. This novel is the record of the relatively unmediated influence of Feuerbach, and the offending class of deceptive fictions is symbolically eliminated. Like Feuerbach, Keller also substitutes a fiction for the one he seeks to remove: that of an individual's "real" social vocation—the novel of development's grail. This is a distinct personal "calling," which, if heeded, will lead to the rock-hard reality-involvement of a properly pragmatic life. Heinrich's false choice of a painting career, a choice abetted by literary fictions, is a deviation from the "true" path of honest work and bourgeois responsibility, which robs him of such authenticity as was available to him. Thus, the first version of the novel, written in the first moment of Keller's Feuerbach reception, constitutes a close intellectual mimicry of the philosopher's methods, as well as a literal incorporation of the principles of his philosophy.

Later work preserves this intense interest in fictions, and the "grandiose monotony" that Keller perceived in Feuerbach's teachings is matched by a conspicuous thematic monotony in his own writings: an almost obsessive concentration on fictions as seducers of men and women who might otherwise be contributing to a healthy economy, entering civil service, or responsibly tending the home fires. Keller repeatedly addresses the question of life-alternative fictions, those various codes, systems, fantasies, and life-lies (including Peter Gilgus's Feuerbach fanaticism) that define another existence enhanced by wish-fulfillment.

Whereas Feuerbach sought to demonstrate that the religious image is actually an image of man, transformed by the imagination into a (superior) Other, Keller portrays these fictions and life-lies as images of (transfigured) desire. The self-alienation of consciousness decried by Feuerbach becomes the self-alienation of desire for Keller. Heinrich's "discovery," in the complete works of Goethe, of an imperative that he go to Germany and study painting is an obvious example of the subject's desire objectified in his interpretation of a literary text. But the most egregious instance of the subject's failure to recognize himself in the alleged Other is the combmakers' triangle: each righteous journeyman finds his own aspirations personified in two Others, who are ultimately identical to himself. This radical self-alienation, a mad desire estranged from its subject and (eventually) detached from its object, causes Jobst and Fridolin to forget their cherished goals for the sake of a purely formal (self-)rivalry. They leave Züs alone with Dietrich in their haste to begin the race, and they bypass the finish line as they try to outrun one another for the privilege of remaining in the master's shop. Afterwards, Jobst, who feels that he has truly lost himself (H 2:212), hangs himself. When Fridolin sees him dangling from the tree, he runs in horror and undergoes a complete self-transformation: "Als [Fridolin] eine Stunde später da vorüberkam und [Jobst] erblickte, faßte ihn ein solches Entsetzen, daß er wie wahnsinnig davonrannte, *sein ganzes Wesen veränderte* und, wie man nachher hörte, ein liederlicher Mensch und alter Handwerksbursch wurde, der keines Menschen Freund war" (H 2:212, my emphasis).

Although the combmakers "lose themselves" to each other, the more typical Keller figure bases his objectification of those desires that represent part of himself on a literary fiction. We will see how Keller's estimation of this particular function of imagination rises with time, as he moves from a condemnation of impossible and impractical wishes in *Der grüne Heinrich* I—where both the complicity of the subject and the malefaction of the fiction are at issue—to a recognition of the heuristic properties of objectified desire in *Das Sinngedicht*, where Reinhart's "literary" quest results in a successful engagement with Lucie, his "weiße Galatea."

Keller's work is often, if not always, described in terms of the opposition of "Sein und Schein," *Schein* referring to a host of fictitious constructs that, like Feuerbach's God, tend to channel psychic, intellectual, and physical energy away from the social tasks to which it might otherwise be applied. Later work, though it does not waver on the importance of these social tasks, is considerably less damning of the fictions that interfere with them. Keller retains the Feuerbachian model, but alters his stance, abandoning the certainty of the polemicist-crusader for the relative open-mindedness of the curious investigator who sees no simple solutions and makes no recommendations. Whereas Feuerbach proceeds to restore to humanity all the assets that it has invested in the deity, Keller depicts a variety of encounters between mind and fiction and the confusion that arises (at whatever primitive level) when the desiring subject is confronted with a fiction that appears to fulfill those very real desires that "reality" frustrates.

Keller and Feuerbach are therefore very similar and very different. Both perceive a widespread alienation from social reality, and both describe this alienation in terms of individual enslavement to fictions, which function as a higher authority in matters of morals, behavior, and personal determination. Initially, Keller reacted to this perception in orthodox Feuerbachian fashion by trying to expose the offending fictions as imaginary constructs with no reliable connection to reality, apparently hoping that such a revelation would work to diminish the damaging effects of excessive imagining—a pedagogical project. However, as Keller promised Baumgartner, he was never to be a "Fanatiker," and in fact his period of discipleship was remarkably brief. After *Der grüne Heinrich* I, Keller took Feuerbach's model and developed it independently as a figural representation of imagination at work in the face of a "reality" that contradicts it. Feuerbach's Keller ceases to exist around 1855, but Keller's Feuerbach perseveres even as the would-be didactic author, whose text is the image of his (didactic) desire, confronts the knowledge that unmasking illusions cannot shake their foundations.

# 2. Pankraz, der Leser:
# Sulking and the Didactic Author

*And surely we should respect the realistic novelist's poignant effort to pro-*
*vide his society with some image of a viable and morally decent order, espe-*
*cially since the work of almost all the most interesting writers of fiction in*
*the nineteenth century amounts to a confession of their failure to find such*
*an order.*[1]

Nearly all of Keller's fiction issues from a single basic situation: an
ordinary person, seized by extraordinary ideals or aspirations, constructs an alternative world of the imagination and lives according to
its values until he is enlightened or eliminated by the "reality" he has
chosen to ignore. Indeed, Keller's novels and novellas are so single-
mindedly devoted to themes of illusion and error that the idea of a
"deluded" or "errant" Keller hero is somehow redundant. All of Keller's heroes err, sometimes spectacularly, and their blunders, crimes,
misapprehensions, misinterpretations, and hallucinations are generally ascribed to the excesses of overactive imaginations—which seek
to revise the world at hand that it might be more faithfully mimetic of
subjective desire.[2]
    This focus on error, as well as overt authorial criticism of "way-
ward" behavior and a corpus of letters, journals, and essays that
resound with unambiguous statements of didactic intention, have
earned Keller a considerable reputation for moral didacticism. Moral-
didactic writing is the most extreme or radical medium for the manufacture of order, inasmuch as the didactic author uses well-established literary conventions of poetic justice to reinforce a rigid hierar-
chy of moral choices, with the intention of persuading readers to
subscribe to this system. His created order (supposedly) reaches beyond the fiction that conveys it and, if successful, duplicates itself to
a certain degree in the reader's world: "daß [das Volk] durch das Bild
auch angeregt zur teilweisen Verwirklichung werde" (*GB* 3/2:196).
Keller is generally held to be guilty of such attempts at moral imperialism, and the image of the bespectacled pedagogue who sugars the
ethical pill with humor is still a presence (if not a focus) in the secondary literature.[3] It would be inadmissibly iconoclastic to argue that
Keller is in no way a didactic author, or, more specifically, that he

does not, on some level and at some times, attempt to influence the actions and moral attitudes of his readership by presenting transparent literary lessons in proper behavior. Such a generalization would, of course, be a misrepresentation of a large body of work that spans roughly forty years—but, as I will argue, a misreprentation of a lesser magnitude than the opposite contention: that Keller's writings are based on a naive faith in the power of his work to reform the citizenry. After *Der grüne Heinrich*, Keller gives strong indications in his fiction that life (inside and outside of literary fictions) is not the kind of orderly procedure that would justify moral didacticism as a viable enterprise.

With the death of Heinrich Lee, the process of imaginative desiring and of resistance to social norms abruptly ceases. The hero has paid for his mistake with his life, and though his problem has not actually been solved, it has been "contained" and made intelligible as *error*—something the reader must now avoid, though he need not address it. This is a properly didactic response to the inscrutable schism between the desired and the available, and, in many ways, the 1855 *Der grüne Heinrich* achieves the reduction of vast mysteries to a simple mandate: cleave unto the bastions of order that we know as empirical and social reality. "Pankraz, der Schmoller," which appeared in 1856 (though it was composed concurrently with the last installment of *Der grüne Heinrich*), is based on an entirely different proposition— namely, that no such reduction is possible.[4] Desire does not terminate with the conclusion of the tale: Pankraz neither dies nor marries, marriage being the other popular nineteenth-century alternative to desire insofar as it represents the "end" of a quest (for love or security) and the beginning of a noneventful period of social integration and living "happily ever after."[5] Somehow, married people (those who do not stray from their partners) have failed to capture and hold the fiction writer's imagination. With relatively few exceptions, marriage has been treated as a kind of determinacy that does not offer especially rich opportunities for intrigue or development—except as the "norm" that makes deviation possible. In any case, Pankraz does not enter this "normal" state. He does accomplish an external reform, metamorphosing into a good son, brother, and civil servant; but this reform, his external socialization, does not entail the resignation or abdication of desire. The "irresponsible imagination" that had impeded reform in his youth persists in spite of material contradiction. *Der grüne Heinrich* and "Pankraz" are Keller's first and second published works of fiction, respectively, and somewhere between the beginning of the first and the conclusion of the second the author shifted from a need to contain (and, perhaps, condemn) imaginative desire to a more open scrutiny of it.

"Pankraz" is nothing if not a close scrutiny of desire. Josef Kunz has remarked that of all Keller's figures, it is Pankraz, "die sich am gründlichsten . . . in das Rätsel . . . des Schönen eingelassen und zugleich am abgründigsten ihre Zweideutigkeit erfahren hat."[6] Indeed, Pankraz seems to have been created to stare directly into the abyss between the character of his desire and the actual nature of the mundane object selected for its fulfillment. Yet, the "knowledge" he brings back from his heroic journey is not of the pedagogically useful variety, recast and revised as it is by the same persistent desires that precipitated the "journey." In point of fact, Pankraz has learned nothing of what he sought—except that he knows nothing of it—and the reader can learn nothing from him—except, perhaps, that confusion is the most appropriate reaction to this situation. This chapter will address two problems of the narrative, both of which undermine its superficial didactic structures and render any "learning" impossible. The first is the conclusion, which smuggles in the continuation of desire (at the last minute), and the second concerns the role of reading and its actual effects on fictional readers and readers of fiction. "Pankraz, der Schmoller" constitutes the self-examination of the didactic author, who constructs his pedagogical edifice in order to topple it. The result is the realistic novelist's "confession of [his] failure to find such an order," and his acknowledgment of the futility of his attempts to exercise significant influence over his public.

In recent (and not so recent) years, a number of scholars have addressed the issue of a fundamental ambivalence in Keller's prose, a trend that runs counter to the practice of discussing him in terms of the value-laden thematic polarities already mentioned. The emphasis on ambivalence naturally works to diminish the image of the *Volkserzieher* who speaks from a position of moral certitude. The rejection of the polar model, whether implicit or explicit, partial or complete, is evident in many branches of the Keller literature and it has been adapted to diverse purposes.[7] Here the work of E. Allen McCormick and of John Ellis will provide the illustrations most relevant to the immediate concerns of this discussion. McCormick's 1962 article, "The Idylls in Keller's *Romeo und Julia*: A Study in Ambivalence," remained for many years unique in "Romeo und Julia" scholarship, which consists, for the most part, of polarizing readings and accounts of the inexorable fate or sins of the fathers that claimed Sali and Vrenchen as innocent victims. McCormick examines the children's three idylls and identifies the "tragic" elements that are interwoven into these episodes of happiness and harmony. He demonstrates the "double value" of Sali's and Vrenchen's idyllic interludes, the "ambivalence rather than polarity of idylls and tragedy,"[8] a double valence that relativizes simple antagonisms (society vs. the lovers, corrupt parents vs. innocent children) and ultimately implicates Sali and Vrenchen in their own destruction. Their responsibility lies in their "inability to reject their idylls,"[9] but this refusal to exit a state of false (imaginary) harmony or wish fulfillment and enter the decidedly nonidyllic "real" world occurs in an atmosphere of authorial ambivalence, which undermines any moral message that might be deduced from their plight.

McCormick did not intend his observations on "Romeo und Julia" as a challenge to the notion of Keller's didacticism in general. On the contrary, he sees the ambivalence of "Romeo und Julia" as an isolated instance, which he describes as "a startling departure from Keller's moralizing, sometimes pedantic optimism."[10] Scholars writing after McCormick, however, have found a similar ambivalence in the more typically Kellerian narratives, those that feature a more apparently decidable plot structure—which transports a figure from error to perception to enlightenment or directly from error to punishment—as well as a judgmental narrator who appears to decide matters for us. The conclusion of "Kleider machen Leute," for example, has often been cited as an instance of ambivalence, an ironic refusal to lead the reader by the nose.[11] Wenzel Strapinski does indeed abandon his misguided masquerade as the romantic Polish count, but he reverts to a "real" self that is hardly attractive, though this impression does not take form until the very last line of the novella: "Aber in Seldwyla ließ er nicht einen Stüber zurück, sei es aus Undank oder aus Rache" (H 2:296). The reader may be uncomfortable with Wenzel's new dullness ("Dabei wurde er rund und stattlich und sah beinah gar nicht mehr so träumerisch aus" [H 2:296]) or suspicious of his "Spekulationen" (often indicative of economic incontinence in Keller), but this final attribution of "Undank oder . . . Rache" relativizes the new, "improved" Wenzel—who is now cured of his desire, "etwas Zierliches und Außergewöhnliches vorzustellen" (H 2:273). Reform, the removal of desire, is not necessarily improvement in this case, and suddenly the process of error-perception-enlightenment, which is completed in Wenzel's marriage, has lost its didactic justification.

Ellis identifies this same ambivalence in "Die drei gerechten Kammacher" as a function of the incompatibility between the narrator's moralistic summarizing of superficial themes and the actual tale that is told.[12] The narrator's opening remarks, that "die drei Kammacher [bewiesen], daß nicht drei Gerechte lang unter einem Dach leben können, ohne sich in die Haare zu geraten," suggest a light-hearted treatment of false or rigid (self-)righteousness. Yet Ellis perceives these remarks as an announcement of the superficial framework within which the narrator will work, a framework that does not reflect "the basic concerns of the story": "For the actual story the narrator then goes on to tell leaves this initial characterization of it far behind."[13] The "actual story" is a serious, even sinister, study of "the way people necessarily live by their aims and of the disasters which befall them in their achieving and in their failing to achieve these arbitrary goals which are their guiding stars."[14]

This is a very important observation because, as Ellis shows, the incompatibility between the narrator's professed aims and the story he tells translates into the simultaneity of a moral judgment (on self-righteousness) and its undoing. It is as if Keller, while writing the novella, repossesses his (or the narrator's) moral and leaves the reader with the "message" that things are not as simple or as orderly as a self-confident didactic narrative would have them—after availing himself of the ordering properties inherent in such a narrative. Order is at issue here, both structurally and thematically, and the didactic framework, which presupposes the symmetry of a generally agreed-upon system of virtue and vice, is often a convenient device for conjuring this ideal of order, which is then called into question.

The conclusion of "Pankraz" is not unlike that of "Kleider," insofar as it represents a last-minute reversal of the apparent didactic movement of the novella. Pankraz, whose sulking is symptomatic of an unwillingness to accept and affirm the random disorder that characterizes material reality, finds this chaos personified in the lovely Lydia, whose external beauty is not complemented by a corresponding beauty of soul. Her cruel rejection of his love—which she herself had solicited—shows the futility of his unrealistic desire for an orderly and comprehensible world (where beautiful women are also good, and where their demonstrations of affection infallibly indicate sincere interest). Lydia's name becomes the token of Pankraz's *Schmollgeist*, his penchant for retreating from an imperfect world and fashioning a compensatory perfection in his imagination. Her rejection and a twelve-hour standoff with a man-eating lion combine to effect his "cure." Pankraz, we are told, ceases to exhibit the gruff, antipathetic behavior that had been indicative of his sulking, and the implication is that he has also ceased to desire (his imaginary Lydia)—though it emerges that the absence of external manifestations does not necessarily portend the end of his sulking. As the story closes,

Pankraz refuses to recall Lydia's name before his mother and sister, who have forgotten it: "Hättet ihr aufgemerkt! Ich nenne diesen Namen nicht mehr!" (H 2:60). The tale then closes with the narrator's teasingly ambivalent summary: "Und er hielt Wort; niemand hörte ihn jemals wieder das Wort aussprechen, und er schien es endlich selbst vergessen zu haben" (H 2:60).

The narrator, whose account of Pankraz throughout is based on observable behavior (some of which he interprets for us), closes with a summary of *appearances*: Pankraz appears to have forgotten Lydia's name and the desire associated with it. Considering the implications of the verb, *scheinen*, as well as the duplicity of Lydia's "appearance," the account of Pankraz's apparent forgetfulness demands to be doubted. Whereas Keller neutralizes Wenzel's conversion (to the good and the true), he denies Pankraz's by so obviously and deliberately refusing to confirm it. Lilian Hoverland also remarks on the odd character of the narrator's report of the ostensible cessation of desire: "In dem die novella abschliessenden satz fällt weiterhin die wiederholung von *Wort* auf. *Wort* statt name im zweiten fall stellt einen etwas ungewöhnlichen gebrauch dar; wenn überdies die beiden verwendungen von *Wort* gleichgesetzt werden, so kann im ersten fall *Wort halten* als 'den namen halten und behalten' verstanden werden. Lydias name und der an ihn geknüpfte traum sind offenbar nicht vergessen."[15]

Unlike John Kabys, "Der Schmied seines Glückes," who abandons his dreams of "forging" his own fortune (in both senses of the word) while learning to forge better nails as a "Nagelschmied," Pankraz does not discharge his desire into some object or activity, but retains it within—just as he has always done. He is still in this sense a sulker because he tenaciously adheres to the word "Lydia," preserving her within, and the "apparent" cure is cast in doubt by virtue of its own "apparentness." Nothing being what it seems for Pankraz, how can the reader accept this account of the "semblance" of a cure? The established suspicion of appearances militates against the apparent end of desire.

A recent study of the German novel presents the following picture of "realism": "Realism insists on the primacy of a unified harmony, where accidents and exceptions are absent and appearance and essence converge (good people look good and the evil are recognizably evil); and realism intends to teach the reader to perceive these laws and to read the world correctly."[16] According to this definition, Pankraz is a "realist" insofar as he does seek harmony by insisting on the coincidence of appearance and essence. However, Keller confronts his hero with Lydia, the ultimate contradiction of this position, and refuses to solve the riddle. Either Keller is not a realist, or such definitions as the one above are too narrow to comprehend the actual *practice* of nineteenth-century German literary realism (the passage quoted is, however, a fair description of nineteenth-century German realist *theory*). Gerhard Plumpe argues compellingly for the "reality" of the imaginary in "Pankraz," demonstrating that certain categories of imaginative fantasy are inescapable and therefore undeniably "real." But he stops short of attributing such thoughts to a *consciously* composing Keller: "Der verdrängte Wunsch ist Motor eines Sprechens, das die Absicht seines Autors durchkreuzt. Insofern artikuliert die Erzählung einen Materialismus des Imaginären, den zu denken Keller verboten war."[17] It seems more likely to me that Keller and the other so-called realists were indeed capable of such conscious thoughts. "Pankraz, der Schmoller" is something of a *Stilbruch* for the author of *Der grüne Heinrich*, who may be describing his own struggle with the limits of art and artificial harmony.

The autobiographical character of "Pankraz" is only slightly less obvious than that of *Der grüne Heinrich*. Once again, the family configuration resembles Keller's own: Pankraz loses his father in early youth, he is raised by an indulgent mother whose kindness he abuses, and he (unlike Heinrich) has a sister, corresponding to Keller's actual sister, Regula.[18] Neither the real nor the fictional sister ever marries. (Regula was already thirty-four when the novella appeared.) Also, Pankraz's rejection by Lydia bears the marks of Keller's disappointed love for Betty Tendering.[19] At this early point in his career, Keller shows a very strong identification with his heroes. He is, if not writing about himself, writing about people very much like him, and it is therefore not surprising that the writer/organizer of the "Pankraz" novella shares his hero's love of order. The basic didactic structure and movement of "Pankraz" imply an authorial *wish* to impose order on experience by presenting it within well-established literary conventions that convey a neat and reassuring teleology. But, just as Pankraz's wishes or desires prove to be misconstructions of a given reality, the author fails to commit himself to the "orderly" solution suggested by his didactic (mis)construction. Furthermore, this particular novella is not so much concerned with orderly moral instruction as with the very possibility of this instruction.

Keller was fond of doubling and tripling his figures and similarly there are many Kellers (as well as sub-Kellers), and it seems that all of them were interested in mixing instruction with delight. On several occasions, Keller expressed the wish (preformulated by F. T. Vischer) "das Didaktische im Poetischen aufzulösen, wie Zucker oder Salz im Wasser."[20] This is a statement, like so many others in the correspondence, of what Keller wished to do, and I would like to stress its status as wish/intention (analogous to imaginative desire) rather than accomplished fact. That Keller *wanted* (or would have liked) to present effective moral examples to his readers is all but certain. Whether he actually believed that he could (or even should) do so is another matter entirely. Moral-didactic writing must be founded on didactic intention (of which Keller may have had plenty) *and* on faith in the (ethical and logistical) feasibility of such a project—in other words, the writer must display his confidence that didactic literature can indeed achieve its end, by reorienting the readership toward the good, the useful, and the true. The example of Pankraz, the reader, illustrates that in 1856 Keller had already lost this faith, that his didacticism was itself ironic and in no way a conscious attempt to influence the behavior of errant readers.

Whereas literature directly influences life to its detriment in the first version of *Der grüne Heinrich*, this influence is impossible to establish in "Pankraz." The transparency of the "Leserfamilie" episode in *Heinrich* (to take the most obvious example), the unreflected or nonironic nature of the message as presented, does not take cognizance of the fact that this is a literary fiction teaching the folly of orienting oneself according to literary fictions, and is therefore a questionable (though not unconventional) medium for that message. The paradox that Lenz evokes in *Die Soldaten* is, however, relevant to "Pankraz," where reading occupies a more central position in a more concentrated framework and where certain deviations from standard renditions of the topos "literature influences life," or "life imitates art," suggest the author's ironic attitude toward it.

In "Pankraz," Keller presents the spectacle of fictional reading in the spirit of Japp's refracted mirror image, that is, as a critique of the notion of the book as undistorted "mirror" of reality. If Heinrich I's books are not accurate mirrors of his world, the book he inhabits is at least presented as such. Whatever its actual effect, behind the 1855 *Der grüne Heinrich* is a more or less naive faith in literature's ability to reflect the world with minimal distortion and therefore to bear pragmatic relevance to the affairs of this world. In condemning Heinrich's faith in fictions within a literary context so that others outside the novel might not make the same mistake, Keller depends on the same questionable equation between literature and life that ruined his hero. Those who read the book are encouraged to act upon its lessons: "Die Moral meines Buches ist: daß derjenige, dem es nicht gelingt, die Verhältnisse seiner Person und seiner Familie im Gleichgewicht zu erhalten, auch unbefähigt sei, im staatlichen Leben eine wirksame und ehrenvolle Stellung einzunehmen."[21] In order to assume one's proper place in society, one must not lose oneself in false (fictional) representations of this society and its alternatives. A book confidently tells its reader to be skeptical of (other) books.

Though the contradiction may have escaped Keller in *Der grüne Heinrich* (or at a certain point during its composition), it emerges as the subject of "Pankraz," where Keller's charges of faith in literature are not leveled against the hero, who really does not confuse literature with life in the final analysis. Rather, criticism is directed against the reader who would look to books for guidelines and plausible simplifications of experience, and against the author (of *Der grüne Heinrich* and of the orderly, superficial framework of "Pankraz") who would subscribe to and (so deviously) promote the notion of the book as mirror for the sake of reforming reader attitudes and behavior—thus imposing his will to order on the world as defined by his readership.

The mysterious Shakespeare episode at the center of the novella, where Pankraz reads the complete plays of Shakespeare in the midst of his fascination with Lydia, constitutes an awkward and deliberate interruption of the pedagogical process, and it raises serious questions about Pankraz's actual susceptibility to literature. From the very beginning, Pankraz appears as a likely candidate for seduction by literature. He rejects his mundane environment, longs for a more beautiful and orderly world, and retreats from family and society. He is not a typical Seldwylan, nor does Keller write of the typical in his collection: "Doch nicht solche Geschichten, wie sie in dem beschriebenen Charakter von Seldwyla liegen, will ich eigentlich in diesem Büchlein erzählen, sondern einige sonderbare Abfällsel, die so zwischendurch passierten, gewissermaßen ausnahmsweise, und doch auch gerade nur zu Seldwyla vor sich gehen konnten" (H 2:12).

Pankraz is distinguished from the common herd not only by his uncommonly well developed aptitude for sulking, but also by his inclination toward reading. The Seldwylans do not read—a rather startling revelation that comes in two installments, as background detail in "Pankraz" and in "Die drei gerechten Kammacher." First, in "Pankraz," we encounter a bookbinder, whose sole narrative function is that of crying "Zur Gesundheit!" (H 2:18) in response to a cobbler's thunderous sneeze. Although "Buchbinder" is a thoroughly adequate description of such a minor figure, Keller, by way of giving local color, elaborates: "[Der] Buchbinder gegenüber, *der eigentlich kein Buchbinder war*, sondern nur so aus dem Stegreif allerhand Pappkästchen zusammenleimte und an der Türe ein verwittertes Glaskästchen hängen hatte, in welchem eine Stange Siegellack an der Sonne krumm wurde, dieser Buchbinder rief: Zur Gesundheit!" (H 2:18, my emphasis). Why is the bookbinder not a bookbinder? The matter is not pursued in "Pankraz." But a definite answer is provided later in "Kammacher," where the state of the profession is reviewed in the portrait of the "Buchbindergeselle," who had loved Züs Bünzlin: ". . . arm wie eine Maus und ungeschickt zum Erwerb, der für einen Buchbinder in Seldwyla ohnehin nicht erheblich war, *weil die Leute da nicht lasen* und wenig Bücher binden ließen" (H 2:187, my emphasis). Keller's consistency in preserving this detail from novella to novella (there is otherwise little communication between the tales in this first volume) implies that the communal neglect of literature and the consequent inexperience in the art of contemplating formal fictions form a part of his overall conception of Seldwyla. As a reader, Pankraz is an exception to the rule, but his response to literature may be grounded in this rule, just as the stories of the *Abfällsel* could occur only against the background of Seldwyla. Thus a certain lack of readerly sophistication is to be expected, though it is by no means certain what form this will take.

There are two reports of Pankraz's reading that precede the encounter with Shakespeare. His earliest reading is associated with inaction, but he effectively puts the knowledge gained into action when the time comes. At fourteen, the hero is "ein unansehnlicher Knabe . . . welcher des Morgens lang im Bette lag, dann ein wenig in einem zerrissenen Geschichts- und Geographiebuche las" (H 2:14), who prefers the inert perusal of this single book to the more productive labor that occupies his mother and sister. His geography book proves to be an adequate mirror of topographical reality when a walk through Germany shows the land to be just as it was described in the book: "Da ich nun durch das allmähliche Auswendiglernen unsres Geographiebuches, so einfach dieses war, auch auf dem Erdboden Bescheid wußte, so verstand ich meine Richtung wohl zu nehmen . . ." (H 2:26). Thus far, the equation between book and world is perfectly valid.

As a soldier in the British colonial army in India, Pankraz devotes his free time to the (in)activity of reading his commander's books. He does not, however, regard these unnamed books as unmediated reflections of reality, though he does consider the possibility:

Diese Zeit benutzte ich dazu, das Dutzend Bücher, so der alte Herr besaß, immer wieder durchzulesen und aus denselben, da sie alle dickleibig waren, ein sonderbares Stück von der Welt kennen zu lernen. Ich war so ein eifriger und stiller Leser, der sich eine Weisheit ausbildete, von der er nicht recht wußte, ob sie in der Welt galt oder nicht galt, *wie ich bald erfahren sollte*; denn obschon ich bereits vieles gesehen und erfahren, so war dies doch nur gewissermaßen strichweise, und das meiste, was es gab, lag zur Seite des Striches, den ich passiert.

(H 2:31, my emphasis)

Pankraz's account of his reading is highly ambiguous with regard to his attitude toward the "mirroring" capacity of his books in this case. The imminent "discovery" to which he refers is the knowledge of the world that he supposedly gains from his dealings with Lydia, and he says that neither his books nor life experience had prepared him for it. Pankraz, as hero of his own tale, is soon to learn whether or not the "wisdom" he has derived from his books has any validity in the world, but he has as yet made no firm assumptions. All he says is that he did not know whether or not this wisdom was applicable to life—an attitude that indicates that he was, perhaps, open to the possibility, but was by no means convinced of it. Thus Keller broaches the subject of influence by literature in connection with the Lydia incident, raising expectations that Pankraz may indeed proceed with her according to his understanding of literature, but a close examination of the passage above yields no real foundation for such expectations. It is unclear at this point (though not conspicuously so) just how Pankraz sees the relationship between the world within the book and the world outside it. There is no indication that he reads the commander's books (whatever they are) in the same way he read his geography book, but the question of a practical connection between the "insides" and the "outsides" of these books seems to occupy his mind.

As Pankraz continues, he remarks that his reading of Shakespeare removed any doubts he might have had about the possible correspondence between fictional and real life, and he is quite emphatic on this point. When relating the particulars of his encounter with Shakespeare, Pankraz, like Heinrich Lee before him, tells us exactly what he read, how it influenced his thoughts and actions, and what the sad result of these actions was. He explicitly states that he read the plays of Shakespeare and then expected the world to exhibit the "wholeness," order, and coherence that so delighted him in these fictions. Shakespeare, he says, caused him to assume an honest and selfless motive behind Lydia's attentions to him; that is, he took her to possess the noble soul that would, in a wholly orderly manner, correspond to her flawless exterior beauty. This assumption, he continues, led him into her "trap," causing him to confess his love and suffer her scorn. Cursing Shakespeare, he remarks: "Dieser verführerische, falsche Prophet führte mich schön in die Patsche. Er schildert nämlich die Welt nach allen Seiten hin durchaus einzig und wahr wie sie ist, aber nur wie sie es in den ganzen Menschen ist, welche im Guten und im Schlechten das Metier ihres Daseins und ihrer Neigungen vollständig und charakteristisch betreiben . . ." (H 2:40). Pankraz has obviously read Shakespeare selectively, or else he has failed to appreciate the role played by hindsight in his assessment of these characters. But, according to this account, the vividly realistic character portrayals in Shakespeare's plays persuaded him that these dramas were a reliable guide to human nature, one that he could safely act upon:

> Ich aber las die ganze Nacht in diesem Buche und verfing mich ganz in demselben, da es mir gar so gründlich und sachgemäß geschrieben schien und mir außerdem eine solche Arbeit ebenso neu als verdienstlich vorkam. Weil nun alles übrige so trefflich, wahr und ganz erschien *und ich es für die eigentliche und richtige Welt hielt*, so verließ ich mich insbesondere auch bei den Weibern, die es vorbrachte, ganz auf ihn, verlockt und geleitet von dem schönen Sterne Lydia, und ich glaubte, hier ginge mir ein Licht auf und sei die Lösung meiner zweifelvollen Verwirrung und Qual zu finden.          (H 2:41, my emphasis)

This is a direct confession of "literary influence," and Pankraz's two-page discourse on Shakespeare works toward establishing his reading as the motivating factor in his confession of love to Lydia, whom he claims to have assumed to be thoroughly beautiful, inside and out. Oddly enough, this assertion of literature's influence on life is not borne out by the events of the tale as narrated by Pankraz. If we test his contention against his narration, we find that Shakespeare is neither the source of his illusion nor the incentive for its reality testing.

The frame narrator who introduces and concludes the novella makes it clear that even as a child Pankraz sustained an inner ideal of order and justice. Pankraz scrupulously abstains from exposing his ideal to the dangers posed by his (disorderly and unjust) surroundings; the only external sign he gives is his characteristic sulking, a kind of implosive withdrawal from events that contradict his personal code. After an uneventful and unsatisfactory childhood, he comes home one evening to find that his sister has eaten his dinner. When she refuses to show contrition (quite the contrary), the offense takes on the proportions of an intolerable injustice and Pankraz slips away without informing his mother or sister, who do not see him again for fifteen years.

When he returns to his family he is a responsible, capable, and somewhat prosperous adult, bearing little resemblance to the lazy, despicable child who ran away from them. Obviously, some explanation is needed, and Pankraz begins to give the women a general account of his travels and reform. He proposes a carefully structured tale, geared toward the transmission of surface phenomena and specifically designed to achieve closure in a matter that (we suspect) defies such symmetry: "Für heute will ich aber nur einige Umrisse angeben, soviel als nötig ist, um auf den Schluß zu kommen, nämlich auf meine Wiederkehr und die Art, wie diese veranlaßt wurde, da sie eigentlich das rechte Seitenstück bildet zu meiner ehemaligen Flucht und aus dem gleichen Grundtone geht" (H 2:24–25). The flight of the sulker and the "hero's" return constitute the beginning and end of a tale whose middle Pankraz intends to withhold; in his words, they are "Seitenstücke," and their match or balance is assured by the omission of the intervening material. Naturally, his recollections, organized for and conditioned by a particular audience, are not a specimen of pure nonfiction (within fiction). Just like any retrospective account of significant personal history, this narrative is colored by the subjectivity of the narrator.[22]

Pankraz's modest proposal, as outlined above, resembles nothing so much as the moral-didactic story his author *would like* to tell. Its ingredients are error, reform, and only those elements that are absolutely necessary ("soviel als nötig ist") to bridge the gap between them. Such a tale does not become mired in reflection, nor does it address the unalterably enigmatic disproportion between imaginable harmony and available chaos. Indeed it actively represses these elements, which could undermine the certainty of purpose necessary to the moral-didactic mode.

Yet neither Pankraz nor Keller succeeds in telling this tidy tale. With the first mention of Lydia, whose name embodies impenetrable mysteries, Pankraz's audience falls asleep—a development that he fails to notice—and the hero lapses into a long, confused narration of his shattering experience of love. Keller has gone to great lengths to call attention to this part of Pankraz's tale,[23] and the "missing" narrative, which will be missed by its sleeping audience, appears—thus highlighted—as a missive to Keller's audience, which is presumably now wide awake. As if the threat of withholding were not enough to focus attention on that which was nearly withheld, Keller's frame narrator announces: "Zum Glück für *unsere* Neugierde bemerkte [Pankraz] dies [mother and sister falling asleep] nicht, hatte überhaupt vergessen, vor wem er erzählte, und fuhr, ohne die niedergeschlagenen Augen zu erheben, fort, vor den schlafenden Frauen zu erzählen, wie einer, der etwas lange Verschwiegenes endlich mitzuteilen sich nicht mehr enthalten kann" (H 2:33, my emphasis). What follows is a lengthy, detailed, and somewhat tedious account of Pankraz's spiritual struggle: the attempt to comprehend the noncorrespondence of his personal ideal of order to the "objective correlative" he has chosen for it—an account that fails to corroborate his claims for his reading.

When Pankraz meets Lydia, an extended tactical struggle ensues. Stimulated by her beauty and charm, he creates a mental image of womanly perfection that he correlates with her physical appearance, having now found a vessel in the external world worthy of containing his subjective ideal.[24] But he carefully guards this ideal against the woman herself and avoids encounters. Stimulated by Pankraz's apparent indifference, Lydia seeks to gratify her vanity and sense of sportsmanship by making yet another conquest, to which end she must extract some statement of admiration from the taciturn man who resists her. Lydia thrusts, and Pankraz parries. She follows him and lingers in his presence; he redoubles his efforts to avoid her. She assaults him with charm and flattery; he rallies his sulking skills and feigns a lack of interest. She changes tactics and appears pale, hurt, and distressed; through mighty effort, he succeeds in registering no reaction. She gives him the works of Shakespeare; he reads them and continues to avoid her. Ultimately, she confronts him with tears and recriminations.

It is *this* gesture that effects his capitulation. Pankraz's experience of Shakespeare, as he tells it in the story, has not in itself brought him any closer to the breaking point—it has merely allowed him to continue on the course he had already been pursuing for some time. Immediately after describing his reading of Shakespeare, he notes: "So ging ich wohl ein halbes Jahr lang herum wie ein Nachtwandler . . . alles ohne mit Lydia um einen Schritt weiter zu kommen" (H 2:42). At the end of six months, he decides to leave, feeling that his sanity is endangered, and it is this decision that forces Lydia's hand, causing her to produce tears and prevail.

The fact that Pankraz makes an issue of his reading of Shakespeare and then fails to substantiate his claims of Shakespeare's influence points to what I consider a deliberate inconsistency in Keller's text. Pankraz, while narrating his adventures with Lydia, suddenly digresses on British drama, blames his reading for his conduct, and then picks up his narration and demonstrates that it was slick maneuvering on Lydia's part and not his reading of Shakespeare that caused him to lose the struggle by confessing his love. Had he been convinced by Shakespeare that the appearance of love is identical to love itself, he would not have hesitated to declare his own. Instead, he maintained a resistance, which threatened to drive him mad, for an additional six months.

By introducing the topos "literature influences life" so plainly and allowing the rest of Pankraz's tale to contradict it, Keller subverts the didactic thrust of a traditional instructive device—which he himself had used in the recently completed *Der grüne Heinrich*—and goes so far as to question literature's ability to influence life at all. The corollary assumptions for a didactic author are all too obvious. Whereas Shakespeare allegedly led Pankraz into a trap, Keller has set one for any reader who would claim to have learned that literary fictions pose a danger to his volition. Keller has, in effect, made a Pankraz out of the reader who feels that he has been instructed (that literary fictions are not to be trusted), since, like his hero, the instructed reader would assume that literature has had a determining effect on his outlook or behavior—an effect that can hardly be attributed to the text in question (where this influence is spurious).

There is also a certain amount of authorial self-irony involved. Keller, who in *Der grüne Heinrich* wrote of the power of literature to bring about lives of promiscuity and crime and tried to avail himself of that power on behalf of goodness, qualifies his sermon in "Pankraz, der Schmoller" by exposing his hero's perception of this power as an illusion. I believe that Keller deliberately inserted the Shakespeare episode into "Pankraz, der Schmoller" in order to raise these issues and to reflect on and moderate his position as educator and author of literary fictions. There is no other explanation for the otherwise gratuitous presence of Pankraz's discourse on Shakespeare. It is entirely superfluous to the requirements of plot and action: there are four additional significant moments in the Pankraz-Lydia exchange, and the intrusion of Shakespeare only serves to prolong the (already prolonged) tactical struggle. Furthermore, except for a chance remark during Pankraz's account of his later life in India, there are no references to it and no echoes of it in this rather lengthy novella. Indeed, the entire two-page discussion of Shakespeare can be neatly excised from the surrounding text without disturbing the flow of narration or requiring that a single word be changed![25]

Shakespeare's presence in Pankraz's tale is an obvious intrusion into an otherwise coherent text, and it shows a lack of primary relevance and integration that Keller could not reasonably have overlooked. The didactic structure of Keller's tale, which is endangered by the plunge into reflection on Pankraz's change of heart, is destroyed by this deliberate subterfuge—an appended episode that reflects on and casts into doubt the very processes the reader of a didactic tale would ideally be engaged in.

The exemplary tale created by the right hand is undone by the left. The disruption (like the ending) foils what might have been a simple lesson, where reality-consciousness is put forward as being morally superior to dreaming and desiring. It makes Pankraz unreliable—not only as Shakespearean hermeneut, but as interpreter of his own actions and motivations—and hence shifts our attention from his relation of events to his palpable confusion about the possible meaning of these events. The spontaneous, naive account of Pankraz's transformation from a solipsistic sulker to a devoted son and civil servant is thus recast in the form of a bewildered man's (bungling) attempt to order experience by revising it. Pankraz's attempt to "author" an orderly version of his life succeeds insofar as his audience sleeps through all but "einige Umrisse" (which do make uncomplicated sense), but it fails as an explanation to himself (the only internal audience for his Lydia story), within Keller's deliberate failure to execute a didactic novella.

"Pankraz, der Schmoller" is a story about confusion rather than reform—which Pankraz feels occurred during his standoff with the lion[26]—and though the poles of this confusion may indeed be something like "Sein und Schein" (I would incline toward "Schein und Schein"), it is not a matter of making the correct choice between them. Had a choice been possible, as in the tidy tale of reform that is never told, Pankraz would not now be confused. By disrupting and undermining Pankraz's superficial tale of error-(perception)-reform, Keller does not indulge in a romantic reversal of the "Sein-Schein" opposition, exalting imaginative fancy over mundane reality. Rather, he takes an ambivalent position and—at least here—denies the possibility of choosing sides. This is neither a true reform nor tenacious adherence to a dream—though this dream persists—but rather the (paradoxically) well-defined confusion of a sensibility (be it Keller's or Pankraz's) that thinks in these terms but can neither unite nor distinctly separate the two in practice.

Thus the nonlesson of "Pankraz" is not merely a self-conscious presentation of a convoluted version of the lesson of *Der grüne Heinrich*:—that literary fictions, whatever they seem to be, are not accurate mirrors of empirical reality—it is also a significant admission on the part of the author that readers are not necessarily subject to direct and calculated pedagogical influence. While Keller does not overtly abjure didacticism, he realistically considers the treacherous synapse between an author's text and an author's text's reader, as well as the fact that the utterly garbled impulse that may succeed in crossing this abyss may have no discernible (or calculable) effect on attitudes and actions. The effect of Pankraz's reading of Shakespeare is merely an illusion (or fabrication) of the reader, who in this case is interested in justifying his ideal of order by assigning blame to Shakespeare and not to his own conception of the world. In "Pankraz," Keller escapes the paradox of a literary fiction that teaches that one should not behave according to the teachings of literary fictions, precisely because he is conscious of it. The perception of this double bind involves the broader perception that the writer, while he may promote certain superficial standards of propriety and good taste by observing them, cannot envision a specific moral improvement for his audience and effectively implement it through literature.

However, it is not only the practical futility of "utility" that Keller acknowledges here, but also the self-interest behind such utility. Pankraz, whose very active contemplative life fulfills the desires that the external world frustrates, is an impotent, but megalomaniacal, sulker and a conspicuous analogue to the didactic writer. Unable to make the world, or Lydia (the distinction is immaterial), submit to his desires, he is forced to internalize his "Schmollen"—that is, his will to an orderly world that will reflect and fulfill his desires—and to behave as a proper citizen with private recourse to the dream preserved. His last act with regard to Lydia is his narrative, an attempt to organize his confusion and to "rewrite" the past as intelligible error— namely, seduction by literature. This project closely resembles that of the 1855 *Der grüne Heinrich*, where Keller ordered and fictionalized his own past and attributed his hero's failures to an early inability and later unwillingness to distinguish between fiction/fantasy and life. The act of narrating in both cases serves as a means of reprocessing experience and endowing it with meaning according to literary conventions, thereby identifying the problem, solving it, and creating a past "as it should be." Both Keller (the writer) and Pankraz (the storyteller) are sulkers who retreat from the scene of action that they might impose order on it.

That Keller regarded writing as a kind of "Schmollen" is clear from an 1843 diary entry where he designates his personal journal as his "Schmollwinkel":

> Aber nicht bloß in Tagen der Mutlosigkeit—nein! Auch in Tagen der festlichen, rauschenden Freude will ich stille Momente verweilen und ausruhen *im traulichen Schmollwinkel meines Tagebuches*. Ich will die schönsten Blüten erlebter Freude hineinlegen, wie die Kinder Rosen- und Tulpenblätter in ihre Gebetbücher legen; und wie sie sich dann in späteren Jahren wehmütig erfreuen, wann ihnen so ein verblichenes Blumenblatt in einem alten Buche zufällig wieder in die Hände fällt: so will ich mich in meinen letzten Erdentagen erfreuen an den Bildern entschwundener Freuden.          (H 3:852, my emphasis)

He adds: "Wann dann zwischen dreihundertfünfundsechzig Regentagen des Leidens nur *ein* Sonnentag der heiteren Freude und des Mutes hervorlacht, so will ich alle jene Regentage vergessen und mein dankbares Auge nur auf diesen sonnigen Freudentag heften . . ." (H 3:852, Keller's emphasis). The diary was to be the repository of selected images from life, images ordered, transformed, and recorded in writing. It was conceived as a retreat, where the writer could go to "sulk," that is, to make the literary effort to banish the unpleasant "Regentage" and collect those images of fulfillment that would one day appeal to the desiring imagination—no longer able to experience the particular "Freuden" on which they are based.

Keller's keeping of the diary, as described in 1843, is essentially the same act as Pankraz's retention of the name Lydia: both consign their prettified and unified images of beauty to private storage, from which they will be recalled from time to time for solitary contemplation. Writing, like sulking, serves to isolate, enclose, and protect the imaginary harmony that is threatened by material contradiction. The respective narratives of Pankraz and Keller ("Pankraz") tell the "poignant" story of an abortive attempt to unify disparate elements of an imaginary plenitude. Whereas Pankraz tries to unite both "halves" (roughly, body and soul, or appearance and essence) of a potentially perfect, if imaginary, woman, Keller, in his (aborted) didactic framework, attempts to join or align book and world for the sake of realization (*Verwirklichung*) of the former within the latter.

In "Pankraz," however, Keller also creates a scenario for the defeat of his own desires for order and control. Yet, just as Pankraz's image of Lydia survives its defeat and endures as abstract wish, so do the author's desires find expression in his subsequent work, in the (pseudo)didactic form of his tales. The shape of Keller's fiction never changes: each hero proceeds from transgression to punishment, or from error to perception of error to enlightenment. In a very few cases the moral "message" is not mitigated by irony; however, in the majority of cases, this morally logical universe is constructed not for the sake of the reader's improvement, but as the representation of a wish, similar to Pankraz's, for order and coherence. It is a quixotic project.

# 3. "Romeo und Julia auf dem Dorfe": The Romance of Realism?

Given that this study follows a more or less chronological path, I should remark that it is not known whether "Romeo und Julia" was composed before, after, or during the work on "Pankraz." The exact sequence of composition for the first volume of Seldwyla stories cannot be divined, and it is doubtful that Keller did compose them one by one in any particular or deliberate order. According to the correspondence, he worked on the five novellas from 3 April to 6 October 1855, though bits and pieces of various stories had been deposited in journals and notebooks during—and in some cases previous to—the early 1850s.[1] Apparently the Seldwyla novellas and the projected "Galatea" novellas (which were not completed until 1880) provided Keller with a productive diversion from the grim task of writing the long overdue conclusion to *Der grüne Heinrich*. He had promised his rather patient publisher, the much maligned Eduard Vieweg, that he would give his undivided attention to *Heinrich* and postpone all other projects until the novel was completed.[2] Acting on Keller's original assurances of quick delivery, Vieweg had already printed, bound, and distributed the early volumes of the novel. The postponement of the conclusion was, Vieweg argued, hurting the book's sales, because lending libraries were not buying installments but awaiting the finished product—with diminishing interest. Mindful of this partial *Schreibverbot*, Keller claimed that his work on the Seldwyla collection during this period was purely mental planning (*aushecken*)—but these plans must have reached a rather advanced stage, because he told Vieweg on 2 April 1855 that he would begin writing on the next day and finish by 1 May.[3] Keller's projections in such matters were always optimistic (he also expected to finish his "Galatea" novellas the following month), but it is more than likely that large sections of *Seldwyla* I already existed either on paper or in his mind.

Thus the first Seldwyla stories are, for all we know, virtually simultaneous and do not in any way form a five-step progression in Keller's gradual ascension to a mature tolerance of chaos and uncertainty. Nevertheless, there is much to suggest that the work on "Romeo und Julia" may have spanned a greater period of Keller's career than the other projects—both in the records pertaining to the theme, and in the various attitudes toward the interaction of life and literature that emerge in the text itself. With regard to Keller's concern with the excesses of imagination and the demands of social reality, "Romeo und Julia" is an intellectual hybrid: it argues both for and against the notion that human actions are determined by literary fictions, and it registers both approval and disapproval of the protagonists' surrender to fantasy. This equivocation is a consequence of the theme itself—raising the question of whether there can be such a thing as a *village* Romeo and Juliet—and of the collision of earlier and later authorial attitudes, resulting from an extended period of planning and composition.

Though "Romeo und Julia" was written during the same brief period as "Pankraz," its "hatching" began back in 1847, when Keller read an account of the double suicide of two young laborers in the 3 September issue of the *Züricher Freitagszeitung*. Inspired by this "real" event, he composed a sketch for the plowing scene and recorded it in his diary in late September: two farmers plowing on either side of a neglected field discuss the wasted land and subsequently plow into it, each pretending not to notice the other's incursion.[4] By early 1849, he had expanded and rewritten the scene in verse—a sample of which follows:

> Drei Äcker, eine wahre Augenweide
> Für jeden, der geführt schon einen Pflug,
> Die laufen nebeneinander über die Heide
> In grader Flucht vor unsres Auges Flug.[5]

Keller was apparently thinking of Goethe's *Hermann und Dorothea*,[6] itself an experiment with real (historical) events, but these verses with their forced rhythms and rhymes, flying eyes and running fields remind one of the parody verses in "Der Apotheker von Chamounix," where Keller was deliberately aiming for a comically stilted effect. It is not necessary to pass judgment on something that Keller abandoned, but apparently his decision to adopt a more prosaic form was a prudent one. This preference for prose and the prosaic is also reflected in the development of the material.

Whatever the genesis of "Romeo und Julia," it represents, to use McCormick's phrase, a "startling departure" from "Pankraz" as well as from anything else Keller had written (or was to write). Although its position on the college *Novelle* syllabus, as the crowning achievement of poetic realism, is unshakable, it is something of a generic and stylistic anomaly, insofar as it combines elements of romance with a more realistic milieu in a manner that is only partially accounted for by the term "poetic realism." We can make any number of qualifications on realism (and, in fact, we are never completely clear on exactly what it is we are qualifying) and posit any variety of realisms, but even within this rather broad Spielraum, "Romeo und Julia" is unique for several reasons.[7] If poetic realism is a nineteenth-century German way of blending the (poetic) universal with the (realistic) particular, which begins in "realistic" circumstances and then overlays this humble, but familiar, background with symbolic action and "transcendent meaning," then "Romeo und Julia" is certifiably a specimen of poetic realism.[8] Yet within this apparent harmonizing of the poetic and the realistic, the protagonists juxtapose their highly "poetic" conception of love—which resembles that of poets' fictions —to their real circumstances and effect a clean division. The lovers follow Keller's typical pattern of abdication of reality for a more appealing figment of the imagination. But in this case we have two distinct fictions: the novella itself, and the "love story" that Sali and Vrenchen enact within it. Unlike the quirks and fantasies of other Keller figures, their fiction gains independent existence as an idealization of mutual affection, which arises in a world where such ideals are reserved for poetry.

Sali's and Vrenchen's love story occasionally achieves independence of the realistic narrative that encloses it largely because of the great difficulties involved in integrating it into this narrative—either as imaginative excess or as a "higher" alternative to "realistic" society—and these difficulties stem from an extraordinarily ambivalent narrative stance. Whereas Keller's typical narrator will identify and evaluate a figure's guiding obsession as error, the narrator of "Romeo und Julia" is something of a fence-sitter: sometimes he speaks in favor of the lovers' dreamy ideals, while at other times he seems to recognize only the reality that contradicts them. Thus the contrast between the "realistic" (rational, sober, nonmagical) background world created by the narrator—where flights of fancy are confined to the purchase of lottery tickets—and the quasi-magical love story of the protagonists often dissolves into narrative recognition of the validity of their emotions, which is then followed by a reinstitution of the original, more sober, standards.

The narrator leans in both directions, sometimes simultaneously, and does so according to no discoverable logic. Gerhard Kaiser attempts to chart this shifting perspective and to account for it, but he is not specific with regard to the textual location of these shifts. He speaks of "die eigentliche Mischung von Humor und Verklärung in der Erzählung," and he notes: "Die Liebenden werden ernst genommen, wie ihr Spiel bewußt ist, und sie werden belächelt, weil sie sich doch auch an den Traum verlieren; sie werden verklärt, soweit ihr Traumleben das Vollkommene ist, und sie werden humoristisch relativiert, soweit dieses Vollkommene bloß folgenlose Innerlichkeit ist."[9] No examples are given, and I believe that Kaiser oversimplifies (uncharacteristically) by implying such orderly procedure—though he and others have recognized that the narrator's views are not fixed.

A prominent instance of this narrative fluctuation is the following comment on the lovers' questionable perception of music in the deserted field on their last night together: "Sie horchten ein Weilchen auf diese eingebildeten *oder* wirklichen Töne, welche von der großen Stille herrührten *oder* welche sie mit den magischen Wirkungen des Mondlichtes verwechselten" (H 2:125, my emphasis). Here the distinction between real and imaginary is not substantive: either will do. The lovers appear to be lost in their dream, but the narrator does not register amusement (as Kaiser's model would suggest); instead, he allows that the music might be real (*wirklich*), and he implies that it is of no great consequence if the storybook aspects of their love are illusory or imaginary. However, two pages later the same voice compares the lovers, who are about to enter the water, with a "Leichtsinniger" who consumes his last effects without thought of the future:

Aller Sorgen ledig gingen sie am Ufer hinunter und überholten die eilenden Wasser, so hastig suchten sie eine Stätte, um sich niederzulassen; denn ihre Leidenschaft sah jetzt nur den Rausch der Seligkeit, der in ihrer Vereinigung lag, und der ganze Wert und Inhalt des übrigen Lebens drängte sich in diesem zusammen; was danach kam, Tod und Untergang, war ihnen ein Hauch, ein Nichts, und sie dachten weniger daran, als ein Leichtsinniger denkt, wie er den andern Tag leben will, wenn er seine letzte Habe verzehrt. (H 2:126–27)

This appeal to hard pragmatic criteria is firmly anchored in a "realistic" view of their behavior. As Lee B. Jennings notes: "Keller, however sympathetic toward his characters' state of mind, emphasizes their frivolity. . . ."[10] It is a mild judgment, considering that they plan to kill themselves, but it is a judgment nonetheless. Keller's narrator behaves much like a spectator who is often charmed, even mesmerized, by the lovers' fantasies, though he usually regards them from an "objective" distance.

Genre expectations, or expectations of consistency of style, are curiously frustrated by Keller's novella, which I can only describe as the story of two young people who behave as if they were the protagonists of romance while operating in a sometimes realistic world, told by a narrator who oscillates between distance from and involvement in their "other-worldly" love. The constitution of this "other world" is an issue that involves Keller's early concern with the effects of imaginative literature on human spontaneity and self-determination. One of the most striking characteristics of Sali's and Vrenchen's conception of their love is its resemblance to romantic fictions, like the one invoked in the title—a resemblance that both corroborates and contradicts the author's or narrator's opening statements about literature's indebtedness to life: "Diese Geschichte zu erzählen würde eine müßige Nachahmung sein, wenn sie nicht auf einem wirklichen Vorfall beruhte, zum Beweise, wie tief im Menschenleben jede jener Fabeln wurzelt, auf welche die großen alten Werke gebaut sind. Die Zahl solcher Fabeln ist mäßig; aber stets treten sie in neuem Gewande wieder in die Erscheinung und zwingen alsdann die Hand sie festzuhalten" (H 2:61). It appears that "real" human behavior determines the great plots of fiction, but these plots themselves recur "in neuem Gewande" in the context of "real" human behavior. In other words, the human behavior that generates fictions also styles itself after fictions.

As the narrator drifts in and out of the lovers' "fiction" while spinning his own, which he insists is a direct reflection of life, it is often difficult to decide exactly what it is we are reading; and the novella, while supposedly demonstrating life's influence on literature, reveals the reciprocal relations in a way that suggests that literature is at least equally influential. This gives rise to a number of questions. Assuming that Seldwyla is reality, what can the position of Sali's and Vrenchen's absolute love be with regard to it? Or, to put it plainly, where did they get these ideas? If it is a romance, the question is absurd. This kind of absolute love is indigenous to romance, but not to realism. There are not many "realistic" people who would rather die than work for a few years and hope for improvement. When Wenzel Strapinski, Keller's later creation, resists Nettchen's suggestion that they return to Seldwyla and insists on his original plan of a brief period of bliss to be followed by his suicide—even though the suicide may no longer be necessary—Nettchen cries: "Keine Romane mehr!" (H 2:292). Romantic indulgence and death for love are thus banished to storybooks or novels, which, Nettchen insists, have nothing to do with life in the world. This is a prosaic observation, but not entirely inapplicable, for "Romeo und Julia" is, at least in part, a prosaic novella—though without the unequivocal force of Nettchen's prosaic good sense.

On the other hand, Keller may be attempting, in "Romeo und Julia," to verify the "realistic" status of such emotions as his protagonists express, insofar as he claims to be writing the novella precisely because the Romeo and Juliet motif has repeated itself once again in real life, "zum Beweise wie tief im Menschenleben jede jener Fabeln wurzelt, auf welche die großen alten Werke gebaut sind." Nevertheless, it is not quite clear whether these motifs are rooted in life or whether they take root. I believe that "Romeo und Julia" is an extended meditation on life and literature by an author who wishes to emphasize or discover that life is the source of (beautiful) literary plots, but who cannot abandon the notion that the literary operations performed on real sources do themselves alter and transform these events in a way that subsequently affects human relations. If Pankraz is confused by the schism between his literary experience and his actual dealings with Lydia, Keller appears in this case to be no less confused about another possible link between life and literature. He seems to be attempting (for the second time) to import Shakespeare into Seldwyla and to legitimize the beautiful themes of romance as plausible representations of human behavior, but the result is so ambiguous that no such statement emerges. Despite its celebrated symbolic consistencies, "Romeo und Julia" is fraught with profound indecision concerning the matters addressed in its introductory paragraph. However, I believe that the novella does advance the notion that, like Heinrich Lee, Sali and Vrenchen have fallen under the spell of a (literary) life-alternative fiction as they develop a storybook ideal of love, which they fulfill in death.

A century of secondary literature has taken little notice of this phenomenon, which suggests a reversal of the position taken in "Pankraz" (if the latter novella is indeed temporally anterior to "Romeo und Julia"), but a very qualified—and obfuscating—reversal. "Romeo und Julia" is a rich and complex (not to mention beloved) novella, and no single reading can claim priority. It would be an exercise in futility to argue that it is *about* the pernicious influence of literary/ cultural fictions or even that the topic is consistently high on its agenda. My specialized reading is therefore not intended to replace or refute more general (and less interested) commentaries, though it does rest on the (possibly polemical) assumption that the lovers' actions are not entirely spontaneous. My purpose is to offer a different perspective on certain matters, including the suicide, and to follow Keller's preoccupation with imagination and fictions through his most popular work, here regarded as a transitional piece.

Returning to the question of generic expectations, at least one contemporary of Keller's complained of an incongruous mixing of genres in "Romeo und Julia." In his review of the novella, Theodor Fontane pointed to two distinct styles and faulted Keller for his inability to sustain a realistic narrative: "[Der] Effekt dieser wundervollen Erzäh- lung . . . [wird] dadurch beeinträchtigt, daß die erste Hälfte ganz im Realismus, die zweite Hälfte ganz im Romantizismus steckt; die erste Hälfte ist eine das echteste Volksleben bis ins kleinste hinein wieder- gebende Novelle, die zweite Hälfte ist, wenn nicht ein Märchen, so doch durchaus märchenhaft."[11] Fontane, who proudly called himself a realist,[12] would naturally be disappointed to see *Realismus* deterio- rate into *Romantizismus*; but the idea of Keller's failure to sustain his realism, as remarked by Fontane, recurs as recently as 1981 in Clifford Bernd's comments on "Romeo und Julia": "The novella is divided into two parts which are wholly irreconcilable: the first dominated by two farmers' selfish real-estate interests, and the second—so discor- dantly different—by two young adolescents' fairy-tale-like love for one another. The initial description of simple peasants, centered around their greed and cutthroat competition for land possession, is superseded by their children's pursuit of a quixotic dream of love."[13] Keller, it should be noted, objected strenuously to Vieweg's sugges- tion that the novella be divided into two parts for the sake of the bookbinder's convenience: "Dies schiene mir aber bei einer so kleinen einfachen Geschichte höchst possierlich und affektiert zu sein."[14] Whether Keller really considered the tale too plain or simple to war- rant such a division is doubtful, but it appears that he did regard it as a unit. He eventually changed the order of the five novellas, so that "Romeo und Julia" might appear in one piece.

I think that Fontane and Bernd exaggerate somewhat in apportion- ing all realism to the first half of the story. Nevertheless, their objec- tions are grounded in a perception of a startling inconsistency be- tween the protagonists' love story and its setting, and they are help- ful in evoking a basic problem with reading "Romeo und Julia," namely that of determining the generic ground on which it stands. If this is a realistic tale, where natural laws and the bourgeois mo- rality that informs social reality are not suspended, then Sali's and Vrenchen's suicide may be perceived as somehow analogous to a real death in a real world and therefore repulsive, regrettable, and per- haps erroneous and immoral.[15] Even in a piece of bourgeois self- criticism, it would be difficult to introduce suicide as a value, regard- less of motivation. If, however, this is some form of romance, then we would not be any more inclined to feel repulsion toward or to mourn the deaths of Sali and Vrenchen than we would those of Tristan and Isolde. Fontane and Bernd perceive both styles and resolve this conflict by dividing the novella into two stylistic halves, which, they indicate, are incompatible. It is the incompatibility of the real and the romantic and the fact of their coexistence that prod the reader, or at least the critic, to make some sort of choice: either to privilege one style over the other, or to subdivide the novella into individual stylistic domains. The radical gesture of suicide—performed by unlikely candidates—calls for some reaction, and this reaction is usually founded on a perception of genre or style. I will argue for division, but on different grounds than those given by Fontane and Bernd.

Though Keller referred to "Romeo und Julia" as an "einfache Geschichte," it is actually a rather baffling one, which has gathered to itself a secondary literature of awesome proportions. As Hermann Boeschenstein notes in his 1969 *Forschungsbericht* on the "Romeo und Julia" literature: "Es scheint unmöglich, alle ins Licht gehobenen Vorzüge der Gestalt und des Gehaltes in einem Gesamteindruck zusammenzuziehen, Wissenschaft schlägt bei dem Versuch wieder in Staunen und Verehren um."[16]

Short of astonishment and reverence, there is at least one way to characterize the reams of critical commentary on Keller's novella, and that is to observe attitudes toward the suicide—as they are conditioned by perceptions of the generic atmosphere in which it occurs. Nearly everyone who has ever written on "Romeo und Julia" has registered a strong reaction to the suicide and has commented on it, in nearly every case attempting to demonstrate briefly or at length that such an action was inevitable, inescapable, and somehow "right." In fact, the repetition of this demonstration over the last century is itself astonishing—not least for the fact that it is rarely clear who is arguing the other side.[17] Within this framework, genre expectations —romance, tragedy, myth, fairy tale, "slice of life," social criticism, or uncertain mixture of the above—provide a foundation for judgment, as critics examine what Otto Ludwig called Keller's "gehäufte Motivierung"[18] and conclude that in the presence of such factors Sali and Vrenchen could not have done otherwise, or that Keller could not have done otherwise with them.

Actually, the first comments on the suicide come from within the novella. In the original conclusion, Keller's narrator gives his own interpretation and explanation of the event. This is the 1856 version, and it differs from the one published by Paul Heyse in 1871 in his *Deutscher Novellenschatz*, which is the standard version as we know it today. In the 1856 version, the newspaper report of the suicide as another example of "Entsittlichung und Verwilderung der Leidenschaften" (H 2:128) is followed by these remarks:

Was die Sittlichkeit betrifft, so bezweckt diese Erzählung keines-
wegs, die Tat zu beschönigen und zu verherrlichen; denn höher
als diese verzweifelte Hingebung wäre jedenfalls ein entsagen-
des Zusammenraffen und ein stilles Leben voll treuer Mühe und
Arbeit gewesen, und da diese die mächtigsten Zauberer sind in
Verbindung mit der Zeit, so hätten sie vielleicht noch alles
möglich gemacht; denn sie verändern mit ihrem unmerklichen
Einflusse die Dinge, vernichten die Vorurteile, stellen die Ehre
her und erneuen das Gewissen, so daß die wahre Treue nie ohne
Hoffnung ist. (H 2:1257–58)

This represents a reversal of the process of "Pankraz" and "Kleider."
Once again, Keller deliberately grafts on a discordant element. This
time, however, instead of interrupting the pedagogical process implied in his tale, he appends a directly didactic summary to what
otherwise might have been a morally neutral tale—though the farmers transgress and suffer punishment, they are not the focus. Yet,
having made his point that they perhaps should not have killed
themselves, Keller reverses himself again:

Was aber die Verwilderung der Leidenschaften angeht, so betrachten wir diesen und ähnliche Vorfälle, welche alle Tage im
niedern Volke vorkommen, nur als ein weiteres Zeugnis, daß
dieses allein es ist, welches die Flamme der kräftigen Empfin-
dung und Leidenschaft nährt und wenigstens die Fähigkeit des
Sterbens für eine Herzenssache aufbewahrt, daß sie zum Troste
der Romanzendichter nicht aus der Welt verschwindet. Das
gleichgültige Eingehen und Lösen von "Verhältnissen" unter
den gebildeten Ständen von heute, das selbstsüchtige frivole
Spiel mit denselben, die große Leichtigkeit, mit welcher heutzutage junge Leutchen zu trennen und auseinander zu bringen
sind, wenn ihre Neigung irgend außer der Berechnung liegt,
sind zehnmal widerwärtiger als jene Unglücksfälle, welche jetzt
die Protokolle der Polizeibehörden füllen und ehedem die
Schreibtafeln der Balladensänger füllten. . . . (H 2:1258)

This is ambivalence *in excelsis*, a condemnation by the Moralist, followed by a panegyric from the *Romanzendichter*. The division of styles
perceived by Fontane and Bernd seems to be rooted in a more fundamental authorial "division." This conclusion sounds less like the
work of the poetic realist than that of the poet and of the (moralizing)
realist, each of whom has his say. Keller's instructions to Heyse concerning the removal of the offending conclusion, given fifteen years
later, are equally ambivalent:

Ich bitte Sie also, in dem Exemplar, das Sie gebrauchen werden, entweder nach dem Satze "abermals ein Zeichen von der um sich greifenden Entsittlichung und Verwilderung der Leidenschaften" den Schwanz zu kappen, was sich maliti̇ös und ironisch ausnehmen würde; oder den folgenden Absatz noch aufzunehmen und nach den Worten: "so daß die wahre Treue nie ohne Hoffnung ist" abzuschneiden, was dann mehr tugendhaft und wohlmeinend klänge. . . . Sollten Sie wider Erwarten finden, daß die übrige Schlußnergelei doch stehen bleiben sollte (es war eine verjährte Stimmungssache) so können Sie's ganz stehenlassen.[19]

Thus, the story as it stands is in part Heyse's invention, born of the necessity of Keller's indecision. Though fifteen years had passed, Keller was unable or unwilling to resolve the problem of the beauty of such a romance and its skewed relationship to reality as he had posed it.

Keller's wavering and waffling are generally not acknowledged, but rather integrated into one of a number of recognizable forms. A brief sampling of selected descriptions of the suicide and the generic assumptions upon which they rest will provide an illustration. Rudolf Maier is perhaps most extreme in his reading of "Romeo und Julia" as tragedy, in its early natural-mystical sense—that is, as a sacrifice of the protagonist Dionysus for the sake of the renewal of the world and its bounty: "In dem Augenblick, da die Wogen des aufrauschenden Wassers sich geglättet haben, hat sich diese Ruhe aller Welt mitgeteilt: auf dem Steinacker ist wieder Stille, und Mohn und Disteln blühn. Wieder werden Bauern kommen, die die Äcker umpflügen. Die entzweite Welt ist geeinigt, das Zerbrochene geheilt, das Vergiftete entgiftet. . . . Dieser Untergang . . . ist bedeutsamer, gewichtiger als ein alltäglicher Tod."[20] Suggestions of the tragic are certainly present in "Romeo und Julia auf dem Dorfe": the action is integrated into natural cycles, the transgression of the farmers constitutes violence against the land and patriarchal property rights, which culminates in a (modest) rift in the world that needs to be healed. But Maier extrapolates from these suggestions and concludes that Sali and Vrenchen are sacrificial victims, whose death ensures the renewal of the world around them. Keller, however, gives no indication that the suicide has actually had the effects Maier imputes to it. On the contrary, he closes with a mean-spirited newspaper report that expresses nothing but moral indignation. Nonetheless, his tale seems to possess a kind of mythic power that tends to supply its own conclusion in accordance with literary models—not the least of which is the reconciliation of the Capulets and the Montagues at the end of *Romeo and Juliet*.[21]

Harold Dickerson regards "Romeo und Julia" as "a love story and nothing more" and maintains that " 'Romeo und Julia auf dem Dorfe' is not a *Lebensbild*: it is the lyrical evocation of a *perfect* love that triumphs in an imperfect world. . . . The lovers' death is an epiphany, the perfect harmony of two souls with themselves and with the world around them."[22] He adds: "This return to the elements is hardly a suicide in the accepted sense of the word but rather a fading away, a benign transition from one state of being into another.[23] If it is a "love story," we need ask it no further questions. Death is "benign" as a function of our good will toward the lovers, who are now fixed like stars in the firmament of romance.[24] But to label Keller's tale as nothing more than a love story is to disregard large sections of it—at least one-half, by Fontane's and Bernd's reckonings—that are devoted to the "imperfect world."

Other critics have focused on this imperfection and have treated the novella as social commentary, stressing its social-critical aspect. Seldwyla society banishes the black fiddler and withholds his inheritance for purely bureaucratic reasons—he has no baptismal certificate—and Manz's and Marti's unquestioning acceptance of this judgment is a self-interested confusion of the letter and the spirit of the law. They each annex a large portion of the abandoned field furrow by furrow, "was zwei Drittel der übrigen [Seldwyler] unter diesen Umständen auch getan haben würden" (H 2:69), and the fiddler is forced to take the loss. This is the social "order" into which Sali and Vrenchen are born, and their love is at odds with it. As Helmut Rehder notes:

> Whether on a grand or a small scale, Romeo and Julia become the victims of a society in which such pretensions of "Gerechtigkeit" are possible. . . . [Even] the principle of "honor" is no longer valid for them; and what society considers "Verwilderung der Leidenschaften" is in them the fulfillment of their nature. . . . Sali and Vrenchen, therefore, find mercy before the poet, although they have failed in "Mäßigung," but society is implicitly condemned, because it has not attempted it.[25]

The lovers' suicide is frequently viewed as a critique of the social order that presumably made it necessary; their death then highlights the inflexibility of a social group that should approve "love" but appears to have forgotten the putative basis for its own morality. Similarly, Robin Clouser refers to their death as "a symptom of social decay and a plea for reform," which Seldwyla society fails to recognize.[26] The novella is, he writes, Keller's "challenge . . . to his fellow believers in democracy to reform their houses before the plague is upon them."[27]

Others believe that Sali and Vrenchen preserve the ideals of their society in their pure form and that the lovers' departure from a corrupt social order and their rejection of an antisocial alternative is an example of these ideals in practice. Hildegarde Fife praises their reluctance to join the countersociety of the black fiddler and his band of vagabonds, and she observes that Sali's and Vrenchen's death is a victory over these forces of social chaos: "The young lovers, in rejecting a life of immorality [with the fiddler], rise above adverse circumstances by an act of free will, and though this act destroys them it also confirms the power of youth and the influence of society at its best." According to Fife, their action indicates that "strong moral forces are alive elsewhere in Swiss society."[28] Barry G. Thomas states that "society itself [is] to a large extent the real cause of the tragedy" and that its "false concept of order . . . ultimately forces Sali and Vrenchen to their death."[29] He explains:

> Sali and Vrenchen can resolve their dilemma only by going beyond the alternatives of separation within society or love outside society. . . . The only means of reconciliation is to accept the consequences of their passion: they fulfill their own individuality in the consummation of their love, and through a voluntary death they pay the price of preserving a social order, which, although it cannot encompass the force of their passion, they are still unable to deny completely.[30]

Yet the lovers' secession from society (which is their suicide) is hardly a protest gesture, nor is it an exemplary deed that counters decayed social values—or even antisocial values, for that matter. This secession is asocial in the extreme and as such inimical to anything resembling a social group, be it the vagabond community or "greater" Seldwyla (the city and its agrarian surroundings). Sali and Vrenchen choose to pursue an ideal of love, which by virtue of its exclusivity and intensity defies communal ethics as well as temporal duration. Whereas the implications for society are not good—since the protagonists who have our sympathy choose to leave it—their suicide is at best an indirect comment on social conditions.

All of the arguments cited above are carefully considered and based on suggestions in the text. I reproduce them only to point out that there are many avenues to pursue in reading "Romeo und Julia."

The text, which has no generic ancestors, imitates or resembles a number of familiar forms or formulas, and in some cases the expectations raised by these forms do take on a life of their own. For these commentators and many others, the suicide implies its own necessity and occasions the search for a plausible explanation.

Kaiser, who also assumes the necessity of the suicide, devotes considerable space to Sali's and Vrenchen's dream of love and the isolation it engenders. He describes their dream and Seldwyla society as two parallel universes, the former representing the perfection of the latter: "Die jungen Liebenden tragen die Unbedingtheit eines Ideals in sich, die sich quer zu Welt und Gesellschaft stellt und ihr voraus ist, ähnlich wie die regulative Idee sich zur empirischen Wirklichkeit verhält. . . . Ihre Idealität trägt so nicht nur den Tod für sie; sie wirft als Herausforderung zur Vollkommenheit zugleich auch einen Todesschatten in die Welt des Vorhandenen."[31] As Kaiser implies, Sali and Vrenchen, originally conceived on the model of *Hermann und Dorothea*, are rustic classicists in their own right. Like Pankraz, they know intuitively that the world is not "as it should be," and that things are "nicht so hübsch beisammen, wie in jenen Gedichten" (H 2:41), but they abandon this world for a better one of their own making, which Kaiser praises as the "Entwurf der vollkommenen Gesellschaft, soweit sie in der Intimgemeinschaft der Liebe präformierbar ist."[32] Yet their world "as it should be" is more than an untested idea, as in the case of "Pankraz" (and less than the social theory mentioned by Kaiser). Their "regulative Idee" is like a poetic fiction, a full-blown scenario for life (and death), coauthored by the protagonists who actually become "Romeo und Julia auf dem Dorfe" in a literal sense—not because of external circumstances, but by virtue of their active participation in a love story of their own devising. The model for their scenario is not Shakespeare's play, but the cultural narrative behind it—that of the preordained course that absolute love must take in order to preserve its purity and intensity.

In order to mount an argument for the suicide on these grounds—that is, as the conclusion of Sali's and Vrenchen's artfully and artificially intensified love relationship—it will be necessary to argue against its being a consequence of the circumstances cited by these scholars and by Sali and Vrenchen themselves. Many reasons are given for the suicide, but nowhere is the necessity of this drastic deed convincingly established. The lovers' "reasons" are summarized in Sali's "verwirrten Gedanken" at the *Paradiesgärtlein*:

Seine verwirrten Gedanken rangen nach einem Ausweg, aber er sah keinen. Wenn auch das Elend und die Hoffnungslosigkeit seiner Herkunft zu überwinden gewesen wären, so war seine Jugend und unerfahrene Leidenschaft nicht beschaffen, sich eine lange Zeit der Prüfung und Entsagung vorzunehmen und zu überstehen, und dann wäre erst noch Vrenchens Vater dagewesen, welchen er zeitlebens elend gemacht. Das Gefühl, in der bürgerlichen Welt nur in einer ganz ehrlichen und gewissensfreien Ehe glücklich sein zu können, war in ihm ebenso lebendig wie in Vrenchen, und in beiden verlassenen Wesen war es die letzte Flamme der Ehre, die in früheren Zeiten in ihren Häusern geglüht hatte und welche die sich sicher fühlenden Väter durch einen unscheinbaren Mißgriff ausgeblasen und zerstört hatten. (H 2:121)

Of all their problems, Sali's injury to Marti is presented as the most insuperable, and it is an act that scholars have judged more harshly than the double suicide.[33] Yet of all the events of the novella, it is perhaps the most confusing in its consequences. Whereas the initial transgression of the farmers can be morally and logically linked to their demise, Sali's action stands in a somewhat incongruous relation to its presumed effects. To recapitulate, Marti has just interrupted the couple's idyllic reunion in the field, threatened to strangle Sali, and assaulted his daughter with alarming violence. The narrator describes the scene from Sali's point of view: "[Er] sah, daß der Alte statt seiner nun das zitternde Mädchen faßte, ihm eine Ohrfeige gab, daß der rote Kranz herunterflog, und seine Haare um die Hand wickelte, um es mit sich fortzureißen und weiter zu mißhandeln" (H 2:95). Sali instinctively grabs a stone and deals the wild intruder a heavy blow to the head, a reaction that is certainly not disproportionate to the stimulus.[34] Marti loses consciousness, and the children initially take him for dead. Their horror diminishes as they discover that he is still breathing, but Vrenchen nonetheless declares: "Es ist aus, es ist ewig aus, wir können nicht zusammenkommen!" (H 2:96). Vrenchen's unrelenting insistence that she cannot wed the man who injured her father seems doubly unreasonable when, weeks later, a robust and healthy Marti, who has lost his bitter memories of the feud and the contested field, frolics on the pleasant grounds of a home for the insane and cries: "Geh heim, Vrenggel und sag der Mutter, ich komme nicht mehr nach Haus, hier gefällts mir bei Gott! . . . Du siehst ja aus wie der Tod im Häfelein und geht es mir doch so erfreulich!" (H 2:98). Marti is a very happy man. In spite of the pathos of insanity, his transformation has an undeniably positive aspect: because he is freed from the obsession that caused his dissipation and ruin, his insanity is in this sense a redemption rather than a misfortune—and the white-robed community in the "freundliche[n] Garten" (H 2:98) of the asylum does seem to be a secularized version of the heavenly host. Though heaven is not usually represented as a mental hospital, Keller does emphasize the bright side of Marti's injury, and the apparently tonic effects of Sali's stone on the wild man have even inspired a clinical evaluation of the latter's symptoms. As Harry Tucker, Jr., notes: "This condition represents the attainment of a goal, albeit by a pathological route, which Marti had sought before he became ill: an anxiety-free state, to be attained by the concession of the disputed land. His post-traumatic picture gives evidence of this secondary gain, freedom from anxiety, mediated by a symptomatology resembling that of the schizophrenic in his breaking with reality."[35] The merits of clinical inquiry may be questionable where no patient exists; nevertheless, Keller is certainly ambivalent in this portrayal of mental affliction, and the positive attributes work to undermine Vrenchen's unilateral insistence that this is the paramount obstacle to their happiness: "Ich werde es aber nicht aushalten ohne dich, und doch kann ich dich nie bekommen, auch wenn alles andere nicht wäre, bloß weil du meinen Vater geschlagen und um den Verstand gebracht hast!" (H 2:100). Marti's loss of mental capacity and his "living burial" recall, furthermore, the fate of Vrenchen's doll during the childhood idyll—an offense for which she quickly forgave Sali.[36]

Certainly there are other factors that speak against the union of Sali and Vrenchen, and it might be interesting to consider these singly. The spectre of the families' feud is an obstacle. Marriage would enrage Manz, but then Sali's opinion of his parents is at its nadir when he and Vrenchen resume relations. A wedding would probably cause quite a stir in the community, but we have no clear indication that the reactions would be negative—the woman who buys Vrenchen's bed, and the "gaffende Gesichter" at the church festivities do not appear to bear them any ill will. Also, the lovers lack the economic means to set up a household, and it would take time, perhaps years, to acquire the necessary capital. Sali is convinced that he cannot work and wait for a long period of time and Vrenchen is likewise disinclined, for the passionate temper of their love is attuned more to intensity than duration. The alternative life of the vagabond fiddler is specifically rejected by Vrenchen on the grounds that she might succumb to the temptation of infidelity—an interesting comment on their "perfect love" and the expected effects of time. Finally, the element of their "bürgerliches Ehrgefühl" prevents them from marrying on any but the most conventional of terms, and Sali's question, "wie entfliehen wir uns selbst?" is then answered by suicide. Ironically, the "bürgerliches Ehrgefühl" that deters them from violating standards of middle-class good taste (by marrying without means in the shadow of a feud, or by joining the vagabonds) does not cause them to question their rashness and choose "ein stilles Leben voll treuer Mühe und Arbeit," the solution proposed in the original version of the novella.

Thus, Sali's assault on Marti, the feud, poverty, the infeasibility of a long separation, the danger of infidelity in an unstructured society, and a sense of middle-class integrity prevent the couple from marrying or planning to marry.[37] At least five more reasons (all of which are left open to question) are added to the paramount cause, which alone is sufficient, according to Vrenchen, for rejecting marriage and happiness. Wherever multiple explanations are offered for a single action—as they are here offered in the thoughts and conversations of the protagonists—causality becomes confused and perhaps questionable; rather than sealing Sali and Vrenchen's fate, this superfluity of causal factors makes it all the more obscure. The lovers, who lament their inability to marry, as they resist any suggestion to the contrary, seem to aspire to something beyond bourgeois (or lower-class) marriage, and they pursue this indistinct goal with single-minded tenacity. In this they resemble Heinrich's "Leserfamilie" who seek a "better world" than that provided by "die Wirklichkeit" (H 1:132). Sali and Vrenchen are apparently interested only in absolute love—that is, love as it exists within the prescribed limits of romantic-idyllic fables—and their decision to end their lives appears, in many ways, to be dictated by a sense for these fictions. This is not to agree with Dickerson that the work bearing the title "Romeo und Julia auf dem Dorfe" is a "love story." Keller's novella is, rather, the conflict between a storybook ideal of love, which motivates the protagonists, and a world that cannot accommodate such otherworldliness. Yet, "Romeo und Julia" is not an argument for accommodation *or* otherworldliness—though it occasionally moves in each direction. Sali's and Vrenchen's dream of love, a "rusticized" grand passion, is as kitsch-ridden as Emma Bovary's wildest book-inspired fantasies and as fraught with "metaphysical desire" as Julien Sorel's Napoleonic conquests. It is a play-within-a-novella, authored by its own protagonists, designed to infuse the tragic beauty of literary fictions into their bleak and unpromising lives—just the type of fantasy that Keller condemned in *Der grüne Heinrich.* If Keller has attempted to reproduce tragic love in rustic garb ("im neuen Gewande"), his insistence on a realistic milieu has led him to undermine the mythic or tragic character of the love depicted.

Sali's and Vrenchen's love, rooted in childhood and their fond memories of better times, begins in earnest on a bridge above the water as they attempt to avert a fistfight between their fathers: "Darüber waren die jungen Leute, sich mehr zwischen die Alten schiebend, in dichte Berührung gekommen, und in diesem Augenblicke erhellte ein Wolkenriß, der den grellen Abendschein durchließ, das nahe Gesicht des Mädchens, und Sali sah in dies ihm so wohl bekannte und doch so viel anders und schöner gewordene Gesicht" (H 2:84). H. H. H. Remak has called this scene "Hollywoodish,"[38] and Keller does seem to have anticipated the techniques of sentimental popular films. The mysterious music the lovers hear in the fields would also fit into this tradition.

Though the renewal of Sali's and Vrenchen's affection is apparently spontaneous, the course of their brief life together is dictated by Vrenchen's (nocturnal) dream of a wedding and by the light verse they read at the church fair. The dream occurs on the evening following Marti's commitment to the asylum as the two sleep "wie zwei Kinder in einer Wiege" (H 2:100) in Vrenchen's house. She dreams of dancing at a wedding feast, and the focal point of her dream is the couple's longing to kiss and the repeated frustration of their efforts to do so. Yet, when Sali awakens her *with a kiss*, she identifies him as the agent of their separation: "Da wollten wir uns endlich küssen . . . und dürsteten darnach, aber immer zog uns etwas auseinander, und nun du bist es selbst gewesen, der uns gestört und gehindert hat" (H 2:100). She recoils when the wish arising from the dream is fulfilled in reality and insists on a reinstatement of the dream: " 'Morgen abend muß ich also aus diesem Haus fort,' sagte es, 'und ein anderes Obdach suchen. Vorher aber möchte ich einmal, nur einmal recht lustig sein, und zwar mit dir; ich möchte recht herzlich und fleißig mit dir tanzen irgendwo, denn das Tanzen aus dem Traume steckt mir immerfort im Sinn!' " (H 2:101). Both Sali and Vrenchen prefer their dreams to the dreary and inauspicious reality of their daily lives, and their final day together is conceived literally as a dream replacement. Yet the elements of the dream that Vrenchen intends to "realize" are the dancing (not the wedding), and the separation (not the nuptial kiss). They agree to go to a church fair where they will not be recognized and to act as if they were a properly betrothed couple. Vrenchen even insists on the proper costume when she announces that she cannot go without new shoes, which Sali then procures. The day begins with a compatible fiction, Vrenchen's spontaneous and absurd tale of prosperity, the *Lügenmärchen*[39] told to the peasant woman who buys her bed: "Sali ist mein Hochzeiter! . . . und er ist ein reicher Herr, er hat hunderttausend Gulden in der Lotterie gewonnen! . . . [In] drei Wochen halten wir die Hochzeit! . . . Das schönste Haus hat er schon gekauft in Seldwyl mit einem großen Garten und Weinberg; . . . [Wir] müssen jetzt augenblicklich gehen . . . um vornehme Verwandte zu besuchen, die sich jetzt gezeigt haben, seit wir reich sind!" (H 2:106–8). Vrenchen shows an impressive knowledge of novelistic or fairy tale endings. The woman who hears her tale is at first skeptical, but as Vrenchen expands the story to include some benefit for her (gifts and loans of money), she begins to believe and offers her sincere congratulations to her future benefactress.

Keller's lovers are not overt consumers of the popular literature that conveys these kinds of fantasies. The lone, but significant, indication we have that they are even able to read comes when the two visit a village market and steep themselves in the sentimental verses attached to bakery goods: "Sie lasen eifrig die Sprüche und nie ist etwas Gereimtes und Gedrucktes schöner befunden und tiefer empfunden worden als diese Pfefferkuchensprüche; *sie hielten, was sie lasen, in besonderer Absicht auf sich gemacht, so gut schien es ihnen zu passen*" (H 2:115, my emphasis). Like Heinrich Lee, Sali and Vrenchen mistake literary texts for accounts of their own emotions. In this case they read a series of versified platitudes concerning idealized love, which derive their general appeal from a broad applicability extending to even the most common imaginative fantasies. But the *Pfefferkuchensprüche* not only apply to the lovers' thoughts and behavior, they also determine them: "Doch wußten sie nicht, daß sie in ihren Reden eben solche Witze machten, als auf den vielfach geformten Lebkuchen zu lesen waren, und fuhren fort, diese süße einfache Liebesliteratur zu studieren" (H 2:115–16).

This is the only reading that they do, and their love as such precedes the experience of the *Pfefferkuchensprüche*, but the idea of love unto death that determines the course of their romance gains prominence only after this scene. Sali has earlier remarked that his love, fortified by misery, is a matter of life and death ("so daß es um Leben und Tod geht" [H 2:100]), but the matter is quickly dropped and the idyll resumes. Though symbols of death are ubiquitous almost from the beginning of the novella, the kitsch-verses at the fair represent the lovers' first exposure to a codified and organized presentation of the ultimate consequences of love, and the experience apparently fortifies their own indistinct sense of love as an emotion that supersedes the will to live. It is interesting that these lofty ideals, which presumably make the lovers' story so "beautifully tragic," are concretized as cute inscriptions on pieces of sculpted gingerbread. What a difference there is between the physical vehicle of Pankraz's significant reading, "wie eine Handbibel . . . in schwarzes Leder gebunden und vergoldet" (H 2:40), and Sali's *Liebeshaus:*

> [Ein] großes Haus von Lebkuchen, das mit Zuckerguß freundlich geweißt war, mit einem grünen Dach, auf welchem weiße Tauben saßen und aus dessen Schornstein ein Amörchen guckte als Kaminfeger; an den offenen Fenstern umarmten sich pausbäckige Leutchen mit winzig kleinen roten Mündchen, die sich recht eigentlich küßten, da der flüchtige praktische Maler mit einem Kleckschen gleich zwei Mündchen gemacht, die so ineinander verflossen. Schwarze Pünktchen stellten muntere Äuglein vor. (H 2:114)

Whatever message Sali and Vrenchen extract from the gingerbread confections has been "pretrivialized" by the physical medium that conveys it. *Der grüne Heinrich* has taught us to beware of sweet things bearing verses and, as it turns out, the poems that Sali and Vrenchen read at the fair are both silly and sinister.

The verses that appear on the *Liebeshaus* are Keller's reworking of the "Inschrift auf dem Haus des Dichters" from the "Diwan des Abu Nuwas":

1. Wer dieses Haus betritt, sei sorgenlos,
   Nur Küsse muß er dulden und Gekos.—
2. Sie sprach: "Wir kamen dieses Umstands wegen."
   Nun denn, so tretet ein mit Glück und Segen![40]

As Heinrich Richartz points out, Keller's version paraphrases the first and last verses, but inserts a middle verse that introduces the "Ausschließlichkeitsanspruch ihrer Liebe"[41] or, in other words, the absolute love to which they aspire. In Keller's rendition the happy speakers make a much more binding commitment:

> Tritt in mein Haus, o Liebste!
> Doch sei Dir unverhehlt:
> Drin wird allein nach Küssen
> Gerechnet und gezählt.
>
> Die Liebste sprach: "O Liebster,
> *Mich schrecket nichts zurück!*

*Hab alles wohl erwogen:*
*In Dir nur lebt mein Glück!*
"Und wenn ichs recht bedenke,
Kam ich deswegen auch!"
Nun denn, spazier mit Segen
Herein und üb den Brauch!                    (H 2:114–15, my emphasis)

The inscription, which suggests secession from the world and entry into the *Liebeshaus* at any cost, is a light-hearted trifle when viewed as a piece of popular love poetry. But Sali and Vrenchen, who dutifully *study* this *Liebesliteratur* and "eben solche Witze mach[t]en," seem to take the conventions and conceits of the genre quite literally. Vrenchen also makes a purchase, a heart-shaped cookie with the following lines attached:

Ein süßer Mandelkern steckt in dem Herze hier,
Doch süßer als der Mandelkern ist meine Lieb zu Dir!

Wenn Du dies Herz gegessen, vergiß dies Sprüchlein nicht:
Viel eh'r als meine Liebe mein braunes Auge bricht!          (H 2:115)

Her poem combines a sweet and silly observation with a pledge that the speaker's love will outlive him/her. Later, as she is about to enter the water, she renews this pledge, by repeating the verse: " 'Meine Blumen gehen mir voraus,' rief Vrenchen, 'sieh, sie sind ganz dahin und verwelkt!' Es nahm sie von der Brust, warf sie ins Wasser und sang laut dazu: *'Doch süßer als ein Mandelkern ist meine Lieb zu dir!'* " (H 2:127, my emphasis). Sali and Vrenchen plan to die physically and to perpetuate their love as "zwei schöne große [Fische]" (H 2:127), and immediately before the suicide, Vrenchen's words reveal a preoccupation with the love poetry she read at the fair.

Their decision to die is intimately linked with the *Pfefferkuchensprüche*, which Keller portrays most conspicuously as kitsch, without the slightest bit of restraint in his use of diminutives. The notion of love's radical exclusivity derived from Sali's *Liebeshaus* combines with the complementary notion of love's ability to survive the lover's death, and both factors add up to a concept of love that, though it may require the ultimate sacrifice, will not conclude at death. That these ideas derive from a literary form that Keller considered to be among the lowest, does not tend to endorse Sali's and Vrenchen's behavior—nor does it dispose the reader to regard the lovers as self-determining individuals or social critics. The appeal of a brief, intense "literary" romance far exceeds that of a long monotonous servitude without the definite assurance of eventual union—neither is certain that their love will last that long—and the combination of their own desperation and predisposition with the *Pfefferkuchensprüche*, which offer an alternative course, drives them to the water. It is not clear that the *Pfefferkuchensprüche* directly inspired the suicide, only that literature played a major role in the course of a love that had already come to resemble a literary fiction.

The lovers' final day is spent between "forgetting" (their troubles) and "awakening" (from their dream):

Das liebende Paar vergaß, was am Ende dieses Tages werden sollte.                                                               (H 2:110)

Endlich erwachten sie aus diesen vergeblichen Träumen.
                                                                       (H 2:110)

[S]ie vergaßen, woher sie kamen und wohin sie gingen. (H 2:111)

[A]lles . . . sah mit Verwunderung auf das wohlgeputzte Paar, welches in andächtiger Innigkeit die Welt um sich her zu vergessen schien.                                                         (H 2:116)

Als sie daher endlich aufwachten und um sich sahen, erschauten sie nichts als gaffende Gesichter von allen Seiten.      (H 2:117)

The "gaffende Gesichter" at the church fair wrench Vrenchen out of her dream and she decides to reenter the dreary world that awaits her, but Sali dissuades her and "rewrites" the scene, transferring the locale for their dancing to the irreal *Paradiesgärtlein*.

Yet, Sali "awakens" later as they dance over the fields in procession with the *Heimatlosen*, and they must once again make the choice of whether or not to pursue their dream to its novelistic conclusion. If marriage and death are their only alternatives within the fiction or within the dream, and if marriage is understood in terms of Vrenchen's *Lügenmärchen*, then death, understood in terms of the *Pfefferkuchenspruch* that Vrenchen now enunciates, must be the logical choice. Whether this is necessary depends to a great extent on which fiction we are now reading, the protagonists' love story or Keller's tale of love and enmity on the outskirts of Seldwyla. I would not presume to decide which fiction we *should* be reading, but I do believe that *necessity*, such as it is, belongs entirely to Sali's and Vrenchen's tale of romance. As McCormick, who examines ambivalence in "Romeo und Julia," points out: "Their destruction is of course in keeping with the 'plot of a genuine "middle class tragedy"' and with Keller's concern for the weakness of human society. But it is also a deeper reflection of their own guilt and failure, of the inherent ambivalence created by Sali's and Vrenchen's inability to reject their idylls—into which they themselves put no small part of the destructive and tragic element."[42] McCormick concludes his essay with this observation and therefore does not take it any further, but both he and Kaiser perceive Sali's and Vrenchen's dream of love as a well-developed alternative to the reality they reject. It is clearly one of the life-alternative fictions that occupied Keller throughout his career as a writer. But it is also a "literary" fiction, conforming to certain accepted conventions, which assumes control of the protagonists' lives and so fascinates the narrator/author that it threatens to prevail over the fiction that conveys it; that it sometimes does prevail is obvious from the secondary literature. If "Pankraz" reveals the writer as *Schmoller*, "Romeo und Julia," with its indecisive narrator, suggests the presence of the writer as fellow reader, who occasionally takes great pleasure in the romantic aspects of his own tale.[43]

Keller's introduction declares that the basic plots of fiction, appearing in new forms, "force the hand" to record them or, more properly, to seize them ("sie festzuhalten").[44] I have argued that not only the narrator/writer but also the protagonists seize the fable that forms the basis of Shakespeare's *Romeo and Juliet*, and that "Romeo und Julia" records both of these seizures. Interestingly, the background of Keller's story suggests a similar seizure. As noted, he read of the incident that inspired his novella in the *Züricher Freitagszeitung*. The newspaper's report of the suicide of the two young people itself reads suspiciously like a literary fiction:

> Im Dorfe Altsellershausen bei Leipzig liebten sich ein Jüngling von neunzehn Jahren und ein Mädchen von siebzehn Jahren, beide Kinder armer Leute, die aber in einer tödlichen Feindschaft lebten und nicht in eine Vereinigung des Paares willigen wollten. Am 15. August begaben sich die Verliebten in eine Wirtschaft, wo sich arme Leute vergnügen, tanzten daselbst bis nachts ein Uhr und entfernten sich hierauf. Am Morgen fand man die Leichen beider Liebenden auf dem Felde liegen: sie hatten sich durch den Kopf geschossen.[45]

This report sounds less like a specimen of objective journalism than like the Boccaccian synopses that precede the novellas in the *Decameron*. Paul Heyse was later to cite these same synopses as examples of the "profiled" action that is characteristic of the novella (and, for what it is worth, Shakespeare drew his Romeo and Juliet theme from a pre-Boccaccian Italian novella). In any case, Keller encountered this particular "heading" and eventually supplied the novella. He even paraphrases the *Freitagszeitung* article at the end of "Romeo und Julia," where the narrator recounts the report of another, less sympathetic, newspaper: "... zwei junge Leute, die Kinder zweier blutarmen zugrunde gegangenen Familien, welche in unversöhnlicher Feindschaft lebten, hätten im Wasser den Tod gesucht, nachdem sie einen ganzen Nachmittag herzlich miteinander getanzt und sich belustigt auf einer Kirchweih" (H 2:128).

The news report that came to Keller's attention was not the original account of the event, according to Ermatinger, whose biography of Keller (based on an earlier effort by Jakob Baechthold) is a model of critical and philological diligence. Ermatinger notes that the *Freitagszeitung* account was based on earlier local reports, one of which he reproduces: "Im 'Leipziger Kreisblatt' Nr 105 vom 2. September 1847 stand folgende Notiz: 'Volkmarsdorf. Am 16. August hat der achtzehnjährige Handarbeiter Gustav Wilhelm von hier durch einen Pistolenschuß die sechzehnjährige Auguste Abicht, Wollarbeiterin, getötet und sodann sich selbst erschossen.' "[46] The facts and tenor of the event are significantly altered in the *Freitagszeitung* report, which seems to have been rewritten in the spirit of *Romeo and Juliet*—which may explain its conspicuous resemblance to literature. Thus, the notorious "wirklicher Vorfall" (H 2:61) that inspired the novella had already passed into a vaguely romancelike form (possibly influenced by Shakespeare's tragedy) by the time it came to Keller's attention. Keller then based his story *not* on a real event that re-creates one of those "Fabeln . . . auf welche die großen alten Werke gebaut sind," but on a second- or thirdhand report of that event. The *report* re-creates the Romeo and Juliet theme in its assumption that Gustav shot Auguste because a union was impossible in this world. The assumption may be correct, but it could just as easily be false. For all we know, Gustav and Auguste may have been repeating an entirely different basic plot of fiction—that of *Othello*, for example—or none at all. It does not necessarily matter what they were doing, but it is highly interesting that Keller's knowledge of the incident whose "reality" justifies his tale is itself probably tainted by fiction—or at least by assumptions that recast events in a familiar fictional form. It is furthermore difficult to believe that he did not recognize this.

The real reason for Gustav's and Auguste's deaths is inaccessible to us at this point, but their demise appears to have triggered a sequence of events in which the Romeo and Juliet theme plays a major part, "forcing the hand" on several levels to make sense of matters in terms of its own requirements. Two bodies are found, the facts are recorded (*Kreisblatt*), and the facts are interpreted (*Freitagszeitung*). The interpreted facts are then deliberately and overtly linked to Shakespeare's play and transformed into a novella in which the theme itself (in the more generalized form of the *Pfefferkuchensprüche*) translates into (fictional) human behavior and two more bodies.

In "Romeo und Julia," Keller betrays a desire to bring romance into reality (as Gustav and Auguste are suspected of doing) by bringing realism to romance in his insistence that the Romeo and Juliet archetype has actually recurred and that this recurrence inspired his tale. Interestingly, Keller's comments in the correspondence indicate that he adapted Shakespeare's title and mentioned the actual incident in his introduction in order that he not be considered an imitator of Shakespeare. In 1856, he defends his title and introduction against Auerbach's objections by noting: "Hätte ich keine Bemerkung über die wirkliche Vorkommenheit der Anekdote und über die Ähnlichkeit mit dem Shakespearischen Stoffe gemacht, so hätte man mich einer gesuchten und dämlichen Wiederholung beschuldigt" (*GB* 3/2: 186).[47] He adds, "Shakespeare, obgleich gedruckt, [ist] . . . das Leben selbst" (ibid.). Yet he demonstrates, I think, not that the archetype used by Shakespeare is life itself but rather that it is one of life's imaginative pleasures, a way of redefining and exalting desire that finds expression in such love poetry as Sali and Vrenchen read at the fair. This would be typical of the early Keller's (Feuerbachian) crusade against life-alternative fictions, and Sali's and Vrenchen's quest for realization of their otherworldly desires does indeed appear as a misunderstanding on their part that carries "tragic" consequences. The "realistic" fiction that encloses their improbable one relativizes their ideals and presents the lovers to some extent as dupes of poetic fictions.

As noted earlier, Keller may not have set out to make such a statement. The poetic beauty of the lovers' idylls and the "gehäufte Motivierung"—though it ultimately breaks down—might also be taken as a sign that he had a perfectly legitimate *Liebestod* in mind. If so, then "Romeo und Julia" is a failure by an author who (like Hamlet) could not make up his mind.[48] Keller becomes tangled in his own web of realism and romance, *Wirklichkeit* and *Einbildung*, as he attempts to forge a convincing link between romance, or tragedy, and convincingly realistic human interaction. Success might have yielded a genuine poetic realism and a solution to Heinrich's vexing problem of an imagination whose demands in no way correspond to that which is available to him. But Keller is not successful. He appears to be divided between a will to synthesize the imaginary and the mundane (based on the mundane origin of the imaginary) and a will to undermine his own attempts at synthesis. By allowing for (trivial) "literary influence" in "Romeo und Julia," Keller subverts romance and keeps the two realms of life and literature distinct. Paradoxically, the invasion of reality by romantic fictions (*Pfefferkuchensprüche* and the love story) works to emphasize their separation, though this separation is not a happy one.

# 4. *Züricher Novellen:*
# Didactic Literature
# and Unreceptive Life

After his productive Berlin years (1850–55) and the appearance of *Seldwyla* I, Keller labored in Zurich and Hottingen as a "freier Schriftsteller" and political journalist until his election in 1861 to the post of "erster Staatsschreiber" of the cantonal government. He served for fifteen years as a paid bureaucrat, producing, among other documents, annual "Bettagsmandate" for the (serious) edification of the canton, and his literary output was relatively sparse. *Sieben Legenden* appeared in 1872 and a second volume of *Seldwyla* stories followed in 1874. By 1876, the year of his resignation, he had completed the *Züricher Novellen*, where he returns (perhaps via the "Bettagsmandate") to the question of didactic literature and its questionable potency in "Herr Jacques."

Keller himself set the tone for scholarly commentary on his "Herr Jacques" when, in 1877, he dismissed it as "eine Randzeichnung" (*GB* 3/2:380).[1] In a recent introduction to the collection Gert Sautermeister offers a succinct summary of scholars' reactions to the narrative that frames the first three *Züricher Novellen*: "Bei aller Wertschätzung, der sich die 'Züricher Novellen' in der literaturwissenschaftlichen Zunft erfreuen, pflegt man doch eins an ihnen zu kritisieren: ihre Rahmenhandlung."[2] Actually, "Herr Jacques" has been more frequently ignored than criticized. Much has been written on individual *Züricher Novellen* and on the collection as a whole, but the frame has been the object of diligent neglect—itself an effective form of criticism.[3] Of course there are reasons for this neglect. Keller consistently chose to publish his novellas in thematically "unified" cycles but he only twice attempted to create a *Rahmenhandlung* for this purpose, and the somewhat clumsy chronicle of the education of Herr Jacques does not offer nearly as many points of access for scholars as do the novellas it encloses. The (well-wrought) narrative fencing match between Reinhart and Lucie, which provides the occasion for the many tales in *Das Sinngedicht*, has also generated much more respect (and much more research) than "Herr Jacques." Yet, though its narration is relentlessly linear, though it lacks complex development and is occasionally blighted by the author's ill-concealed disgust for the small-minded philistine who is its subject, "Herr Jacques" is nonetheless intriguing in its bearing on the pedagogical value of the three novellas that are (structurally) subordinated to it. Keller's *Randzeichnung* is really a "marginal" exercise in subversion, which undermines the avowed purpose of the three novellas within.

Due to the canonizing effects of anthologies, college syllabi, and scholarly essays, "Hadlaub" and "Der Landvogt von Greifensee" have escaped obscurity, whereas "Jacques" and "Der Narr auf Manegg" have been situated firmly within the netherworld of unread or unreadable matter: while two of the "framed" stories have gained in prominence, the frame itself (along with the middle tale) has receded and faded from view. Without making any claims for (or against) "Herr Jacques" this chapter proposes to take the first cycle of *Züricher Novellen* at face value and to shift focus from the novellas to the frame narrative. Whatever their respective artistic merits, the four tales are organized and presented as a primary narrative with three dependent narratives, each of which addresses a problem in the development of the frame's adolescent hero.[4]

Whereas "Pankraz" creates a scenario for the defeat of the author's desire for order and exposes the pedagogic urge as quixotic, "Herr Jacques" makes much the same point by depicting the direct practical application of didactic fiction and the failure of such fiction to achieve its intended effect. Here literature influences life insofar as it prompts Jacques to redefine his awakening sexuality as the urge to do something "original" in the field of literature. It is utterly ineffectual, however, when applied as a corrective to this situation. Herr Jacques's godfather relates three exemplary tales to cure the boy of his misplaced ambitions, but it is ultimately "life" itself, in the unmistakable form of a newborn baby, that causes him to renounce literature and grudgingly to accept his sexuality.[5]

"Herr Jacques" is a writer's tale in which three literary projects intertwine. Keller creates the didactic fiction and its foil, the godfather implements "his" didactic tales, and Herr Jacques unwittingly pursues maturity—and progeny—by means of his quest for literary distinction. That this quest for distinction, based as it is on creativity and imagination as values, leads him directly to the symbolic enactment of his manifest biological destiny—he becomes the baby's godfather—suggests that the antagonism between imagination and reality that fuels *Der grüne Heinrich* had diminished considerably for Keller by 1877. In "Jacques" allegiance to imagination, even though it involves a turning away from the "real," never causes the boy to stray far from his own reality—but it must be admitted that Jacques has little imagination. The boy's obsession with writing and the course he devises for himself form a personalized allegory of maturation and reproduction that allows Keller's rather stiff bourgeois hero to ease into his adult role. In fact, the only one who truly suffers from excesses of the imagination is Buz Falätscher, "Der Narr auf Manegg," and his excesses are attributed to his madness, which has its material basis in his "bad" genes. Imagination, or desire, that reaches beyond the given and assumes fulfillment on the strength of its intensity or conviction, is no longer a hazard to life and limb, but it is still one of the wellsprings of error—and it is error that fuels Keller's narratives. In this case, however, we have three candidates for errant hero, and a determination of protagonist is purely a matter of perspective. Jacques, who cannot write but wishes to, is only the most obvious choice. It is his godfather who makes the greater error of presuming that the didactic fiction he is able to write (and relate) will affect and reform its "recipient" according to plan. And, finally, it is Keller, writing of his own urges to control and reform the world outside his books ("das Volk zeigt sich plastisch"), who is once again denying and denouncing the desires of the pedagogue by indulging them.

Rolf Engelsing describes the end of the eighteenth century and the beginning of the nineteenth as a time of great crisis for the bourgeois reader. As the popularity of clearly prescriptive religious-didactic works and the *Erbauungsliteratur*, which overtly defined and reinforced bourgeois values, diminished, bookstores and lending libraries were flooded with works of fiction and philosophy that made fewer decisions for the general reader—leaving him with (more of) the task of processing his own impressions and integrating them into his now "individual" world-view. Though literature did not necessarily exert a direct influence on behavior, as might a code of law, it nonetheless provided a number of what Engelsing calls "Garderoben für die verschiedensten Vorstellungen, Haltungen und Tätigkeiten."[6] Jacques's experience seems to fall within this general pattern as he reads one day in the late 1820s, "daß es heutzutage keine ursprünglichen Menschen, keine Originale mehr gebe, sondern nur noch Dutzendleute und gleichmäßig abgedrehte Tausendspersonen" (H 2: 611). The meaning of "Original" is highly ambiguous (at worst it is condescending), but its aura is irresistible, and Jacques is able to define and adapt the word to his growing perception of his task in life.

Whereas Heinrich Lee finds "Gestalt und Namen" for his emotions in chivalric novels and textual authority for his plans to study painting in Goethe, Jacques encounters corroboration of his long-standing desire for distinction and a name for the feelings that trouble him in a single sentence: "Mit Lesung dieses Satzes hatte er aber gleichzeitig entdeckt, daß die sanft aufregenden Gefühle, die er seit einiger Zeit in Schule und Haus und auf Spaziergängen verspürt, gar nichts anderes gewesen, als der unbewußte Trieb ein Original zu sein oder eines zu werden, das heißt, sich über die runden Köpfe seiner guten Mitschüler zu erheben" (H 2:611).[7] Having thus stumbled on his apparent "Trieb zur Originalität," Jacques redefines his nascent procreative urge as the creative urge to write highly original works of fiction. Yet up to this point he has experienced considerable difficulty in generating even imitations of great literary models. His "Der neue Ovid" a series of modern metamorphoses involving the transformation of nymphs and humans into the plants that form the basis of colonial trade, has not progressed beyond the title stage. Keller has rarely been less kind in his treatment of the ungifted writer, and we are given to understand that Jacques's presumption is an unseemly vice that must be eradicated. This is the given purpose of the first cycle of *Züricher Novellen*.

Jacques's godfather, the would-be exterminator of vice in this case, proposes to cure the boy of his immodest ambitions by means of the historical fiction he, the godfather, has written. Here, Keller pits literature against literature in a struggle for the soul of the rigid philistine who would presume to write. The self-deception involved in Jacques's "Trieb zur Originalität," the substitution of literary endeavor for a clear-eyed acceptance of adulthood and its functions, is never directly identified in this consciously Victorian narrative. However, the unmentionable persists as a subterranean *Leitmotiv*, surfacing occasionally in gestures such as Jacques's blushing, the cracking of his voice, his horror when directly confronted with the face of his future wife (whom he always regards out of the corner of his eye), and the eight-day laxative cleansing cure that precedes his wedding.

Jacques has "misread" his "unbewußten Trieb" and created an acceptable conscious alternative that is not, however, acceptable to his godfather, nor is it necessarily therapeutic in terms of his capacities. He consistently fails to reproduce his thoughts in prose or verse, while distancing himself from thoughts of biological reproduction. Karl Reichert's allegations of haphazard construction of the first cycle and its internal connections are, to a great extent, justified. In this particular case, Keller seems to have implanted conspicuous references to fertility and reproduction in the first two novellas. Hadlaub and Fides, for example, unite in the presence of a child: "Indessen hatten sie unbewußt begonnen, das Kind gemeinsam zu liebkosen

und zögerten über diesem Spiele nicht länger, ihre Ehe zu beschlie-
ßen und zu besprechen" (H 2:694). Hadlaub nearly misses his chance
to marry and multiply because he pursues his goal as a poet and not
as a man. The loathsome Buz, who has no fixed identity and eventually poses as a poet, is sterile; his wife leaves him "da sie keine
Kinder von ihm bekam" (H 2:711). Those who project themselves
into roles, it seems, are not capable of reproducing themselves in the
"real" world. These communications between the tales and the frame
are awkwardly contrived, but they imply that for Jacques, who projects himself into the role of writer, fertility is at stake. Thus it is
somewhat odd that the highest example of good "originality" offered
for Jacques's consideration is that of Salomon Landolt, who fails to
marry and sire children.

Reichert has identified "Hadlaub" as a pedagogical error on the
part of the godfather: "Um einen im Grunde unbegabten Jüngling,
der sich einbildet, Dichter werden zu können oder zu müssen, auf
den rechten Weg zu führen, darf man ihm nicht ausgerechnet das
Beispiel eines Dichters vor Augen stellen."[8] Yet, "Landvogt" may be
the same kind of mistake. If Jacques is fleeing his "sanft aufregenden Gefühle" which incline him toward (reproductive) contact with
women, the story of a man who also fled women (despite his gallant
protestations of rejection) might not induce the boy to acknowledge
and address those urges concealed by his "Trieb zur Originalität." But
this may be asking too many questions of a text whose compositional
principles include—as Reichert charges—expediency. In a letter to
Theodor Storm, Keller apologizes for the state of the collection, especially of the fifth novella, "Ursula": "Wegen der 'Züricher Novellen'
hab' ich auch ein schlechtes Gewissen, sie sind zu schematisch, und
man merkt es gewiß. Die 'Ursula' haben Sie richtig erkannt, sie ist
einfach nicht fertig, und schuld daran ist der buchhändlerische Weih-
nachtstrafik, der mir auf dem Nacken saß" (GB 3/1:420).[9]

In any case, the education of Herr Jacques toward marriage and
progeny is not purely a process of his coming into possession of an
unambiguously coveted grail. Tensions between fertility and sterility,
and the relative merits of each, emerge in the frame itself. The godfather, for example, is a bachelor, albeit apparently not by choice.
Rejected by Herr Jacques's mother years before, he still carries a
grudge—"Er . . . führte . . . seither stets einen kleinen Bosheitskrieg
gegen sie" (H 2:702)—though she has apparently made at least a
godfather out of him. The narrator himself—Keller was an oft-re-
jected bachelor—expresses great bitterness toward women and ideals
of marital bliss when he, in his omniscience, describes a group of
girls, "die an der Grenze der Kindheit noch alle frisch und lieblich

waren und das ihrer wartende Reich der Unschönheit noch nicht gesehen hatten" (H 2:619). In a truly extraordinary fit of vituperation, this narrator digresses on the frightening creatures into which these young virgins will develop. The passage is too long to reproduce in full, but a sample may suffice to suggest its tone: "Ei, und dort das angehende Spitznäschen, das die erhabene Beatrix für einen kommenden Dante zu verkünden scheint und sich zu einem Geierschnabel auswachsen wird, der einem ehelichen Dulder täglich die Leber aufhacket, unversehrt von seinem schweigenden Hasse!" (H 2:619). Given the prevailing misogyny, it is not surprising that Jacques would prefer to understand his yearnings for the opposite sex as a longing to write. When the same girls playfully push his "Jugendflamme" at him, he shoves her back "wie ein unvorhergesehenes großes Übel" (H 2:620). Ironically, "originality," the quality that Jacques equates with literature and imagination and that his godfather seeks to demystify and "domesticate," may have something to do with abstaining from women.

"Originality," nominally the central concern of the first cycle of *Züricher Novellen*, is a surprisingly elastic concept. Though the word retains its positive charge, definitions and illustrations are subject to anarchic variation. Jacques perceives originality as an untamed greatness of soul, whose expression is creative literature. He subscribes to the Storm and Stress cult of the artist as *Originalgenie* and sighs over the river where the Stolbergs "genialisch und pudelnackt gebadet [hatten]" (H 2:613). His godfather, on the other hand, effects the reduction of the original to the exemplary: "Ein gutes Original ist nur, wer Nachahmung verdient! Nachgeahmt zu werden ist aber nur würdig, wer das, was er unternimmt, recht betreibt und immer an seinem Orte etwas Tüchtiges leistet, und wenn dieses auch nichts Unerhörtes und Erzursprüngliches ist!" (H 2:622). The only figure in the godfather's tales who fits this description is Landolt, who is notable primarily for the fact that in spite of five major romantic entanglements, he managed to emerge unscathed and unwed.[10] Yet Jacques's wish for originality runs parallel to his drive to "originate" progeny. Thus the "Original" is the genius-artist, the "author" of exemplary behavior (Landolt, cheerfully resigned to an unattached, childless life), and the progenitor. While Jacques is extending a metaphor ("translating" basic physical urges into the will to another kind of creativity), his godfather is speaking an entirely different language or—to belabor a point—failing to "read" his "reader." He will attempt to persuade Jacques to accept his definition of originality, but this conservative definition bears no relation to the emotional substratum of Jacques's "Trieb," which is his drive to pro-create.

Though the conceptual foundation of "Herr Jacques" is somewhat leaky, the story of reading and writing that it presents is more cohesive, and it is possible that Keller may have paid more attention to this aspect. In order to review the process of Jacques's *Erziehung* in relation to his godfather's *Erzählen*, it will be necessary to consider some of the events of "Herr Jacques" in chronological order. As noted, Jacques's literary ambitions predate the experience of the sentence, and he has not yet succeeded in committing any of his "Der neue Ovid" to his "Heft immer weißbleibenden Papiers" (H 2:612). He complains to his godfather that modern times are foiling his efforts to be original, and the godfather counters with the story of a thirteenth-century epigone, Johannes Hadlaub, who was Zürich's post-*Blütezeit* Minnesinger. Hadlaub sings the praises of his lady, Fides, and her father, who has charged him with collecting old *Minnelieder* for the *Codex Manesse*,[11] is amused at the revival of the quaint tradition of courtly love. The attention bodes well for his daughter who is expected to attract suitors on the strength of this poetic tribute. The family encourages Hadlaub, and Fides, who resists this artifice, is forced to participate in a mock ceremony, awarding the poet *Minnelohn* for his service. Hadlaub fails to win his *frouwe* according to the poetic conventions of courtly love, but happily succeeds when he drops his pretensions. Fides moves to Zurich and becomes a "Bürgersfrau" (H 2:696)—typical of Keller's tendency to *Bürger*-ize everything he touches—and the moral of the tale is articulated by Rüdiger Manesse's (nameless) wife: "Alte Mären lesen wir in den Büchern, aber wir spielen sie nicht selbst wieder ab . . ." (H 2:661).

Either these subtleties are lost on Herr Jacques or he chooses not to replay this particular "alte Mär." The godfather's first experiment in applied pedagogy fails miserably. Contrary to his expectations, his "reader" has paid less attention to the lesson of "Hadlaub" than to the momentous undertaking of the *Codex Manesse*, which excites his "Trieb zur Originalität." Taking his inspiration directly from "Hadlaub," Jacques conceives a new literary project: that of replacing the Manesse manuscript (lost to the city of Paris) with his own "Züricher Ehrenhort," a collection of *original* poems, which will recount the history of Zurich and thus bring glory to the "Athens an der Limmat" (H 2:701). In this case, Jacques produces a grandiose title page, but no poetry follows.

The failure of the gentle *fabula docet* causes the godfather to turn to a more pointed, less ambiguous brand of cautionary tale, "Der Narr auf Manegg." Buz Falätscher, the titular fool, is a grotesque personification of Jacques's "Trieb zur Originalität." Descendent of Rüdiger

Manesse through a series of liaisons between priests and prostitutes, Buz suffers from "die Krankheit, sein zu wollen, was man nicht ist" (H 2:717). Like Jacques, Buz tries to improve on the Manesse manuscript, which he has stolen, but he produces "Verse von jenem schauerlichen Klang, der nur in der Geistesnacht tönt und nicht nachgeahmt werden kann" (H 2:713). The inimitable fool leaves no poetic or biological progeny, and he dies of fright when the nobles come to reclaim the manuscript.

"Der Narr auf Manegg" is a stark exemplary tale, which appears to be tailored specifically to Jacques's psychic distress—as well as to his very ordinary powers of perception. Both Jacques and Buz seek recognition in a literary vein, and each becomes a parasite of the same literary text, the *Codex Manesse*. Herr Jacques has been forced to identify with a repulsive, though "original," author, and the tale does have a certain effect—Jacques abandons his "Züricher Ehrenhort":

> Er bedachte seufzend, ob er auch der Mann dazu sei, das große Werk einem guten Ende entgegen zu führen, und da ihm das immer zweifelhafter schien und der unglückliche Narr von Manegg vor seinen Augen schwebte wie ein Nachtgespenst, ergriff er ein Zänglein und löste, jedoch sorgfältig, das große Pergament [title page] vom Reißbrett. Hiemit gab er den weitausschauenden Plan verloren und beschränkte sich darauf, die Eingangspforte desselben in einen alten Rahmen zu fassen und . . . an die Kammerwand zu hängen.                               (H 2:717)

Jacques's gesture of "resignation" is also one of preservation. His title page, intended as the entry gate to a body of written material, is recycled and implemented as a picture. This gesture indicates a shift of focus from literature to the visual arts for the cycle as a whole. When the godfather next visits his pupil, he brings copies of Michelangelo's paintings from the Sistine chapel for the boy's edification: "Er sollte sein Auge an die wahre Größe gewöhnen und das Erhabene sehen lernen, ohne dabei gleich an sich selbst zu denken" (H 2:717). The method is that prescribed in the Auerbach letter—"wie man schwangeren Frauen etwa schöne Bildwerke vorhält"—and it should be noted that the central motif of the Sistine murals is the creation of man, an obvious analogy to Jacques's ever more manifest destiny.

The "Leserfamilie" severity of "Der Narr auf Manegg" seems to achieve its end, but Keller intrudes and ascribes a lingering "Originalitätsübel" (H 2:717) to Jacques, which necessitates yet another tale. Of the three tales, "Der Landvogt von Greifensee" is the only one that provides a model for imitation, and it is, appropriately enough, given to Jacques in written form, that he might *copy* it. Finally Jacques will be writing something, but it will be exactly the didactic lessons that are intended to save his soul.

"Landvogt" presents a model of serenity. The hero is an extraordinary individual, whose accomplishments range from military brilliance—Frederick the Great had repeatedly sought Landolt's service —to a tenderness of spirit that enables him to comfort a dying child. Interestingly, though we see him associating with the likes of Geßner, Bodmer, and Breitinger, Landolt is not a writer. Even when he tells his housekeeper the story of his five flames (within the context of the godfather's narrative), the godfather interjects, "Wir wollen die Geschichten nacherzählen, jedoch alles ordentlich einteilen, abrunden und für unser Verständnis einrichten" (H 2:727). Landolt's creative outlet is his drawing and painting (the godfather's current medium of instruction): "Seine Malkapelle, wie er sie nannte, bot daher einen ungewöhnlich reichhaltigen Anblick an den Wänden und auf den Staffeleien, und so mannigfaltig die Schildereien waren, . . . so leuchtete doch aus allen derselbe kühne und zugleich still harmonische Geist. Der unablässige Wandel, das Aufglimmen und Verlöschen, Widerhallen und Verklingen der innerlich ruhigen Natur schienen nur die wechselnden Akkorde desselben Tonstückes zu sein" (H 2: 772). The "Malkapelle," a domestic Sistine chapel, creates a link between Michelangelo, artistic genius, and Landolt, good civil servant and Sunday painter, thus allowing the godfather to co-opt the representative of (hypertrophic) creative energy and integrate this energy into his (well-rounded) bourgeois model.

Landolt survives five so-called rejections by women with names like "Grasmücke" and "Distelfink" to settle into his contented bachelorhood. By remaining single, he retains the friendship and memories of his five ladies—possessing them more fully in their absence, one might suppose—and his further life is one of cheerful industry, resignation, and civil service.

At story's end, Jacques is less impressed by the modestly magnificent Landolt than by the mechanics of the novella itself. Intimidated by the literary labor involved in conceiving and executing five instances of rejection by women, "ihm zum Teil widerwärtige Dinge" (H 2:802), he renounces his quest for originality once again, and the literary antidote to his trouble seems to have taken effect: "[er] verzichtete freiwillig und endgültig darauf, ein Originalgenie zu werden, so daß der Herr Pate seinen Part der Erziehungsarbeit als durchgeführt ansehen konnte" (H 2:802). If the frame story were to conclude at this point, it would have demonstrated the efficacy of didactic literature, as it seems to have announced the success of the godfather's project. But Keller foils this impression by extending Jacques's story beyond the ostensible resignation and demonstrating that his hero is busily planning texts in his mind until he is routed by life experience—even though this extension of the novella is in direct contradiction to the announcement of Jacques's resignation.

Jacques develops—in an unnarrated interval—into a successful businessman who pursues his creative interests vicariously as a patron of the arts—though the literary arts are conspicuously absent from the "Künste und Wissenschaften" that enjoy his largesse: "Bei der Einrichtung von Kunstanstalten, Schulen und Ausstellungen, beim Ankaufe von Bildern und dergleichen führte er ein scharfes Wort und wirkte nicht minder in die Ferne, indem er stetsfort an den ausländischen Kunstschulen oder Bildungsstätten hier einen Kupferstecher, dort einen Maler, dort einen Bildhauer, anderswo wieder einen Musikus oder Sterndeuter am Futter hatte" (H 2:802–3). The benefactor is also something of a tyrant, who avenges his own resignation on those whom he supports: "[Das] erste Erfordernis aber, das er in allen Fällen festhalten zu müssen glaubte, war die Bescheidenheit. Da er selber entsagt hatte, so verfuhr er in dem Punkte umso strenger gegen die jungen Schutzbedürftigen; in jedem Zeugnisse, das er verlangte oder selbst ausstellte, mußte das Wort Bescheidenheit einen Platz finden, sonst war die Sache verloren, und bescheiden sein war bei ihm halb gemalt, halb gemeißelt, halb gegeigt und halb gesungen!" (H 2:802). The bourgeois businessman, who controls the flow of cash to hungry artists, exercises a strict normative patronage, demanding modesty from his charges, "da er selber entsagt hatte." Not unlike a didactic author, Jacques has written a scenario for the life of the artist, and he enforces his text by withdrawing support from those who deviate from his norm:

> Da gewährte es ihm denn die höchste Genugtuung, aus dem Briefstil der Überwachten den Grad der Bescheidenheit oder Anmaßung, der unreifen Verwegenheit oder der sanften Ausdauer zu erkennen und jedem Verstoß mit einer Kürzung der Subsidie, mit einem Verschieben der Absendung und einem vierwöchentlichen Hunger zu ahnden und Wind, Wetter, Sonne und Schatten dergestalt eigentlich zu beherrschen, daß die Zöglinge in der Tat etwas erfuhren und zur besseren Charakterausbildung nicht so glatt dahinlebten. (H 2:803)

Whereas the writer of moral-didactic fiction attempts to influence life through art, the patron Jacques attempts to control the circumstances of artistic creation by manipulating the necessities of life. What he has actually learned from his godfather is a method of imposing values on those who are in need of his assistance, and the success of this project, like that of the godfather's, is ultimately illusory.

Jacques's wedding, "das Kunstwerk seiner ersten Lebenshälfte" (H 2:803), provides the occasion for a honeymoon trip to Rome and a surprise visit to a young sculptor whom he supports. As the artist's letters have been a model of humility, Jacques has formed detailed expectations of the scene that awaits him:

> Er war auf ein bescheidenes, aber reinliches und feierlich stilles Atelier gefaßt, in welchem der gelockte Jüngling sinnig vor seinem Marmor stände. Mutig drang er, die Gattin am Arme, in die entlegene Gegend am Tiberflusse vor, auf welchem, wie er ihr erklärte, die Kähne mit den karrarischen Marmorblöcken hergefahren kämen. Schon erblickte er im Geiste den angehenden Thorwaldsen oder Canova, von dem Besuche anständig froh überrascht, sich erstaunt an sein Gerüste lehnen und mit schüchterner Gebärde die Einladung zum Mittagessen anhören; denn er gedachte dem Trefflichen einen guten Tag zu machen; *wußte er doch, daß derselbe den ihm erteilten Vorschriften gemäß sparsam lebte* und, obschon er erst neulich seine Halbjahrs-Pension erhalten, gewiß auch heute noch nicht gefrühstückt habe, der ihm eingeprägten Regel eingedenk, daß es für einen jungen unvermögenden Menschen in der Fremde vollkommen genüge, wenn er im Tag einmal ordentlich esse, was am besten des Abends geschehe.                          (H 2:804, my emphasis)

Jacques's imaginary scene is identified as a "Bildhauernovelle" when the narrator observes that the drunken sculptor is in no shape to serve as its hero: "[Er] war leider nicht vorbereitet, als Held einer der heute so beliebten Bildhauernovellen zu dienen, da er sich eben im unheimlichen Stadium des faulen Hundes befand, dem ja seiner Zeit auch der junge Thorwaldsen nicht entgangen ist" (H 2:807). The studio, supposedly selected and furnished in accordance with the patron's principles of modesty, is actually a commercial laundry filled with a large number of gypsylike peasants, who are celebrating the artist's somewhat belated wedding to one of their own. The narrative of Jacques's expectations of the artist and his home, as quoted above, represents a considerable expansion of its counterpart in the original version of the novella as published in *Die deutsche Rundschau*: "Ausgehängte Wäsche, Kochgeschirre und dergleichen in einem verdächtigen Vorraume wollten nicht recht stimmen *zu dem Bilde* eines sinnig vor dem Marmor stehenden Jünglings, *das er im Kopfe trug.*"[12]

The original Herr Jacques had a picture in mind, whereas in the definitive version he anticipates a fully developed encounter with an ideal pupil. In revising his text Keller changed register from the visual arts and gave narrative/literary form to his hero's thoughts, as befits the character of one who has internalized (and not renounced) strong literary ambitions. The physical description of Jacques on his wedding trip gives further evidence of his continuing preoccupation with literature: "Einen hohen Strohhut auf dem Kopfe, in gelben Nanking gekleidet, mit zurückgeschlagenem Hemdekragen und fliegenden Halstuchzipfeln, führte er die Neuvermählte auf den sieben Hügeln herum" (H 2:803). Though the *Rundschau* version contained the explanatory phrase "a la Byron"[13] (after "Halstuchzipfeln"), Herr Jacques also bears a suspicious resemblance to Tischbein's famous portrait of Goethe in the Roman Campagna. In either case, the patron of all arts except literature has chosen clothing that lends him the aspect of a poet.

Recovering from the initial shock of seeing his "Bildhauernovelle" so basely contradicted, Jacques demands to see the statue he has underwritten. He finds the sculptor's "thirsting faun" (scheduled to have been executed in marble) to be a crude clay study in an advanced state of dessication—covered with dried rags and standing in a heap of potatoes. As the protective rags are removed and body parts fall from the central mass, Jacques reluctantly abandons his "Bildhauernovelle," but he then rallies and decides that the whole experience can be rendered as a "Künstleranekdote": "Hierüber mußte er endlich selbst lachen und es begann ihm die Ahnung aufzudämmern, daß es sich um eine gute Künstleranekdote, um ein prächtiges Naturerlebnis handle. . . . Herr Jacques war ganz Aug und Ohr, um keinen Zug des Gemäldes zu verlieren und wenigstens den ästhetischen Gewinn dieser Erfahrung möglichst vollständig einzuheimsen" (H 2:808). Supposedly, the anecdote will recount the didactic patron's expectations and the actual circumstances that foil them, a distinct analogue to Keller's own "Züricher Ehrenhort," which allows that the best didactic theory has little effect when put into practice.

Jacques is living proof of the failure of his godfather's literary practice. He is obviously still yearning to write as he tries to convert experience into anecdote, a literary form, in order to realize an aesthetic profit. A brief "study" of his literary influences reveals an interesting process: the models he has chosen for imitation (in his quest for originality) move ever closer to his own immediate reality. Beginning with the myths of distant Roman antiquity (Ovid), his model migrates to the Swiss Middle Ages (*Codex Manesse*), to the contemporary light fiction of his social class ("Bildhauernovelle"),[14] and finally to the real events occurring before him.

With each successive model, Jacques moves closer to the original creative act he so fervently desires to perform. "Der neue Ovid" and the "Züricher Ehrenhort" are the works envisioned in puberty. Both relate to specific literary models but are rather vague in concept. Jacques knows what he wants to do (a modern *Metamorphoses* and a verse history of Zurich), but he fails to fill in his framework—though the illustrated title page of the latter represents an advance over the sheaf of blank pages designated for the former.

It is quite different, however, with the projects of his adult life, after he has "renounced" or internalized his ambitions. In this stage, the character of his models is less clear but his own contribution is more substantial. The "Bildhauernovelle" implies no specific precursor but rather a prose subgenre—yet Jacques endows it with precise content and detailed action, beyond what is suggested by the generic heading. The "Künstleranekdote" is even less specific as a category than its predecessor, "Bildhauer" being a definite kind of "Künstler" and "Novelle" a more established and regulated form than "Anekdote." Nevertheless, the "Künstleranekdote" is the most fully developed of Jacques's projects, and he scrutinizes his material to achieve a faithful rendering of this original event. For the first time in his career, Jacques, the would-be writer, is face to face with his text. His will to write now inspires him to reproduce "real" life, and the next logical step in his journey to biological adulthood will be to *create* real life. Here literature and life intersect for Herr Jacques, and it is at this moment that "der Bambino," the sculptor's illegitimate child, emerges to effect his purgation.

Realizing that his efforts at the cocreation of a statue have resulted in the procreation of the sculptor's child—an interesting twist on the Pygmalion legend and an event that obviously preceded the wedding—Jacques grows angry: "Ein größerer Unwille, eine dunklere Entrüstung als je zuvor zogen sich auf dem Antlitze des Herrn Jacques zusammen" (H 2:808). His displacement maneuver has led him down a circuitous path to the very juncture he had sought to avoid, and his instincts dictate flight. But before he can flee the "Höhle der Unbescheidenheit" (H 2:809), he is forced to acknowledge his wife's wish for a similar creation and to accept the godfatherhood of the baby itself. He removes a sheet from his notebook—the token of the writer in Keller's work—wraps a coin in it, and places it under the child's clothing. Thus in a comic-symbolic ceremony, the patron's money is wrapped in the writer's (blank) page and invested in "life." Godfather Jacques then runs off, not to write a "Künstleranekdote" after all, but grudgingly to originate his own progeny.[15]

This final scene is a delightful parody of the naive realist position. Jacques, the aspiring writer and reticent progenitor, finally has his text within his grasp, and this text promises to be a more or less exact duplication of Life Itself—though its subject matter is the Artist, that mythical figure who, at present, is behaving like the most ordinary of men. Yet the appearance of the baby, another version of Life Itself, disrupts the patron's reverie and destroys the literary potential of the scene before him. At this moment, the concerns of "Herr Jacques" shift from literary matters to life matters (or living matter), and it is at this moment that Jacques resigns his dream of originality in order to imitate the (real) artist, whose base behavior he resents. Every literary effort to reform Jacques has failed, but this rude awakening, which cannot be integrated into his literary text, effects his reform. The border has been crossed into life and the ends of (didactic) literature have been accomplished on the other side.

Jacques, who is now "nicht mehr in erster Jugend" (H 2:803) will (we assume) finally indulge those "sanft aufregenden Gefühle" that he earlier perceived as his "Trieb zur Originalität." Insofar as the overt design of the first cycle of Züricher Novellen is that of curing Jacques of his obsession with creative writing (and the corollary avoidance of one of life's functions), the failure of didactic literature to do so must indicate some doubt on the part of the author as to its general potential for success. Though Jacques is initially swayed by a book he reads—actually, by a word in "some" sentence in "some" book (the "effective" text is never specified)—his experience shows that the influence of literature is accidental and unpredictable, and quite possibly a phenomenon better ascribed to adolescence. Indeed, victims of literary influence in Keller are often the young and impressionable, who find their libidinal inclinations recast and legitimized in books. The godfather's tales, all written by Keller of course, do have a moral-didactic thrust in this context, and they seem to assume a parallel process: that the appeal to "higher" inclinations can effect the improvement of character. Yet the godfather's stories are not Keller's stories. Keller's stories are embedded within a context of failed instruction, which undermines the godfather's intent and qualifies the novellas themselves. The godfather's implicit confidence in the power of didactic fictions to improve and reform their audience is not shared by the author, who once again constructs his didactic edifice in order to topple it. This is a strategy that allows for the expression of a quixotic wish to reform readers in the face of a straightforward admission that literature is not the appropriate medium for such a project. Thus Keller's "marginal" tale, which ascribes an extraliterary purpose to "Hadlaub," "Der Narr auf Manegg," and "Der Landvogt von Greifensee" (in which they fail), actually affirms their independence of such utility by subverting their contextual "intent."

# 5. *Das Sinngedicht:*
# Beyond the Futility of Utility

In the fifth canto of Dante's *Inferno,* Francesca of Rimini tells of her brief intimacy with Paolo, a moment of sweet abandon, which resulted in their murder and subsequent eternal damnation. As is well known, she blames the whole affair on a book that they were reading, *Lancelot of the Lake.* As she explains:

> To pass the time one day, we read of Lancelot and how love constrained him. We were alone and suspected nothing. Several times that reading urged our eyes to meet and our faces grew pale. But it was a single passage that overwhelmed us: When we read of how those worshipped lips were kissed by so great a lover, this one, who shall never be parted from me, kissed my mouth all trembling. That book *and its author* were our Gallehault [go-between] and on that day we read no further.[1]

Had Paolo and Francesca been engaged in conversation, embroidery, music, or some other less dangerous medieval leisure-time pursuit, they might never have kissed, Francesca's husband might never have caught them *in flagrante,* and he might never have done away with them so swiftly that they had no occasion to repent and therefore no chance of salvation. Poor Dante faints when he comprehends their monstrous fate, no doubt because this vile punishment is the consequence of a deep and enduring (if suddenly conceived) love. But might he not also be reeling at the thought of the evils wrought by literary fictions *and by their authors*?[2] It is obvious that Keller also considered this problem. Pankraz's designation of Shakespeare as "dieser verführerische falsche Prophet" (though undermined by the conspicuous absence of a causal connection between reading and action) seems to confirm Dante's fears and, however trivially, to endorse his swoon. But Pankraz's blunt formulation of his apparent seduction gives a comic focus to a danger that his author implicitly denies, and this denial becomes a recurring feature of Keller's later fiction.

Although Keller probably did not ever experience a direct report of the damaging effects of fictions (as did the fictional Dante), his first novel reflects a consciousness of the peril of reading and of the author's responsibility both to make readers aware of this peril and to neutralize the danger in his own work. The perception of fiction as a powerful means of direct or directable influence (be it positive or negative) was in the air as Keller began to write—even if that air was growing stale. The gradual "secularization" of popular reading material, which gained momentum in the later eighteenth century, was typical of most secularizing processes in that the "objects" (books) that lost their religious content retained a quasi-religious aura. Literary texts (within literature) still functioned as sacred authorities, and, for authors of the late eighteenth century, there was in principle little difference between Augustine reading the Bible and Werther reading Homer or Anton Reiser reading *Werther*. Literary criticism after the Enlightenment retained its moral vigilance and continued its efforts to discourage the immoral and to elicit works of secular fiction portraying exemplary attitudes or behavior. It is in this climate of desanctified promotion of proper behavior that the novel begins to attain respectability in the public eye. In *Die zweite Wirklichkeit*, Lieselotte Kurth records that Friedrich von Blanckenburg predicted that the novel, as the entertainment of the masses, could be expected to exert influence over mass morals, and that critics recommended novels to young people as being preferable to history books, which often lacked poetic justice.[3] Samuel Richardson was widely read in German translation at the time, though he was occasionally criticized because some of his characters were so good as to be, in a practical sense, inimitable. Blanckenburg, for example, was especially indignant that Richardson had failed to indicate exactly *how* it was that Clarissa had become so virtuous (certainly, family environment had little to do with it).[4] Thus much of German literary criticism from 1750 to 1850 (and beyond) concerned itself primarily with monitoring secular fiction and drama, attending to probability and purity of genre, that these works might have the desired effects on readers and be truly worthy successors to the religious readings they supplanted.

It appears, then, that the book-world equation, which brought so many errant reader-heroes to ruin, was also the basis for normative literary criticism and much literary writing between 1750 and 1850. Later in the nineteenth century, however, this confidence in literary suasion begins to weaken, although the traditional forms persist. In Keller's later work, the figure of the reader-hero, who reads his fiction and obeys it, comes to represent the wish-dream of the epigonal didactic author, the flickering fantasy of fiction's capacity for controlling the world outside it and for effecting change. Keller espouses the traditional faith in *Der grüne Heinrich*, showing how literary fictions can intrude upon daily life and manipulate readers like puppets, but he questions the connection in "Pankraz," creates an obfuscating *mise-en-abîme* in "Romeo und Julia," satirizes the connection in "Herr Jacques," and ultimately renders the notion harmless and amusing in *Das Sinngedicht*. By the time we reach *Das Sinngedicht* in a chronological tour of Keller's work, imaginative literature has lost its sacred aura, and "desecration" is no longer possible. Herr Reinhart is Keller's last reader-hero, and his adventures constitute the author's final remarks on the (fictional) reception of fiction that has served as Keller's figure of preference for the imagination in its rebellion against the drab forms of empirical reality.

Strictly speaking, *Das Sinngedicht* concerns the literal reception of poetry—Logau's couplet at the beginning and Goethe's "Mit einem gemalten Band" at the end—and in both cases the "misapprehension" of verse has a heuristic function: it brings Reinhart and Lucie together and facilitates their engagement. Both poems are literally enacted by their recipients, but each enactment depends on a different method of reception and understanding—and it is the method that is at issue in *Das Sinngedicht*, where the problem of how to understand fictions and language itself (as figurative speech or direct speech) is illustrated in the difficulties that Reinhart and Lucie have in establishing a noncombative rapport. Here Keller creates and resolves a conflict between Reinhart's "scientific" thinking, which is based on experimentation and the observation of empirical data, and the historical-hermeneutical methods of understanding espoused by Lucie.[5] Keller deliberately structures this opposition between "objective" scientific observation and empathic interpretation as a male-female dichotomy, and in so doing, he overcomes (or suspends) his own misogyny, favoring Lucie and making Reinhart appear misguided, ridiculous, and occasionally swinish. Ernst May offers a succinct statement of authorial allegiance in his *Gottfried Kellers Sinngedicht*: "Keller ist durchaus auf Seiten Lucies."[6] In a radical departure from earlier work,[7] Keller parodies the male presumption behind Reinhart's "Galatea ideology" and allows Lucie to prevail on her own terms, privileging the "feminine" toward a cautious leveling of sexual differences. As Lucie observes: "[Es] ist immer lehrreich zu vernehmen, was die Herren hinsichtlich unseres Geschlechtes für wünschenswert und erbaulich halten; ich fürchte, es ist zuweilen nicht viel tiefsinniger als das Ideal, welches unsern Romanschreiberinnen bei Entwerfung ihrer Heldengestalten oder ersten Liebhaber vorschwebt, wegen deren sie so oft ausgelacht werden" (H 2:989).[8]

Another aspect of this opposition between male scientific thought and female understanding is the schism that Keller perceived between contemporary scientific advances, specifically Darwinism, and his own, more spiritual view of human behavior. As Wolfgang Preisendanz has observed, the literary style associated with Darwinism was the then-emerging naturalism, a literary trend that Keller was not prepared to accept—any more than he could embrace Darwinism.[9] Keller had already made light of *The Origin of Species* in the *Züricher Novellen*, where he describes two lions drawn by Herr Jacques as being "auf einer untern Entwicklungsstufe erstarrt" (H 2:700). *Das Sinngedicht* opens with a stab at Darwin: "Vor etwa fünfundzwanzig Jahren, als die Naturwissenschaften eben wieder auf einem höchsten Gipfel standen, obgleich das Gesetz der natürlichen Zuchtwahl noch nicht bekannt war, öffnete Herr Reinhart eines Tages seine Fensterläden und ließ den Morgenglanz . . . in sein Arbeitsgemach" (H 2:935).[10] *Das Sinngedicht* describes the mating of Reinhart and Lucie, but it is a mating dance (oddly analogous to similar procedures in the animal kingdom) facilitated by poetry and storytelling; the specifically (educated) human capacity for creating and reacting to fictions provides them with a channel of communication that eventually leads to methodological harmony and betrothal.

As the collection opens, Reinhart is deeply engrossed in the fictions or hypotheses of natural science, attempting to prove or disprove them by experiment. His experiments with light (Lux, Lucie) threaten literally to blind him: his eyes are growing weak from the observation of light rays as refracted through a prism ("auf die Tortur gespannt" [H 2:936]) in a darkened laboratory. This is the stock figure of the monomaniacal scientist whose exposure to life and light is minimal. Reinhart is a scientific recluse, surrounded by laboratory equipment, and his book collection (an index of character in Keller and elsewhere)[11] is unilaterally scientific in nature: "Wo man ein Buch oder Heft aufschlug, erblickte man nur den lateinischen Gelehrtendruck, Zahlensäulen und Logarithmen. Kein einziges Buch handelte von menschlichen oder moralischen Dingen oder, wie man vor hundert Jahren gesagt haben würde, von Sachen des Herzens und des schönen Geschmackes" (H 2:936).

Lucie's books, on the other hand, reveal an interest in human beings and their history. The core of her collection is a shelf of autobiographies: "Diese Bände enthielten durchweg die eigenen Lebensbeschreibungen oder Briefsammlungen vielerfahrener oder ausgezeichneter Leute. . . . [Überall] kein anderes als das eigene Wort der zur

Ruhe gegangenen Lebensmeister oder Leidensschüler enthaltend" (H 2:956). Whereas Reinhart is preoccupied with mathematical, chemical, and physiological functions, Lucie doggedly pursues an understanding of inner life or mental life:

> Ich suche die Sprache der Menschen zu verstehen, wenn sie von sich selbst reden; aber es kommt mir zuweilen vor, wie wenn ich durch einen Wald ginge und das Gezwitscher der Vögel hörte, ohne ihrer Sprache kundig zu sein. Manchmal scheint mir, daß jeder etwas anderes sagt, als er denkt, oder wenigstens nicht recht sagen kann, was er denkt, und daß dieses sein Schicksal sei. . . . Wenn ich sie nun alle so miteinander vergleiche in ihrer Aufrichtigkeit, die sie für kristallklar halten, so frage ich mich: gibt es überhaupt ein menschliches Leben, an welchem nichts zu verhehlen ist, das heißt unter allen Umständen und zu jeder Zeit? Gibt es einen ganz wahrhaftigen Menschen und kann es ihn geben? (H 2:1161–62)

Lucie's question implies a critique of Reinhart's approach to knowledge, which springs from rational analysis of observable fact, just as his impulsive question, "Warum treiben Sie alle diese Dinge?" (H 2:958), indicates a lack of understanding for her taste in reading. What passes for fact in autobiography can easily be fiction, and in no case are all the facts given. Lucie's unwillingness to accept a clean division between fact and fiction indicates an approach more suited to its object. Autobiography, which gives literary form to life, is another way of making life literary, and Lucie expands her "narrative" knowledge by reading lives as texts rather than tables.

Reinhart begins his odyssey by reading a literary text as life. Prevented from doing further research by his ailing eyes, and seeking some point of departure for his hiatus in textual authority, he climbs to his attic (the spatial semiotics are worth noting) and inspects a pile of old books "die von den halbvergessenen menschlichen Dingen handelten" (H 2:938). He locates a volume of Lachmann's Lessing edition and utters the following panegyric to Lessing: "Komm, tapferer Lessing! es führt dich zwar jede Wäscherin im Munde, aber ohne eine Ahnung von deinem eigentlichen Wesen zu haben, das nichts anderes ist als die ewige Jugend und Geschicklichkeit zu allen Dingen, der unbedingte gute Willen, ohne Falsch und im Feuer vergoldet!" (H 2:938). That bit of "Lessing's" advice, which is not accessible to the laundress but is supposedly transparent to the scientist, appears in the form of a Logau epigram with erotic overtones:

Wie willst du weiße Lilien zu roten Rosen machen?
Küß eine weiße Galathee: sie wird errötend lachen.   (H 2:938)

Reinhart commits the fundamental error of the reader-hero and decides to enact the text he is reading: "Welch ein köstliches Experiment! Wie einfach, wie tief, klar und richtig, so hübsch abgewogen und gemessen!" (H 2:938).

Having found beauty and "truth" in a literary text, Reinhart sets out on a quest for his "weiße Galathee," kissing various women and awaiting the combined reaction (blushing and laughter) that will mark one of them as the woman he can fashion into a bride. His method is purely experimental, and the results—physiological responses occasioned by emotion—will be visible to the observing eye. After several failures, he agrees to deliver a letter to a woman unknown to him, and he finds his way to Lucie, who first appears standing next to a *marble* fountain, dressed in *white*, and occupied with cleaning *roses*: "Je ungewohnter der Anblick dieses Bildes war, das mit seiner Zusammenstellung des Marmorbrunnens und der weißen Frauengestalt eher der idealen Erfindung eines müßigen Schöngeistes als wirklichem Leben glich, umso ängstlicher wurde es . . . Reinhart zu Mut, der wie eine Bildsäule staunend zu Pferde saß" (H 2:951). Obviously Reinhart has reached his destination. Lucie, whose appearance is so poetically contrived, is to be his ideal woman—although she is hardly a Galatea waiting to be acted upon.

Reinhart's experience is not that of the typical reader-hero, who must learn that literary fictions are not an accurate guide to the world. To all intents and purposes, Reinhart's method of literary reception has achieved its aim: he has found the woman he seeks, though he has yet to kiss her. Before he does so (and it will be a long time) he must grapple, not with his faith in fictions, which is only incidental in this case, but with his own scientific literalism—which leads him to confuse the symbol with the symbolized, and the process described by the poem as straightforward instruction (kiss, blush, laughter) with the process it alludes to poetically: that of converting a virgin (white lily) to a woman/wife (red rose). "Aber indem er sich sagte, daß er hier oder nirgends das Sprüchlein des alten Logau erproben möchte, und erst jetzt die tiefere Bedeutung desselben völlig empfand, merkte er auch, mit welch weitläufigen Vorarbeiten und Schwierigkeiten der Versuch verbunden sein dürfte" (H 2:953). The first of these difficulties is the loss of his text. Reinhart, who had absent-mindedly presented the poem and not the letter to

Lucie, once again surrenders the piece of paper to her when she comprehends the nature of his project and desires to burn the Logau epigram, discarding his hypothesis before he can prove it. Like Nettchen, who cries "Keine Romane mehr!" Lucie, who wants no more experiments, delivers the paper up to a candle flame, thus destroying the material medium of the poem Reinhart hopes to enact.

As Preisendanz has carefully demonstrated, the bouts of storytelling that ensue do not involve allegorical reference to a developing romance between Reinhart and Lucie. Rather they address more general problems of "misunderstanding" between partners, including disguise, lack of communication, and the confusion of symbol and symbolized.[12] In each case the protagonists' methodological principles clash, creating the appearance of debate or opposition in the presence of mutual attraction—but love is frequently represented as denial of love in Keller's writings.[13] Lucie, the hermeneut, interprets human behavior and motivation, reading between the lines and merging information from Reinhart's narratives with her own prior experience of such (real or fictional) occurrences, whereas Reinhart, the scientist, literalist, and narrator of most of the tales, presents his stories objectively, often relying on his own alleged personal observation of the narrated proceedings.[14] His story of a *Treppenheirat*, for example, begins quite literally as the eventually-to-be-wed couple meets on the stairs. When Lucie objects that the same tale, "Die arme Baronin," has been artificially structured to make the heroine appear passive, Reinhart cautions her not to read anything into the "facts" as they stand:

> "Kennen Sie die Leute, oder haben Sie sonst schon von der Geschichte gehört?"
> "Ich? Nicht im mindesten! Ich höre heute zum ersten Male davon reden."
> "Nun, wenn Sie also keine andere Quelle kennen, so müssen Sie sich schon an meine Redaktion halten, die ich nach bestem Wissen und Gewissen besorgt habe. Ich beteure, daß auch nicht die leiseste Spur von Koketterie und Schlauheit soll zwischen den Zeilen zu lesen sein, und ich bitte Sie, hochzuverehrendes Fräulein, nichts hineinlegen zu wollen, was hineinzulegen ich nicht die Absicht hatte!" (H 2:1064)

Reinhart's insistence on interpretive restraint in the absence of other sources, and on the sanctity of his version, closes his tale to the prying maneuvers of "feminine" understanding.

Lucie, on the other hand, deliberately leaves much to the imagination in "Die Berlocken." Narrating from a woman's point of view, she refuses to indulge her male audience with a description of the beautiful young Indian woman, Quoneschi or "Libelle":

Ich kann es nicht wagen, eine Beschreibung von dem wunderbaren Wesen zu machen, und muß es den Herren überlassen, sich nach eigenem Geschmacksurteil das Schönste vorzustellen, was man sich damals unter einer eingeborenen Tochter Columbias dachte, sowohl was Körperbau und Hautfarbe als Kostüm und dergleichen betrifft. Ein hoher Turban von Federn wird unerläßlich, ein buntes Papagenakleidchen rätlich sein; doch wie gesagt, ich will mich nicht weiter einmischen. . . .   (H 2:1151)

Her refusal is somewhat ironic, and perhaps vindictive, but she makes her methodological point by forcing her listeners to enter her tale and build on it by exercising their imagination. The "facts" are absent in this case, and the storyteller conceives her story as a participatory fiction. Lucie more than compensates for her reticence, however, in the later description of a man, Quoneschi's beloved Donnerbär:

Wenn ich vorhin bescheiden auf eine Schilderung der schönen Libelle verzichtet habe, behielt ich mir vor, dafür das Äußere dieses jungen Kriegshelden umso ausführlicher darzustellen, soweit meine schwachen Kräfte reichen; denn hier tritt ja das Frauenauge mit seinem Urteile in sein Amt. Denke man sich also einen Komplex herrlich gewachsener riesiger Glieder vom sattesten Kupferrot und vom Kopf bis zu den Füßen mit gelben und blauen Streifen gezeichnet . . . so hat man einen Vorschmack dessen, was noch kommt. . . .   (H 2:1155)

She continues for some time; but even where she supplies the details of appearance, she concedes that they are arbitrary and that they actually originate in the recipient's imagination ("Denke man sich . . ."). Whereas Reinhart tries to erect a barrier between tale and recipient, allowing only for a monodirectional transmission of the literal sense, Lucie insists on two-way traffic in her tales, facilitating "Rezeption" in a more Jaußian sense.

This fundamental difference of approach is mediated not by storytelling, but by the intervention of Lucie's uncle, who begins by revealing to Reinhart the rather frivolous circumstances under which his mother chose between two rival suitors ("Die Geisterseher")—thus making Reinhart the product of a somewhat haphazard "Damen-wahl"[15]—a mild shock for the would-be Pygmalion. Finally, after all tales have been told, the uncle explains how it is that Lucie "receives" Reinhart's tales of so many passive women and why she is piqued by them: "Und merken Sie denn nicht, daß es weniger schmeichelhaft für Sie wäre, wenn sich die Lux [Lucie] gleichgültig dafür zeigte, daß Sie für allerhand unwissende und arme Kreaturen schwärmen, zu denen sie einmal nicht zu zählen das Glück oder Verdienst hat?" (H 2:1157). Lucie has understood Reinhart's narratives as interested tales of exemplary feminine passivity—which indeed they are, but only insofar as they serve him as a firstline defense against the active woman who confronts him. He composes his story of "Don Correa," for example, because "[e]s schien ihm nämlich prächtig zur Abwehr gegen die Überhebung des ebenbürtigen Frauengeschlechtes zu tau-gen" (H 2:1094). Incidentally, the arrogant woman in "Don Correa" is finally hanged for her crimes.[16]

The uncle's explanation comes as a great surprise to Reinhart, who blames figurative speech for the misunderstanding:

"So geht es," sagte er mit unmerklicher Bewegung; "wenn man immer in Bildern und Gleichnissen spricht, so versteht man die Wirklichkeit zuletzt nicht mehr und wird unhöflich. Indessen habe ich natürlich an das Fräulein gar nicht gedacht, so wenig als eigentlich an mich selbst, so wie man auch niemals selber zu halten gedenkt, was man predigt. Es ist Zeit, daß ich abreite, sonst verwickle ich mich noch in Widersprüche und Torheiten mit meinem Geschwätz, wie eine Schnepfe im Garn." (H 2:1157)

Reinhart has intended for his "Bilder und Gleichnisse" to support a very specific argument about worldly and prosperous Pygmalions and the less advanced, impecunious Galateas they choose to educate. But the argument is ultimately a hypothesis that he does not intend to verify in his choice of a spouse. One never considers practicing what one preaches, he notes, and preaching is thus a substitute for practice, just as the "ideal" process of inscribing one's own being and desires on the character of a potential wife is best pursued in com-pensatory fictional tales, like that of Pygmalion and Galatea. This aspect of the author's intention has escaped Lucie's interpretive skills, possibly because she has not recognized that Reinhart himself is the "Galatea" in this context.[17] It is, in fact, Reinhart who is transformed and enlivened through contact with Lucie, who thaws his cold, sci-entific exterior and encourages or inspires an appreciation of the "menschliche Dinge" that he had consigned to his attic.

During the storytelling, Reinhart's narrative style develops from alleged recitation of the facts ("Regine," "Die arme Baronin") to his largely imagined rendition of the historical Don Correa's adventures: "[er] spann und malte . . . den größten Teil der Nacht hindurch das Geschichtchen aus" (H 2:1094). When Reinhart, in his conversation with Lucie's uncle, refers to his several tales as "Geschwätz," which threatens to trap him "wie eine Schnepfe im Garn," he trivializes the Galatea experiments (including his own enactment of the Logau epigram) and denies the validity of the scientific method in matters of the heart. Somewhat later, after Lucie has confessed her girlish fascination with the Catholic Leodegar, who replaced Schiller's Max Piccolomini in her dreams, Reinhart shows a deep emotional appreciation of her involvement and offers his own interpretation:

> Was Sie erlebt haben, ist wohl zu unterscheiden von der ungehörigen Liebesucht verderbter Kinder und widerfährt nur wenigen bevorzugten Wesen, deren edle angeborene Großmut des Herzens der Zeit ungeduldig, unschuldig und unbewußt vorauseilt. Der naive Kinderglauben an die leichtfertigen Scherzworte des Herren Kardinals [Leodegar], an welchem Sie so treulich festgehalten haben, gehört zu dieser Großmut, wie ein Taubenflügel zum andern, und mit solchen Flügeln fliegen die Engel unter den Menschen.                                        (H 2:1181)

He then confesses the inadequacy and inferiority of his own method: "Beschämt ermesse ich an diesem Beispiele des Guten, wie teilnahmslos mein Leben verlaufen ist, wie inhaltslos, und auf wie leichtsinnige Weise ich sogar vor Ihr Angesicht geraten bin!" (H 2:1181). Reinhart has himself converted to Lucie's methodology by developing an interest in the "human sciences" and becoming "human" himself, like the legendary marble statue-woman he thought he was seeking. He recalls his literal reading of Logau with shame.

It is on the basis of Reinhart's distinction between his "Bilder und Gleichnisse" and "die Wirklichkeit" that Preisendanz is able to divorce the content of the tales from the action of the frame itself.[18] The images and figures of the stories are not directly involved in the growing affection between Reinhart and Lucie, although the understanding and interpretation of such images is the paramount issue. This is yet another variation on Keller's monothematics of the reception of fictions, dreams, and fantasies and the problem of what to do with them. However, in *Das Sinngedicht*, for the first time, Keller emphasizes and expatiates on the mode of reception, beginning with Reinhart's experimental use of the Logau couplet and proceeding, via

Lucie's interest in autobiography, to a view of fictions that requires the participation of imagination as a means of avoiding primitive *Selbstbezug*. Danger, despair, death, and the many unpleasant issues that arise in earlier Keller works are in this case confined to the tales themselves; Reinhart and Lucie—like Boccaccio's *Decameron* storytellers—are set apart from all human misery and are able to contemplate method, free from the influence of the stormy vicissitudes of life.

Das Sinngedicht concludes with Reinhart's and Lucie's reception of, or reaction to, Goethe's "Mit einem gemalten Band." The event occurs under the chapter heading "In welchem das Sinngedicht sich bewährt," indicating that a literary text has stood the test of "reality" and proved to be true (within the charming artifice of the collection entitled "Sinngedicht"). Reinhart and Lucie do not read Goethe's poem, but rather they overhear a shoemaker singing it with rustic embellishments:

> [Das Lied] war nichts minderes als Goethes bekanntes Jugendliedchen "Mit einem gemalten Bande," welches zu jener Zeit noch in ältern, auf Löschpapier gedruckten Liederbüchlein für Handwerksbursche statt der jetzt üblichen Arbeitermarseillaisen und dergleichen zu finden war und das er auf der Wanderschaft gelernt hatte. Er sang es nach einer sehr gefühlvollen altväterischen Melodie mit volksmäßigen Verzierungen, die sich aber natürlich rhythmisch seinem Vor- und Rückwärtsschreiten anschmiegen mußten und von den Bewegungen der Arbeit vielfach gehemmt oder übereilt wurde.                    (H 2:1184)

The shoemaker has integrated poetry into his work routine, forcing the meter to follow the rhythm of his work and making the poem a "useful" (because pleasant) accompaniment to the daily drudgery of his occupation. It is worth noting that this image briefly resolves the schism between the imaginary and the mundane, which has hitherto been exacerbated by literature in Keller. This shoemaker knows what to do with his text; work and poem merge and complement each other:

> Wenn er mit leichten Schritten begann:
>     Kleine Blumen, kleine Blätter —ja Blätter
>     Streien wir mit leichter Hand
>     Gude junge Frihlings-Gädder —ja Gädder
>     Tändelnd auf ein luftig Band
> bei dem luftigen Band aber durch einen Knoten im Garn aufgehalten wurde und dasselbe daher um eine ganze Note verlän-

gern und zuletzt doch wiederholen mußte, so war die unbeküm-
merte und unbewußte Treuherzigkeit, womit es geschah, mehr
rührend als komisch.                                  (H 2:1184)

Reinhart and Lucie are fascinated, despite the rural character of the
delivery: "Dazu sang er in einem verdorbenen Dialekte, was die
Leistung noch drolliger machte. Allein die unverwüstliche Seele des
Liedes und die frische Stimme, die Stille des Nachmittages und das
verliebte Gemüt des einsam arbeitenden Meisters [who is engaged to
Lucie's maid] bewirkten das Gegenteil eines lächerlichen Eindruckes"
(H 2:1184).

   This second poem that Reinhart and Lucie experience together, like
Paolo and Francesca reading of Lancelot, also penetrates their "reality" as they arrive at the same "reading" and carry out the instructions it implies:

> Einen Blick, geliebtes Leben!
> Und ich bin belohnt *genuch*.

Reinhart und Lucie *blickten* sich unwillkürlich an. Der Sänger im
kleinen Haus schien für sie mitzusingen, trotz seines abscheu-
lichen Idioms. Welch ein Frieden und welch herzliche Zuversicht
oder Lebenshoffnung pulsierten in diesen Sangeswellen! Am
jenseitigen Fenster stand ein mit Grün behangener Vogelkäficht.
Nun kam die letzte Strophe. Fihle, sang er,

> Fihle, was dies Herz empfindet —ja pfindet,
> Reiche frei mir deine Hand,
> Und das Band, das uns verbindet —ja bindet,
> Sei kein schwaches Rosenband!

. . . Da ein paar Kanarienvögel mit ihrem schmetternden Ge-
sange immer lauter dreinlärmten, war eine Art von Tumult in
der Stube, von welchem hingerissen Lucie und Reinhart sich
küßten. Lucie hatte die Augen voll Wasser und doch lachte sie,
indem sie purpurrot wurde. . . .
                              (H 2:1185, second emphasis mine)

   Reinhart and Lucie, Keller's Paolo and Francesca, are caught un-
awares, "hingerissen," and driven into one another's arms by the
power of literature. Yet their imitation is not their undoing, but rather
a fortuitous integration of poetry into their lives. Why is it that some
readers suffer eternal damnation for their "mimetic" kisses and others
find perfect wedded bliss? Obviously, their respective backgrounds
differ—Francesca was already married, and her husband was apparently a jealous man—but so too do their respective contexts. Though

Dante's *Commedia* does not confine itself to the explication of virtue and vice, right and wrong, it is nonetheless highly conscious of these issues, and the *contrapasso* dealt out to poor Francesca of Rimini and her lover identifies their union as sinful. Their book is also implicated, and Dante can only exit this conundrum by fainting. In contrast to Francesca's infernal narrative, the poetically inspired kiss in *Das Sinngedicht* occurs in an atmosphere of playful artifice, where danger and sin do not exist—except as the subject of tales told for amusement. If anything, *Das Sinngedicht* is a literary joke, a narrative that makes light of the so-called perils of reading, neutralizing them for the case at hand and blithely rejecting other possibilities.

Reinhart's and Lucie's behavior reflects both Goethe's and Logau's poems, which merge in a very specific way to inaugurate the lovers' betrothal. Their mutual "Blick," corresponding to the reference in Goethe's "gemalten Band" ("Einen Blick, geliebtes Leben"), leads to the *kiss*, which in turn effects Lucie's *blush* and *laughter*, all particulars of Logau's couplet. Lucie knows this and she remarks on it: "Bei Gott, jetzt haben wir doch Ihr schlimmes Rezept von dem alten Logau ausgeführt!" (H 2:1186). Reinhart assures her that he had not been thinking of Logau ("Aber ich habe wahrhaftig nicht an das Epigramm gedacht" [H 2:1186]), but he then echoes Goethe's poem by asking for her hand: "Willst du mir deine Hand geben?" (H 2:1186). This is the first "du" that has fallen between them, and it appears to be a quotation of the conspicuously repeated line from the shoemaker's song: "Reiche frei mir deine Hand" (H 2:1186). The sequence of enactments should not be overlooked. The "Blick" from "gemalten Band" precedes the fulfillment of Logau's epigram, which is then followed by Reinhart's "Goethean" request for Lucie's hand. The Goethe poem thus encloses Logau's lines in this sequence of imitative gestures and presents a novel (and idiosyncratic) instance of literature within literature (within literature). Keller's lovers participate in a multitiered joke of the author's: moved by "gemalten Band" to demonstrate Logau, whose Galatea ideology they mutually reject, Reinhart and Lucie acknowledge the fulfillment of the discredited couplet and accede to the final prescription of "gemalten Band." Goethe and Logau are less dangerous Gallehaults than the unnamed author cited by Francesca. Keller accomplishes the *Verharmlosung* of literary fictions by allowing them to exert their influence within this carefully contrived artifice.

Where virtue and vice are not at issue, where no danger to human volition appears, the question of didactic utility does not arise. The strict opposition between the subjective, "selbstbezogene" exercise of imagination and effective membership in the social community that characterized Keller's early prose does not disturb the tranquility of *Das Sinngedicht* because we have no sense of a social community external to the proceedings on Lucie's estate. Certainly there are maids to be supervised, and shoemakers to be spied on, and even an occasional visitor from the outside world, but these are background figures who step forward only to fulfill minor narrative functions. Keller has not only banished danger from the courtship of Reinhart and Lucie, he has also nullified all questions of social responsibility. The protagonists are not necessarily irresponsible—rather, they have nothing to be responsible to. Lucie defends her sex (for her own sake), and Reinhart becomes capable of empathic understanding, but it is unclear how they will apply these skills in the future. One can only conclude that they will continue to delight one another and their near relations and that they will continue to live in this delightful isolation. No future plans for professional, vocational, or civic activities are mentioned, and this is a remarkable omission for Keller, who tends to conclude his prose narratives with an account of the social contributions made, or to be made, by those protagonists who survive.

Keller does not attempt and fail to evoke social reality in *Das Sinngedicht*. On the contrary, he consciously maneuvers to exclude it from consideration, and in so doing he constructs a hermetically sealed "ultraliterary" world where poetry may be put into practice. The "social" realism of *Der grüne Heinrich*, "Pankraz," "Romeo und Julia," and "Herr Jacques," which refers the reader to bourgeois standards of community responsibility, is absent from *Das Sinngedicht*, which makes no pretensions of resemblance to social reality.[19] The premise for the collection, Reinhart's experiment, is purely fanciful. As Keller wrote to Heyse in July 1881:

> Die Unwahrscheinlichkeit betreffend . . . , so ist sie in allen diesen Fällen die gleiche. Auch die Geschichte mit dem Logauschen Sinngedicht, die Ausfahrt Reinharts auf die Kußproben kommt ja nicht vor; niemand unternimmt dergleichen, und doch spielt sie durch mehrere Kapitel. Im stillen nenne ich dergleichen die Reichsunmittelbarkeit der Poesie, d.h. das Recht zu jeder Zeit, auch im Zeitalter des Fracks und der Eisenbahnen, an das Parabelhafte, das Fabelmäßige ohne weiteres anzuknüpfen. . . .
>
> (*GB* 3/1:57)

Not only does Reinhart's experiment bear no resemblance to mundane life outside fiction, but Lucie's estate, the site of his "education," is also a realm apart. It is a mountain retreat, surrounded by dense vegetation and accessible only by a labyrinthine path. Lucie pursues no "useful" occupation, and her uncle the colonel is retired.

Yet it is precisely here, in the rarefied atmosphere of Lucie's domain, where social utility and moral didacticism are superfluous, that Keller stages the resolution of the conflict between imagination and (what passes for) the mundane. Reinhart and Lucie enact literary texts and profit by it, but they do so in the most obvious fiction that Keller ever wrote.[20] Everything works out well for Reinhart and Lucie, but Keller's choice of milieu is itself a comment on the viability of such dreams as readers might draw from literary fictions. The book-world equation holds for these lovers mainly because their world is so unabashedly a book.

Keller's social conscience reasserted itself forcefully in his final prose work, *Martin Salander*, but he was ultimately dissatisfied with the novel, finding it too prosaic. Salander, however, is not a reading hero, and his (considerable) struggles involve the "Sein und Schein" of socioeconomic conditions and dissembling opportunists. Keller, who died in 1890, never wrote about readers again after *Das Sinngedicht*.

The story of reading in Keller's fiction revolves around a core perception of an incommensurability between life and its literary representation (which is overcome only under the special circumstances of *Das Sinngedicht*). This perception contradicts the presupposition of a naive realism—namely, that the literary fiction can be an adequate replacement of, or substitute for, "life" and can therefore teach us useful lessons regarding our lives. The fictions Keller examines are of another order, and their alleged resemblance to "life" is usually a cruel joke. Keller never abandons his traditional format, nor does he cease to search for a compromise between the imaginary and the mundane. But his search consists in the repeated demonstration of the futility of his efforts. He succeeds only in keeping the two realms distinct—thus achieving a certain "realism" on his own terms, though this "realism" strives to subvert the very notion of itself. Only in *Das Sinngedicht* does Keller manage to integrate poetry into practice, and he does so by renouncing any claim to social verisimilitude and by presenting this fusion as a jest, a grand and obvious fiction.

The questionable continuity between literature and life, book and world, language and reality, that has occupied historians of literary modernism and subsequent experimental movements, was also the primary concern of Keller's fiction. Those who would have us believe in a "radical rupture" between realism and modernism assume the existence of a stable and naive realism from which modernism can then differentiate itself—but this assumption is little more than a literary-historical convenience. More plausible is the contention that German-language fiction was "reformed" from within before being subjected to "deformation" or formal experimentation from without. In other words, the later nineteenth century, as exemplified by Keller, was really a transitional period in which new wine was being offered in old bottles. To extend an awkward metaphor, modernist writers poured this wine out of the bottles into a vast and interesting array of irregular vessels. Keller's disappointment at the noncorrespondence between beautiful fictions and ordinary life constitutes his own peculiar recognition of the "divorce" between language and reality. His fictional readers revive and reprise this divorce throughout his career.

# Notes

## Introduction

1. Curtius, *Europäische Literatur*, chap. 16, "Das Buch als Symbol," 306–52. See also Uwe Japp's brief but comprehensive article, "Das Buch im Buch."
2. Jeziorkowski, *Literarität und Historismus*, 9.
3. Wuthenow, *Im Buch die Bücher*, 9.
4. Dante, *La Divina Commedia*, ed. C. H. Grandgent and Charles Singleton (Cambridge, Mass.: Harvard University Press, 1972), 55 (*Inferno* 5:137). Francesca of Rimini explains to Dante: "That book and its author were our Gallehaut." While reading "Lancelot of the Lake," she and Paolo were seized by passion and they kissed. More on this in chapter 5.
5. J. M. R. Lenz, *Die Soldaten* (Leipzig, 1776).
6. The historical J. M. R. Lenz was not a stable being, and his attitudes toward literature and its influence (as well as his ideas on curing society's ills) wavered frequently. Nonetheless, the play, which warns against visits to the comedy while labeling itself a comedy, is an exercise in irony, a *mise en abîme* of the position of literature within literature within literature. . . .
7. Levine, *Realistic Imagination*, 71.
8. Wuthenow, *Im Buch die Bücher*, 9.
9. Japp, "Das Buch im Buch," 658. Wuthenow also mentions the mirroring of the actual reader. His book appears to be heavily indebted to Japp, both for the latter's insights into the nature of fictional reading and for the selection of texts brought forth to illustrate them.
10. For Norman Holland, the process is more ambiguous: "These books-within-books and plays-within-plays create a deeper, inner sense of uncertainty, an uncanny feeling such as seeing my reflection in a mirror move and act by itself would produce. Because we fuse with a work of art, to call its reality into question is to question our own. Because these effects make me uncertain as to whether I am confronting a reality or a fiction . . . I find my own position in reality called into question. Have I mixed up fiction and reality as a madman would?" (*Dynamics of Literary Response*, 99).
11. Japp, "Das Buch im Buch," 658.
12. Lieselotte Kurth gives very convincing evidence in *Die zweite Wirklichkeit* of the eighteenth-century belief that real people did imitate the books they read—this being the underlying assumption of novelistic conduct manuals; see her first section, "Der Roman und die Gesellschaft," 5–114.
13. There is, to be sure, a very small segment of the population that appears to style itself after literary or cinematic fictions (from the alleged rash of suicides in the wake of *Werther* to the recent presidential assassination at-

tempt that was prefigured in the film *Taxi Driver*); but this constitutes a pathological extreme, and a definite connection between fiction and action has never been established.

14. Holland, *Dynamics of Literary Response*, 73.

15. Ibid., 334.

16. Sammons, *Literary Sociology*, 78.

17. Girard, *Deceit*, chap. 1, "Triangular Desire," 1–52.

18. For a discussion of the extraliterary phenomenon, see Girard, *To Double Business Bound*: "human desire really *is* mimetic" (p. ix).

19. Girard, *Deceit*, 2.

20. Ibid., 1.

21. See Girard's comments in the "Discussion" of Georges Poulet's "Criticism and the Experience of Interiority," in *The Languages of Criticism and the Sciences of Man: The Structuralist Controversy*, ed. Richard Macksey and Eugenio Donato, 5th ed. (Baltimore: The Johns Hopkins University Press, 1982), 83. See also Bersani, *Future for Astyanax*.

22. Girard, *Deceit*, 282.

23. Ibid., 65, Girard's emphasis. Girard's explanation of the quest for a mediator is remarkably similar to Kaspar T. Locher's assessment of man's alternatives in Keller: "The most essential choice man has to make, Keller seems to say, is that between exposing himself directly and constantly to the vast mystery of life, or embracing any one of a multitude of forms which have been devised as buffers to soften the impact of the unpredictable on frail man. If he chooses the latter alternative, he will find some security in the apparent reliability of human institutions, in the human meanings which religions, philosophies and sciences impose upon the meaningless. If he chooses unmitigated exposure, he will have to do without the consolations human ingenuity has interposed between man and the universe" ("Keller and the Fate of the Epigone," 183).

24. Feuerbach, *Das Wesen des Christentums*, in *Sämtliche Werke*, ed. Bolin and Jodl, 6:168–69. All quotes are from this edition and will be cited within the text by "F," volume number, and page number.

25. Keller, *Sämtliche Werke*, ed. Heselhaus, 1:477. Subsequent references to this edition will be cited throughout within the text by "H," volume number, and page number. I use primarily this edition because it is far more accessible than the standard critical edition by Fränkel and Helbling (hereafter cited as "FH," volume number, and page number).

26. Girard, *Deceit*, 233.

27. Especially in the last few decades, critical terms such as "subtext" and "poetic subject" have been adapted to substitute for, and in some cases represent, authorial intention. Though this intention/intentionality would ideally reside in the text, it is not uncommon to encounter extraneous biographical detail in the makeup of the subtext or poetic subject. In practice, reports of the "death of the author" may be greatly exaggerated.

28. Muschg, *Gottfried Keller*; Kaiser, *Leben*.

29. Keller, *Gesammelte Briefe*, ed. Helbling, 3/2:195; subsequent references

to this collection will be cited within the text with *"GB,"* volume number, and page number. This passage is quoted and discussed in practically every lengthy study of Keller. See, for example, Ermatinger, *Kellers Leben,* 368; Kaiser, *Leben,* 426; Locher, *Welterfahrung,* 13; Neumann, *Gottfried Keller,* 205.

30. The collection features a considerable amount of "negatives Leben," including that of the savage, deranged, and possibly syphilitic Buz Falätscher.

31. Auerbach made two significant deletions from "Fähnlein," apparently on moral grounds. One of these was announced in advance, whereas the other was made without Keller's knowledge or consent. Keller disagreed with both deletions, but his response was a model of delicacy in both cases. See Auerbach's letter of 21 June 1860: "Die Erinnerung an die Kinderliebe muß ich streichen, so schön sie auch ist. Das geht nicht für einen Kalender, der unverborgen vor den Kindern da liegen muß. Ich habe in meinen Kalendergeschichten sogar den Akzent des Erotischen vermieden aus diesem Grunde" (*GB* 3/2:194). Keller's reaction (25 June 1860) was submissive, but double edged: "Daß Sie die Kindergeschichten streichen müssen, begreife ich jetzt vollkommen, obgleich ich an die Unzulässigkeit erotischer Episoden dachte; aber wunderlicherweise glaubte ich gerade dadurch, daß ich sie in die Kinderschuhe steckte, die Sache unschuldig zu machen" (*GB* 3/2: 196). See Keller's letter of 15 September 1860 for his reaction to Auerbach's unauthorized excision of a kiss (*GB* 3/2:200–201); his anger is clearly apparent, but he concludes the matter by blaming himself for misjudging the context.

32. Gottfried Keller, *Der grüne Heinrich,* ed. Thomas Böning and Gerhard Kaiser (Frankfurt am Main: Deutscher Klassiker Verlag, 1985), "Paralipomena," #18, 923.

33. Richartz, *Literaturkritik,* 161.

34. See Locher, "Kellers wohlwollende Ironie": "Keller, der stets für das Volk schreiben wollte, schreibt tatsächlich für die *happy few* der sprachlich Kultivierten, die ein genügend feines Ohr besitzen, um die . . . leisen Verschiebungen seiner Sprache ins Ironische wahrzunehmen" (p. 88).

35. Mews, "Zur Funktion der Literatur," 394.

36. Ibid., 403.

37. Jeziorkowski's *Literarität und Historismus* also merits mention here, though it does not focus on the specific issues mentioned. Jeziorkowski, finding that Keller's work is "in ganz erstaunlichem Grad literarisiert; auf literarhistorische Realitäten bezogen" (p. 10), uses the latter's work as a prominent example of the nineteenth-century author's tendency to incorporate material from past literature into his own prose. Finally, Theodor Anton Scherrer's *Thema und Funktion der Literatur,* a brief dissertation which has not been widely circulated, examines Heinrich Lee's reading of Goethe as an exemplary moment that provides a set of values for Keller's writing as a whole and also furnishes criteria for the judgment of subsequent encounters between characters and the fictions they read or (wish to) write. Scherrer sees Keller's goal as that of simplifying, unifying, and beautifying the

world (p. 20) for a mass readership (p. 36), whereas I approach him as a writer who emphasizes the bewildering aspects of existence for a more restricted audience. Scherrer's study came to my attention toward the end of my work on this project and I was surprised to find that, in spite of his title and the list of Keller texts he discusses, his work has very little in common with mine.

38. Richartz, *Literaturkritik*, 25.

## Chapter One

1. I give priority to *Entwicklungsroman*, which is actually least commonly used in reference to Keller's novel, because *Bildung* and *Erziehung* imply greater participation by outside agencies (in the hero's maturing process) than one can justly posit in this case. Furthermore, *Entwicklung* is the word repeatedly used by Heinrich himself and by the count in reference to this process. For examples of their usage, see H 1:1028, 1037.

2. The great work on Keller's humor and its mediating properties is (still) Wolfgang Preisendanz's *Humor als dichterische Einbildungskraft*. According to Preisendanz, Keller's humor discovers (or uncovers) the commensurability between apparent polar opposites.

3. Emil Ermatinger refers to the conclusion as "ein hastig errichtetes Notdach" (*Kellers Leben*, 272), and mentions the (contemporary) "laut gewordenen Vorwurf, der Verfasser habe seinen Heinrich vorschnell sterben lassen, bloß um mit dem vierten Band zu Ende zu kommen" (p. 303). Keller confirms these suspicions (in advance) while answering Hermann Hettner's objections in his letter of 25 June 1855: ". . . allein die Sache oder das Buch mußte doch ein Ende nehmen, und ich glaube, dieser Schluß hat mehr Bedeutung bei aller bloßen Andeutung, als ein summarisches Heiratskapitel gehabt hätte" (*GB* 1:415).

4. See Clemens Heselhaus's commentary to the Hanser edition (H 1:1129–33): "Die Jugendgeschichte, mit der die zweite Fassung beginnt, ist im ganzen unverändert geblieben" (p. 1129). Though the decision of the Hanser editors to publish the second version of the novel without the *Jugendgeschichte* (and to refer the reader to the first version, which is published in full) may have been an economic one, it is also based on their perception of a similarity between the original and the revision sufficient to warrant such a move. It is nonetheless an example of the practice that Keller called "Buchbinderpoesie." All quotations from the *Jugendgeschichte* are taken from the first version.

5. Parental intervention in these autodidactic proceedings is minimal, and we are given to understand that such guidance is the duty of a father—a duty that is, at best, poorly discharged by Heinrich's widowed mother.

6. Martin Swales also discusses this schism as it operates in the "Pumpernickel" episode, but with a slightly different emphasis. He identifies the schism as being between the world of the child and that of the un-

sympathetic adult: "The teacher shows no comprehension of the complex psychological processes of a child's mind: capital letters are shapes, words are sounds, mysterious entities in their own right, whose conventional value has not yet been learned or absorbed" (*German Bildungsroman*, 91). In Swales's account, it is the child's application of imagination that remains active in Heinrich, even as he matures, and blocks his socialization. This chapter highlights many of the same episodes discussed by Swales in his remarkably succinct essay on *Der grüne Heinrich* as *Bildungsroman* (pp. 86–104), but I cite these episodes as illustrations of Heinrich's bonds of sympathy with letters and literary fictions, whereas Swales's more ambitious undertaking does not focus on reading at all.

7. Eventually, Heinrich is dismissed from school for his role in the siege of a teacher's house. As he recalls joining the crowd of unruly schoolboys outside the victim's window, he remarks: "Mir schwebten sogleich gelesene Volksbewegungen und Revolutionsszenen vor" (H 1:175). Literature is also implicated in this event, the major trauma of young Heinrich's life.

8. In this spirit, Heinrich later recalls his childhood *Lügengeschichte*, for which his schoolmates were punished, as an instance of the child's indifference to the distinction between good and bad, true and false (H 1:681). This is, however, only a momentary "enlightenment."

9. In a letter to Ferdinand Weibert of 25 November 1879, Keller complains that the 110 unsold copies of the original version, which he has obtained from the original publisher, were in very bad condition. He adds: "Nun sind sie bald verbrannt" (*GB* 3/2:301). See also Sautermeister, "*Der grüne Heinrich*," 81.

10. A more explicit comparison of (wrongheaded) reading with the consumption of sweets occurs in "Die mißbrauchten Liebesbriefe," where Keller lampoons the intellectual pretensions of Kätter Ambach (and, one assumes, women like her): Kätter, returning home with an armful of books, "las aber dort nur die kurzweiligsten Sachen daraus, wie Kinder, welche die Rosinen aus dem Kuchen klauben" (H 2:357).

11. Swales, citing Judith's wisdom and integrity, disagrees: ". . . she will not allow herself to be transformed into some *dea ex machina*, into some spiritual authority divorced from the real world" (*German Bildungsroman*, 101). *She* certainly does not wish this divorce, but her sudden appearance is indeed rather "mechanically" unnatural.

12. For the best available account of this openness to life (and literature), see the writings of Kaspar T. Locher on Keller, especially "Keller and the Fate of the Epigone"; *Gottfried Keller: Der Weg zur Reife*; and *Welterfahrung*.

13. Keller's "Pankraz, der Schmoller" complains of Shakespeare that he depicts "die Welt des Ganzen und Gelungenen in seiner Art, das heißt wie es sein soll . . . und dadurch gute Köpfe in die Irre führt, wenn sie in der Welt dies wesentliche Leben zu sehen und wiederzufinden glauben." He continues: "Ach, *es ist schon in der Welt*, aber nur niemals da, wo wir eben sind, oder dann wann wir leben" (H 2:40, my emphasis).

14. Ellis, *Narration*, 136–54.

15. Ibid., 140.

16. Ibid., 136.

17. For many years, the discussion of the extent and nature of Keller's allegiance to Feuerbach centered on the matter of Keller's atheism—a lack of religion that was unacceptable to many scholars. See Lemke, "Deification of Gottfried Keller," for a summary of scholars' attempts to "rescue" Keller from the taint of atheism. Otherwise, Feuerbach's influence has generally been located in Keller's commitment to *Diesseitigkeit* and his rejection of metaphysics: see especially Ernst Otto, "Die Philosophie Feuerbachs." Gerhard Kaiser, however, discusses Feuerbach in connection with Keller's oedipal struggle: "Von der familialen Urszene Gottfried Kellers her gelesen ist Feuerbach der Mann, der Gottvater . . . verabschiedet und den Rückzug zur ganzen, glühenden, sinnlich zu erfahrenden Mutter Natur weist" (*Leben*, 147).

18. Ludwig Feuerbach, *Vorlesungen über das Wesen der Religion.* Feuerbach concludes the Heidelberg lectures with these words (also quoted by Goldammer in "Ludwig Feuerbach," 315).

19. 28 January 1849.

20. Though this may be a reasonable approach to *Der grüne Heinrich I*, it sometimes leads to unnecessary distortions of both Keller and Feuerbach, such as Edith Runge's contention that Sali's and Vrenchen's precious last day together in "Romeo und Julia auf dem Dorfe" exemplifies Feuerbach's teaching that a consciousness of mortality enhances life ("Ein kleiner Blick in die künstlerische Verwandlung," *Monatshefte* 52 [1960]: 249–52). Keller's lovers progressively withdraw from the social community (and appear to posit an afterlife of "togetherness"), whereas Feuerbach saw the acceptance of mortality and death as a means of channeling consciousness back into the social community.

21. Goldammer, "Ludwig Feuerbach," 316; Locher, *Welterfahrung.*

22. Ermatinger, *Kellers Leben*, 316.

23. Ibid., 189.

24. Otto cites and paraphrases Hans Dünnebier, *Gottfried Keller und Ludwig Feuerbach* (Zurich: Internationaler Verlag für Literatur, 1913), 272: "in Keller's Bibliothek [sei] nur der letzte 1866 erschienene Band von Feuerbachs Werken vorhanden gewesen" ("Die Philosophie Feuerbachs," 106).

25. Keller claims in the Baumgartner letter that he had been thinking in this direction all along: "Mein Gott war längst nur eine Art von Präsident oder erstem Konsul, . . . ich mußte ihn absetzen" (*GB* 1:274).

26. It should be noted that Feuerbach did *not* object to literary fictions as such. In the *Vorlesungen über das Wesen der Religion*, he explains: "Religion ist Poesie . . . aber mit dem Unterschied von der Poesie, von der Kunst überhaupt, daß die Kunst ihre Geschöpfe für nichts Anderes ausgiebt, als sie sind, für Geschöpfe der Kunst, die Religion aber ihre eingebildeten Wesen für *wirkliche* Wesen ausgiebt" (F 8:227, Feuerbach's emphasis). Feuerbach regarded poetic fictions as "honest" fictions, whereas religious fictions were inherently deceptive.

27. This observation, which is really Feuerbach's conclusion, appears in a footnote to the introduction of his argument, illustrating the fervor (and impatience) of the crusading philosopher.

28. Marx Wartofsky remarks this tendency in Feuerbach's written style: "The inversion of religious and theological expression is the hallmark of Feuerbach's style" (*Feuerbach*, 274).

29. "Wir haben ebenso wie den philosophischen, den politischen Idealismus satt; wir wollen jetzt politische Materialisten sein" (*Vorlesungen*, F 8:2). See also Neumann, *Gottfried Keller*, 92. Neumann quotes Alfred Schmidt's *Emanzipatorische Sinnlichkeit* (Munich: Hanser, 1973), which states that Feuerbach's philosophy is the "höchste begriffliche Form der deutschen revolutionären Demokratie" (p. 30).

30. Gerhard Plumpe makes the same observation of "Pankraz, der Schmoller" in "Praxis," 172. His views will be discussed in the coming chapter.

# Chapter Two

1. Bersani, *Future for Astyanax*, 61.

2. There are, of course, cases where the faculty of imagination is completely lacking, and lack of imagination generally carries the same consequences as excessive imagining in Keller's work, though the unimaginative are treated more harshly. They are nonentities who occur in groups where the members are, for all practical purposes, indistinguishable from one another: the Weidelich twins in *Martin Salander*, the three "Kammacher," and the Ruechensteiner in "Dietegen." See Paula Ritzler's taxonomy of Keller figures in "Das Außergewöhnliche."

3. Keller's pedagogical aspirations are no longer a favored topic for scholars, but the image persists. To Winfried Menninghaus, for example, he is "der Didaktiker und Moralist Keller" (*Artistische Schrift*, 132); and Locher traces recurring challenges to Keller's contemporary relevance to the "didaktischen Ernst, der in seinem ganzen Werk zutage tritt" (*Welterfahrung*, 7).

4. Keller was highly critical of his first novel, and in 1854 he complained to Hermann Hettner that he was not, by nature, a novelist: "diese weitschichtige, unabsehbare Strickstrumpfform [liegt] nicht in meiner Natur" (*GB* 1:397). A year later, he intimated that his eagerness to conclude the novel and the pressure from his publisher contributed to the sudden, and largely unexplained, death of Heinrich Lee: "allein die Sache oder das Buch mußte doch ein Ende nehmen, und ich glaube, dieser Schluß hat mehr Bedeutung bei aller bloßen Andeutung, als ein summarisches Heiratskapitel gehabt hätte" (*GB* 1:415). Whereas "Pankraz" was conceived and executed rather quickly toward the end of the Berlin years, Keller spent more than a decade developing and writing *Der grüne Heinrich*, and he was, furthermore, limited in what he could do in the later volumes, having allowed the earlier volumes to be published before he began to write his conclusion.

Thus the shift in Keller's attitudes toward didactic writing was probably not quite as sudden as the publication dates would suggest.

5. See Bersani on marriage and death at the end of nineteenth-century novels: *Future for Astyanax*, 54–55.

6. Kunz, *Die deutsche Novelle*, 98–99.

7. As early as 1906, Hugo von Hofmannsthal implicitly rejects this model when he has his speaker in "Unterhaltungen über die Schriften von Gottfried Keller" locate the essence of Keller's writing "in der unbegreiflich feinen und sicheren Schilderung gemischter Zustände" (*Gesammelte Werke*, 2 [Berlin: Fischer, 1924], 268). Wolfgang Preisendanz, always polemically explicit on the matter of thematic polarities, stresses humor as a fundamental principle of form that mediates between "Maske und Wesen" (*Humor*, 146). Locher also argues against polarities: "[Keller] mißtraut dem Entweder-Oder; seine Vorliebe gilt dem Sowohl-Als-auch" (*Welterfahrung*, 21).

8. McCormick, "Idylls," 266.

9. Ibid., 279.

10. Ibid., 265.

11. Locher remarks that Keller's conclusions often frustrate reader expectations, which are "allzu fazil," noting that "aus dem romantischen aber frischen, echten . . . Wenzel ein typischer Goldacher Plutokrat mit Schmerbauch wird . . ." (*Welterfahrung*, 159). Kaiser finds Wenzel's conversion to be the one dark spot in the novella: "denn an dieser Stelle . . . breitet sich schließlich doch der Dunstschleier der Melancholie aus; besser ein Macher als ein Träumer sein, aber doch nicht ganz gut" (*Leben*, 353).

12. Ellis, *Narration*, 136. See also Locher's remarks in *Welterfahrung* on the noncorrespondence of chapter titles in *Der grüne Heinrich* to the material of the chapters they head (142–43).

13. Ibid., 139.

14. Ibid., 154.

15. Hoverland, "Kellers 'Pankraz, der Schmoller,' " 32; Hoverland's emphasis and orthography. Kaiser and Sautermeister disagree with this perspective on the ending. Kaiser believes that by killing the lion, Pankraz has also killed his yearnings, and that with Lydia's name he also forgets love: "Um ein liebevoller Mensch zu werden, muß er die Liebe vergessen—sogar das Wort, den Namen der Geliebten. Der Verlust ihres Namens wiederholt auf der Ebene der Sprache die Tötung" (*Leben*, 292). Sautermeister sees a complete conversion for Pankraz, stemming from the intensification of his sulking before the lion: "Die Entfremdung von sich selbst und von den Menschen schlägt, auf die unerträgliche Spitze getrieben, in eine Selbstgewinnung um, die als 'unverwüstliche ruhige Freundlichkeit' in den praktischen Dienst von Familie und Gesellschaft tritt" ("Pankraz"). Neumann writes that forgetting Lydia's name is the precondition of the social stability that, he believes, Pankraz achieves: "Anamnese hat nicht nur statt, sondern bürgerliches Leben gründet sich hier auf die zuverlässige Verdrängung der Erinnerung an das Verlorene" (*Gottfried Keller*, 127). Kaiser, Sautermeister, and Neumann all understand "Pankraz," to some extent, as a pedagogical exercise.

16. Berman, *Modern German Novel*, 60–61. Similar statements occur throughout. Berman's book is a learned and provocative study of the novel, but his comments on realism are excessively polemical.

17. Plumpe, "Praxis," 172.

18. Regula had actually complained that she had been omitted from *Der grüne Heinrich*. Recognizing Gottfried's life story in the novel, she concluded that the absence of a sister for Heinrich Lee meant that her brother was ashamed of her. Frau Keller reports this to her son in her letter of 11 March 1854: "Regula wurde zwar empfindlich, daß nirgends keine Erwähnung von einer Schwester sich findet. Man könnte daraus schließen, als würdest Du Dich schämen, sie als Deine Schwester zu betrachten!" (*GB* 1:119).

19. Betty Tendering (1831–1902) has been associated with the figures of both Dortchen Schönfund and Lydia. David Jackson gives a detailed account of the Betty affair in "Pankraz, der Schmoller." Frau Keller also mentions the incident in her letter to Gottfried of 20 November 1855: "Wir mußten uns sehr verwundern über Deine Gemütsbewegungen. Es ist uns unerklärlich, wie ein Frauenzimmer so viel über Dich vermag, um Dich so weit in Kummer und Verdruß zu versetzen" (*GB* 1:135). It is interesting, if not entirely pertinent, to note that Keller was consistently unsuccessful in winning the affection of the women he loved. After numerous rejections, he finally succeeded in becoming engaged to the somewhat reluctant Luise Scheidegger in 1866. Shortly after the formal engagement, however, Scheidegger committed suicide, and Keller seems to have had no significant dealings with women after that.

20. Letter to Berthold Auerbach, 25 February 1860 (*GB* 3/2:190). As noted, Auerbach is the recipient of most of Keller's clearly formulated statements of didactic intention, and it is possible that this intention becomes more pronounced when Keller addresses the more prominent poet's related concerns.

21. Letter to Eduard Vieweg, 3 May 1850 (*GB* 3/2:15).

22. Plumpe remarks: "Indem Pankraz seine Erlebnisse a posteriori . . . erzählt, erhält sein Bericht eine außerordentliche Ambivalenz; es ist vorab kaum auszumachen, ob er neutrales Referat eines objektiven Geschehens oder aber—das andere Extrem—bloße Fiktion sein wird" ("Praxis," 166). The very situation of the narrator raises doubts about the veracity of his tale.

23. Keller also alludes to the first book of *Wilhelm Meisters Lehrjahre*, where Marianne falls asleep while listening to Wilhelm's tale of his past. See Ermatinger, *Kellers Leben*, 312–13; Kaiser, *Leben*, 688.

24. Plumpe suggests an analogy between Pankraz's Lydia and Feuerbach's God, observing that Pankraz projects all the goodness and beauty he can imagine into her, and he notes that Pankraz actually compares her with God during their argument in the garden ("Praxis," 169). Plumpe feels that Feuerbach's presence in the novella is so strong that "man behaupten kann, in ihr die narrative Artikulation zentraler Feuerbachscher Konzepte zu sehen" (p. 171). One of Plumpe's examples is Pankraz's reading of Shakespeare, which he compares to a Christian's (naive) reading of the Bible.

25. If one were to take an eraser to vol. 2 of the Hanser edition and eradicate p. 40, l. 12, through p. 42, l. 26, the result would be a smooth description of Pankraz's general struggle in the absence of Shakespeare (with some intervening white space). Shakespeare is not mentioned, nor is the experience recalled, until p. 54, where Pankraz tentatively (and I would say gratuitously) attributes his overactive imagination to his reading of Shakespeare. This remark could likewise be erased without disturbing the continuity. I do not make these observations in order to tamper with Keller's text, but to point out certain prominent "seams" between the Shakespeare episode and the novella in which it is so awkwardly embedded.

26. Pankraz refers to the lion as his "Lehrer und Bekehrer" (H 2:22), but the suddenness of his alleged conversion undermines its plausibility. See R. Boeschenstein, "Pankraz und sein Tier."

## Chapter Three

1. See the correspondence with Eduard Vieweg (GB 3/2:9–164; especially 58–59, 61, 67, 70, 74, 76–77, 80–81, 87), where Keller and Vieweg refer to preliminary work on the Seldwyla and Galatea novellas. See also Ermatinger, *Kellers Leben*, 306–8 for sketches of novellas from 1851–52, although only one of these, "Geschichte von drei Schreinergesellen," figures in *Seldwyla* (as "Die drei gerechten Kammacher").

2. Both Keller and Vieweg refer repeatedly to the author's *Ehrenwort* in their letters of this period; see GB 3/2:74, 76–77, 91, 96, and passim.

3. 96. At that time, Keller intended to send *Die Leute von Seldwyla* to Hugo Scheube for publication and to send Vieweg the Galatea novellas. However, he soon came to regard Scheube as insolvent and sold *Seldwyla* to Vieweg.

4. See FH 7:391–92.

5. FH 7:393.

6. See Ermatinger, *Kellers Leben*, 320. Keller mentions his epic poem in a letter to Wilhelm Baumgartner of 28 January 1849: "Jenes epische Gedicht von den zwei jungen Leutchen und den Bauern, welche pflügen, habe ich auch angefangen . . ." (GB 1:276–77).

7. Several good discussions of realism and "Romeo und Julia" have appeared in recent years. August Obermayer's "Kellers 'Romeo und Julia' " identifies "naturgesetzliche Kausalität" as an important element of the nineteenth-century version of "das Selbstverständliche" that characterizes realism in any era. Robert Holub, in "Realism, Repetition, Repression," stresses the convention of "repetition" in nineteenth-century German realistic fiction, but he sees Keller's (over)emphasis on his own purported repetition of an actual event as misleading on the surface. Holub makes a compelling, if occasionally shocking, argument for a kind of psychic realism in "Romeo und Julia" by pointing out "structures of incest" in the text.

8. See Preisendanz, *Humor*, and Bernd, *German Poetic Realism*, for more thorough and authoritative accounts of poetic realism.

9. Kaiser, "Sündenfall," 40.

10. Jennings, "Keller's Prose," 205. Jennings's extraordinary article, which examines Keller's depiction of soul or spirit according to "extrinsic" and "intrinsic" models of the self, is one of the finest essays on Keller to appear in the last twenty years.

11. Theodor Fontane, *Sämtliche Werke*, ed. Walter Keitel (Munich: Hanser, 1966), Abt. 3, vol. 1, 495.

12. While Fontane considered himself a realist, he considered Keller "au fond ein Märchenerzähler" (*Theodor Fontane, Schriften zur Literatur*, ed. Hans Heinrich Reuter [Berlin: Aufbau, 1960], 94). See also Obermayer, "Kellers 'Romeo und Julia,' " 247.

13. Bernd, *German Poetic Realism*, 41. Obermayer considers "Romeo und Julia" to be something of a "realistisches Märchen" (as his title suggests). It is Obermayer's opinion that Keller managed to integrate "Märchenzüge" ("Kellers 'Romeo und Julia,' " 251) into his realism "und so vielleicht für das 19. Jahrhundert den Begriff der Wirklichkeit modifizierte, indem er ihm Bereiche eingliederte, die man bislang als nicht dazugehörend empfand" (p. 255).

14. Letter to Vieweg, 6 October 1855, *GB* 3/2:120–21.

15. In Goethe's *Die Leiden des jungen Werthers*, the hero's rival, Albert, states the bourgeois position on suicide quite succinctly as he reacts to Werther's pointing a gun to his own temple: "Ich kann mir nicht vorstellen, wie ein Mensch so töricht sein kann, sich zu erschießen; der bloße Gedanke erregt mir Widerwillen" (Erstes Buch: Am 12. August). In Keller's own time, the suicide of Charlotte Stieglitz in 1834 (intended to provide poetic inspiration to her husband, Heinrich) was hotly debated as a most shocking event; see Sammons, *Six Essays on the Young German Novel*, 63–67, and Promies, "Der ungereimte Tod."

16. Hermann Boeschenstein, *Gottfried Keller*, 48.

17. Lionel Thomas and Robin Clouser actually produce some evidence of counterpositions. Thomas quotes an 1858 English review: "It is vexatious to think that a man of genius should write a story which, because of a few sentences that might perfectly well have been omitted without destroying the interest or reality of the picture, cannot be read aloud in the family circle" ("Keller's *Romeo und Julia*, 132); however, he is "not certain which sentences are meant," although he believes the review refers to Keller's "condemnation of accepted values" (ibid.). Clouser ("*Romeo und Julia*") criticizes those who attribute the suicide to "character flaws," but he cites only Helmut Rehder, who primarily blames society ("Romeo und Julia"), and McCormick, who does indeed blame the lovers, though he does not expatiate. It is likely that some of those who are arguing for the necessity of the suicide are really addressing their own doubts as to this necessity.

18. Otto Ludwig, unpublished review of "Romeo und Julia," in *Gesammelte Schriften*, 6 (Leipzig: Grunnow, 1891), 50. This phrase constituted high praise from Ludwig, who maintained: "man wünscht auch nicht, daß die Katastrophe ausbliebe" (p. 49).

19. Letter to Heyse, 10 June 1870, *GB* 3/1:16–17.

20. Maier, "Gottfried Keller," 60.

21. Menninghaus also understands "Romeo und Julia" in terms of antique tragedy, but he stresses Fate and the theme of inherited guilt and makes a sophisticated argument for Keller's "Kritik des Rechts" (*Artistische Schrift*, 91–144).

22. Dickerson, "Music," 48, 49 (Dickerson's emphasis).

23. Ibid., 52.

24. A. T. Cooke, in a very sensitive and appreciative reading, agrees that Keller is trying to evoke perfect love, stating that Keller, "in having his heroine die for love, . . . creates something more beautifully tragic, more romantic than anything her quest for a new life could have offered her" ("Keller's 'Romeo und Julia,' " 239). This is an interesting twist on the general emphasis on causality, inasmuch as it assumes that tragic beauty was *Keller's* goal and that both he and Vrenchen benefit from the suicide.

25. Rehder, "Romeo und Julia," 434.

26. Clouser, "*Romeo und Julia*," 182. See also Obermayer, who perceives "heftige Gesellschaftskritik" in the novella in general, but notes: "Die Gesellschaft wird zwar kritisiert, aber nicht prinzipiell in Frage gestellt" ("Kellers 'Romeo und Julia,' " 254).

27. Clouser, "*Romeo und Julia*," 182.

28. Fife, "Keller's Dark Fiddler," 124.

29. Barry G. Thomas, "Paradise Lost," 75.

30. Ibid., 76.

31. Kaiser, "Sündenfall," 30.

32. Ibid., 42.

33. Rehder calls it "the gravest revolt against the order of life with children raising their hand against their progenitor" ("Romeo und Julia," 422) and Clouser notes that "Sali's deed has been judged more severely than Romeo's [killing of Tybalt]" ("*Romeo und Julia*," 172).

34. Clouser asks: "how would we judge Sali had he stood passively by while his beloved Vrenchen is beaten, even if by her own father?" ("*Romeo und Julia*," 172).

35. Tucker, "Post-Traumatic Psychosis," 251.

36. Sali's deed and Vrenchen's reaction recall yet another *Fabel*, that of *Le Cid* as dramatized by Corneille. Rodrigue avenges an insult to his father by killing his beloved Chimène's father in a duel. Chimène insists on justice for her father's death, but in this case the heroine relents and agrees to marry Rodrigue after a suitable period of time has passed.

37. See Hart, "The Irresponsible Imagination," and Holub, "Realism, Repetition, Repression," for similar considerations of the novella's apparent chain of causality.

38. Remak, "Vinegar and Water," 49; see also Hermann Boeschenstein, *Gottfried Keller*, 50.

39. McCormick's term; see "Idylls," 275–76, for his discussion of Vrenchen's story and its relation to her dream world.

40. FH 7:394; Richartz, *Literaturkritik*, 107.
41. Richartz, *Literaturkritik*, 108.
42. McCormick, "Idylls," 279.
43. Ernst Feise states in *Xenion* that Keller is in love with Vrenchen (p. 164), and, unlikely as this sounds, there is much to support this contention—especially in the strangely pathetic tone in which he describes her suffering at her father's hands: "[Vrenchen] war aufgelegt zu Scherz und Spiel . . . wenn es nicht zu sehr gequält wurde und nicht zu viel Sorgen ausstand. Diese plagten es aber häufig genug; denn nicht nur hatte es den Kummer und das wachsende Elend des Hauses mit zu tragen, sondern es mußte noch sich selber in acht nehmen und mochte sich gern halbwegs ordentlich und reinlich kleiden, ohne daß der Vater ihm die geringsten Mittel dazu geben wollte" (H 2:75); see also H 2:97. The fairy-tale pathos of these passages contrasts sharply with the rest of the narration.
44. Fränkel also gives the original version of the introduction: "Auch diese Geschichte zu erzählen würde eine müßige Erfindung sein, wenn sie nicht auf einem wahren Vorfall beruhte, zum Beweise, wie tief im Menschenleben jede der schönen Fabeln wurzelt, auf welche ein großes Dichterwerk gegründet ist. Die Zahl solcher Fabeln ist mäßig, gleich der Zahl der Metalle, aber sie ereignen sich immer wieder aufs neue mit veränderten Umständen und in der wunderlichsten Verkleidung" (FH 7:394). For discussions of the changes that Keller made in his introduction, see Holub, "Realism, Repetition, Repression," 466–69 and Wells, "Kellers Erzählkunst in 'Romeo und Julia auf dem Dorfe,' " 169–70.
45. Ermatinger, *Kellers Leben*, 319.
46. Ibid.
47. Letter to Berthold Auerbach, 3 June 1856 (*GB* 3/2:186). Keller reaffirms his position in his letter to Ferdinand Weibert of 29 August 1875 (*GB* 3/2: 262), where he emphatically states that he is not an imitator, but mentions that others have imitated him in this vein, particularly Alfred Hartmann, whose "Lear auf dem Dorfe" (actually "Lyrenhans und seine drei Töchter") appeared shortly after "Romeo und Julia."
48. In the interest of thoroughness, it should be noted that Keller may have been especially inclined toward thoughts of romance at this time because of his involvement with Betty Tendering. The famous "Betty blotter," to which the lovesick and forsaken Keller committed a number of drawings, poems, and amorous exclamations, repeats the dates "1855" and "Mai 1855" without explanation. Apparently something significant for his relationship with Betty (probably rejection) occurred in May 1855, and it is likely that he was working on "Romeo und Julia" at that time or shortly afterwards. He did finish the novella between April and October of that same year. The blotter, with its endless repetitions of the name "Betty," also contains verbal and pictorial references to "Romeo und Julia." There are two separate drawings of a skeleton playing the fiddle with a star above his head (recalling the black fiddler who predicts the lovers' deaths and the star imagery), and behind one of them is a poppylike flower with its own star (poppies grow

on the ill-starred abandoned field). Furthermore, just beneath an iron gate bearing Betty's initials, Keller copied the "Inschrift auf dem Haus des Dichters" from Abu Nuwas—the very verses on which Sali's *Pfefferkuchenspruch* is based. A smitten Keller, compensating for forced resignation, may account to some extent for the strangely inconsistent narrator.

## Chapter Four

1. Letter to Ferdinand Weibert, 18 September 1877. Keller also refers to the novella as "ein humoristisches Akkompagnement" in his letter to Julius Rodenberg of 6 June 1876 (*GB* 3/2:341).

2. Sautermeister, "Nachwort," 308.

3. Most books and essays that deal with the *Züricher Novellen* make some mention of "Herr Jacques." The few scholars who actually dwell on the novella or address it in detail include: Agnes Waldhausen, *Die Technik der Rahmenerzählung*; Ermatinger, *Kellers Leben*, 495–97; Kaiser, *Dichtung*, 135–41, and *Leben*, 423–38; Scherrer, *Thema und Funktion der Literatur*, 77–81; and Sautermeister, "Nachwort," 308–15.

4. See Reichert, "Entstehung." Reichert explains the loose and somewhat clumsy structure of the collection by positing a specific order of conception and composition for the five novellas and sections of the frame, and by identifying the problems Keller may have faced in integrating them: "In den 'Züricher Novellen' scheinen sich zwei Baugedanken oder 'Ordnungslinien' zu durchkreuzen: erstens die Erziehung des jungen Jacques durch Beispielgeschichten von echten und falschen 'Originalen,' zweitens die chronologische Anordnung kulturhistorischer Erzählungen aus der Geschichte Zürichs vom Mittelalter bis zur Gegenwart, vom Meister Hadlaub bis zum Meister Hediger" (p. 473).

5. Waldhausen remarked on this in 1911: "Menschen, wie Herr Jakobus [können] weder durch mündliche, noch literarische Lehren, sondern allein durch das Leben dauernd und vollständig geheilt werden" (*Die Technik der Rahmenerzählung*, 58).

6. Engelsing, *Der Bürger als Leser*, 184.

7. See Kaiser, *Dichtung*, 164, and *Leben*, 430–35, for a discussion of the "vorlautes Buch" in which Jacques finds the fateful sentence. Kaiser speculates that it may be the work of Jean *Jacques* Rousseau.

8. Reichert, "Entstehung," 477.

9. 25 June 1878.

10. Actually, both notions of originality partake of paradox insofar as (more than most) they suggest that originality is attained by means of imitation (of those who are original).

11. For the purposes of Keller's story, Hadlaub did the copying, though this is not a historical certainty.

12. FH 9:351, my emphasis.

13. FH 9:352.

14. The "Bildhauernovelle" is a hackneyed account of the modest genius whose patient industry and asceticism are the conditions of artistic creation—a vision not unrelated to popular conceptions of Michelangelo. It is also an attempt—as is Jacques's patronage—to erase distinctions between the bourgeois and the Artist.

15. Both Kaiser and Bernd Neumann see problems with the didactic structure of the frame, but they argue that the second cycle of *Züricher Novellen* (published together with the first, but independent of the frame) relativizes or "transcends" any failure that may occur in the first. Kaiser believes that the "pädagogische Wirkungsmöglichkeit des Bandes . . . *fast* zurückgenommen [wird]" (*Leben*, 434, my emphasis), but that the frame concludes prematurely to prevent this from happening: "Ein umfassender Rahmen müßte umfassend desillusionieren" (p. 438). See also Neumann, for a discussion of the "prosaic" conclusion to "Herr Jacques" and its effects on Keller's message (*Gottfried Keller*, 206ff).

# Chapter Five

1. Dante, *Inferno* 5:127–38, my emphasis. The translation is my own, based on that of Charles S. Singleton (Princeton: Princeton University Press, 1970), 55.

2. See Girard, "The Mimetic Desire of Paolo and Francesca," in *To Double Business Bound*, 1–8. Girard cites Francesco D'Ovidio, who believes that the penultimate line of the passage quoted, "Galeotto fu 'l libro e chi lo scrisse," expresses Dante's "fear that he too might become a Galehalt" (Girard, p. 8, quoting D'Ovidio, *Nuovi Studii Danteschi* [Milan: Università Hoepli, 1907], 531).

3. Kurth, *Die zweite Wirklichkeit*, 15–25. Kurth also notes that Gottsched advised his niece, Victoria, to model her behavior on that of Henriette in Richardson's *Grandison* (p. 63).

4. Ibid., 81.

5. See Kaiser, *Leben*, 512, 514; also Neumann, *Gottfried Keller*, 239.

6. May, *Kellers "Sinngedicht,"* 29.

7. Keller's celebrated "strong" female characters (Judith, Regel Amrain, Gritli) tend to draw their strength from ignorance insofar as they are unable to fathom—much less to experience—the existential ills that "weaken" the men they exist to assist. Dortchen Schönfund, though she barely emerges as a character, is a possible exception to the rule and a definite predecessor of Lucie. While I disagree with May's assessment of Lucie in the beginning as a "farblose Emanzipierte" who is not up to narrating the "bedeutenderen und tieferen" stories that Reinhart relates, I believe that he is making the same point when he remarks that Lucie acquires a more human dimension when she confesses the illusions and errors of her youth: "Durch ihr tiefes

Fühlen und ihre Mängel wird sie menschlich und somit Reinhart gleich-
wertig" (ibid., 13–14). Somehow, error confers rank in Keller's scheme of
things.

8. The Fränkel-Helbling edition includes the following variant from an
earlier manuscript: "[es ist immer lehrreich zu vernehmen] wie wir ja auch,
sobald wir Romane schreiben, nach den Helden beurtheilt werden, die wir
unsern Idealen gemäß ausstaffiren, und man hat uns schon oft genug darüber ausgelacht" (FH 11:403). The revised version serves to distinguish and
distance Lucie from the *Romanschreiberinnen*, a group that Keller probably
did not care to elevate or "rescue."

9. Preisendanz, "Kellers 'Sinngedicht,' " 156–57.

10. Neumann writes that this reference to *The Origin of Species* has "nur
wenig mit einer Polemik Kellers gegen den Darwinismus als Wissenschafts-
lehre zu tun; [es] bezeichnet vielmehr eine gesellschaftliche Welt, in der die
Gesetze des *Sozial*darwinismus noch nicht in Kraft sind" (*Gottfried Keller*,
242). Neumann argues that *Das Sinngedicht* is a "Handwerkeridylle," set in a
time previous to widespread capitalism.

11. The most prominent example is that of Züs Bünzlin's "Häufchen un-
terschiedlicher Bücher" in "Die drei gerechten Kammacher" (H 2:186–87).

12. Preisendanz, "Kellers 'Sinngedicht,' " 142ff.

13. Heinrich Lee, for example, disguises his love for Judith and Dortchen,
and Pankraz conceals his feelings from Lydia.

14. Neumann notes, "diese Gleichgerichtetheit mit Wilhelm Diltheys gei-
steswissenschaftlicher Hermeneutik mag zufällig sein" (*Gottfried Keller*, 241),
and indeed Keller does not appear to be evoking Dilthey.

15. This is Kaiser's term, from his chapter heading " 'Das Sinngedicht'
oder die Damenwahl" (*Leben*, 503).

16. Neumann also remarks on this: "Die den Mann beherrschende, ihn
physisch in Beschlag nehmende, promiskuitive Frau hat sich also in die
Hexe, der der tödliche Prozeß gemacht werden muß, verwandelt (bei welcher Gelegenheit der Admiral Don Correa seinerseits die gesamte männ-
liche Pracht der Macht, mit der ihn der "Vater Staat" als Statthalter der
Männer-Gesellschaft ausgestattet hat, entfaltet: an dieser Stelle ein
todbringender Pfau des Krieges und der Gerichtsbarkeit)" (*Gottfried Keller*,
255).

17. Kaiser writes, "Die Geschichten von bildenden Männern entpuppen
sich als die Geschichten von triumphierenden Frauen," but he maintains
that Reinhart plays Pygmalion's role, although he notes that the "vermeint-
lichen Experimentalobjekte . . . lebendiger als die Experimentatoren [sind]"
(*Leben*, 517).

18. Preisendanz, "Kellers 'Sinngedicht,' " 149–50.

19. As noted, Neumann regards the isolated setting of *Das Sinngedicht* as
an appeal to cultural nostalgia, a "Handwerkeridylle." Yet the scarcity of
"Handwerker" and Reinhart's and Lucie's benevolent disdain for this class
suggest that the emphasis lies elsewhere—not on economic conditions, but

on the freedom from social restraints that allows them to lead a life of storytelling.

20. Even the *Sieben Legenden* and "Spiegel, das Kätzchen" are more "realistic" in a social sense, because they deal with "real" dangers and often with profound problems. "Das Tanzlegendchen," for example, describes a life wasted by the heroine who is duped into postponing all pleasure until the afterlife.

# Bibliography

## Primary Sources

Feuerbach, Ludwig. *Sämtliche Werke*. Edited by Wilhelm Bolin and Friedrich Jodl. 13 vols. Stuttgart: Frommann, 1960.

Keller, Gottfried. *Gesammelte Briefe*. Edited by Carl Helbling. 4 vols. Bern: Benteli, 1950–54.

———. *Sämtliche Werke*. Edited by Jonas Fränkel and Carl Helbling. 22 vols. Zurich: Eugen Rentsch, 1926–49.

———. *Sämtliche Werke und ausgewählte Briefe*. Edited by Clemens Heselhaus. 4th ed. 3 vols. Munich: Hanser, 1978–79.

## Secondary Sources

Berman, Russell. *The Rise of the Modern German Novel: Crisis and Charisma*. Cambridge, Mass.: Harvard University Press, 1986.

Bernd, Clifford Albrecht. *German Poetic Realism*. Boston: Twayne, 1981.

Bersani, Leo. *A Future for Astyanax: Character and Desire in Literature*. New York: Columbia University Press, 1984.

Boeschenstein, Hermann. *Gottfried Keller*. Stuttgart: Metzler, 1969.

Boeschenstein, R. "Pankraz und sein Tier: Zur Darstellung psychischer Prozesse um die Mitte des 19. Jahrhunderts." In *Formen realistischer Erzählkunst*. Edited by Jörg Thunecke, 146–58. Nottingham: Sherwood Press, 1979.

Clouser, Robin. "*Romeo und Julia auf dem Dorfe*: Keller's Variations upon Shakespeare." *Journal of English and Germanic Philology* 77 (1978): 161–82.

Cooke, A. T. "Gottfried Keller's 'Romeo und Julia auf dem Dorfe.'" *German Life and Letters* 24 (1970–71): 235–43.

Curtius, Ernst Robert. *Europäische Literatur und lateinisches Mittelalter*. 5th ed. Bern: Francke, 1965.

Dickerson, Harold. "The Music of *This* Sphere in Keller's *Romeo und Julia auf dem Dorfe*." *The German Quarterly* 51 (1978): 47–59.

Ellis, John M. *Narration in the German Novelle*. Cambridge: Cambridge University Press, 1974.

Engelsing, Rolf. *Der Bürger als Leser: Lesergeschichte in Deutschland, 1500–1800*. Stuttgart: Metzler, 1974.

Ermatinger, Emil. *Gottfried Kellers Leben*. 8th ed. Zurich: Artemis, 1950.

Feise, Ernst. *Xenion: Essays in German Literature*. Baltimore: The Johns Hopkins University Press, 1950.

Fife, Hildegarde Wichert. "Keller's Dark Fiddler in Nineteenth-Century Symbolism of Evil." *German Life and Letters* 16 (1963): 117–27.

Girard, René. *Deceit, Desire, and the Novel: Self and Other in Literary Structure.* Translated by Yvonne Freccero. Baltimore: The Johns Hopkins University Press, 1965. (Originally published Paris: Grasset, 1961.)

———. *To Double Business Bound: Essays on Literature, Mimesis, and Anthropology.* Baltimore: The Johns Hopkins University Press, 1978.

Goldammer, Peter. "Ludwig Feuerbach und die 'Sieben Legenden' Gottfried Kellers." *Weimarer Beiträge* 4 (1958): 311–25.

Hart, Gail K. "The Irresponsible Imagination." Ph.D. dissertation, University of Virginia, 1983.

Holland, Norman. *The Dynamics of Literary Response.* New York: Norton, 1975. (Originally published Oxford: Oxford University Press, 1968.)

Holub, Robert C. "Realism, Repetition, Repression: The Nature of Desire in *Romeo und Julia auf dem Dorfe.*" *Modern Language Notes* 100 (1985): 461–97.

Hoverland, Lilian. "Gottfried Kellers 'Pankraz, der Schmoller': Eine Neuwertung." *Wirkendes Wort* 1 (1975): 27–37.

Jackson, David. "Pankraz, der Schmoller and Gottfried Keller's Sentimental Education." *German Life and Letters* 30 (1976): 52–64.

Japp, Uwe. "Das Buch im Buch: Eine Figur des literarischen Hermetismus." *Neue Rundschau* 4 (1975): 651–70.

Jennings, Lee B. "The Model of the Self in Gottfried Keller's Prose." *The German Quarterly* 56 (1983): 196–230.

Jeziorkowski, Klaus. *Literarität und Historismus: Beobachtungen zu ihrer Erscheinungsform im neunzehnten Jahrhundert am Beispiel Gottfried Kellers.* Heidelberg: Winter, 1979.

Kaiser, Gerhard. *Dichtung als Sozialisationsspiel.* Göttingen: Vandenhoeck und Ruprecht, 1978.

———. *Gottfried Keller: Das gedichtete Leben.* Frankfurt: Insel, 1981.

———. "Sündenfall, Paradies und himmlisches Jerusalem in Kellers *Romeo und Julia auf dem Dorfe.*" *Euphorion* 65 (1971): 21–48.

Kunz, Josef. *Die deutsche Novelle im 19. Jahrhundert.* Berlin: Erich Schmidt, 1970.

Kurth, Lieselotte. *Die zweite Wirklichkeit.* Studies in the Germanic Languages and Literatures, no. 62. Chapel Hill: University of North Carolina Press, 1969.

Lemke, Victor. "The Deification of Gottfried Keller." *Monatshefte* 48 (1956): 119–26.

Levine, George. *The Realistic Imagination.* Chicago: University of Chicago Press, 1981.

Locher, Kaspar T. "Gottfried Keller and the Fate of the Epigone." *The Germanic Review* 35 (1960): 164–84.

———. *Gottfried Keller: Der Weg zur Reife.* Bern: Francke, 1969.

———. *Gottfried Keller: Welterfahrung, Wertstruktur und Stil.* Bern: Francke, 1985.

———. "Gottfried Kellers wohlwollende Ironie." *Selecta* 3 (1982): 84–89.

McCormick, E. Allen. "The Idylls in Keller's *Romeo und Julia*: A Study in Ambivalence." *The German Quarterly* 35 (1962): 265–79.

Maier, Rudolf. "Gottfried Keller: Romeo und Julia auf dem Dorfe." *Der Deutschunterricht* 3 (1951): 49–63.

May, Ernst. *Gottfried Kellers "Sinngedicht": Eine Interpretation.* Bern: Francke, 1969.

Menninghaus, Winfried. *Artistische Schrift: Studien zur Kompositionskunst Gottfried Kellers.* Frankfurt/Main: Suhrkamp, 1982.

Mews, Siegfried. "Zur Funktion der Literatur in Kellers *Die Leute von Seldwyla*." *The German Quarterly* 43 (1970): 394–405.

Meyer, Hermann. *Das Zitat in der Erzählkunst.* Stuttgart: Metzler, 1961.

Muschg, Adolf. *Gottfried Keller.* Munich: Kindler, 1977.

Neumann, Bernd. *Gottfried Keller: Eine Einführung in sein Werk.* Königstein/Ts.: Athenäum, 1982.

Obermayer, August, "Gottfried Kellers 'Romeo und Julia auf dem Dorfe': Ein realistisches Märchen?" *Jahrbuch der Grillparzer-Gesellschaft* 3. Folge, 12 (1976): 235–55.

Otto, Ernst. "Die Philosophie Feuerbachs in Gottfried Kellers Roman, 'Der grüne Heinrich,' " *Weimarer Beiträge* 6 (1960): 76–111.

Plumpe, Gerhard. "Die Praxis des Erzählens als Realität des Imaginären." In *Wege der Literaturwissenschaft*, edited by Jutta Kolkenbrock-Netz, 163–73. Bonn: Bouvier, 1985.

Preisendanz, Wolfgang. "Gottfried Kellers 'Sinngedicht.' " In *Zu Gottfried Keller*, edited by Hartmut Steinecke, 139–57. Stuttgart: Klett, 1984. (First published in *Zeitschrift für deutsche Philologie* 82 [1963]: 129–51.)

———. *Humor als dichterische Einbildungskraft.* Munich: Eidos, 1963.

Promies, Wolfgang. "Der ungereimte Tod, oder wie man Dichter macht: Zum 150. Todestag von Charlotte Stieglitz." *Akzente* 32 (1985): 560–75.

Rehder, Helmut. "Romeo und Julia auf dem Dorfe: An Analysis." *Monatshefte* 35 (1943): 416–34.

Reichert, Karl. "Die Entstehung der 'Züricher Novellen' von Gottfried Keller." *Zeitschrift für deutsche Philologie* 82 (1963): 471–500.

Remak, H. H. H. "Vinegar and Water: Allegory and Symbolism in the German Novelle between Keller and Bergengruen." In *Literary Symbolism*, edited by Helmut Rehder, 33–62. Austin: University of Texas Press, 1965.

Richartz, Heinrich. *Literaturkritik als Gesellschaftskritik: Darstellungsweise und politisch-didaktische Intention in Gottfried Kellers Erzählkunst.* Bonn: Bouvier, 1975.

Ritzler, Paula. "Das Außergewöhnliche und das Bestehende in Gottfried Kellers Novellen." *Deutsche Vierteljahrsschrift* 28 (1954): 373–83.

Sammons, Jeffrey L. *Literary Sociology and Practical Criticism: An Inquiry.* Bloomington: Indiana University Press, 1977.

———. *Six Essays on the Young German Novel.* Studies in the Germanic Languages and Literatures, no. 75. Chapel Hill: University of North Carolina Press, 1972.

Sautermeister, Gert. "*Der grüne Heinrich*: Gesellschaftsroman, Seelendrama,

Romankunst." In *Romane und Erzählungen des Bürgerlichen Realismus,* edited by Horst Denkler, 80–123. Stuttgart: Reclam, 1980.

————. "Nachwort." In Gottfried Keller, *Züricher Novellen,* edited by Gert Sautermeister, 308–15. Munich: Goldmann, 1983.

————. "Pankraz, der Schmoller." *Kindlers Literatur Lexikon* 5, col. 1325. Zurich, 1969.

Scherrer, Theodor Anton. "Thema und Funktion der Literatur in Gottfried Kellers Prosawerken." Ph.D. dissertation, University of Zurich, 1978.

Swales, Martin. *The German Bildungsroman from Wieland to Hesse.* Princeton: Princeton University Press, 1978.

Thomas, Barry G. "Paradise Lost: The Search for Order in Three Tales by Gottfried Keller." *Germanic Review* 46 (1971): 63–76.

Thomas, Lionel. "An Approach to Keller's *Romeo und Julia auf dem Dorfe.*" *Modern Languages* 54 (1973): 131–38.

Tucker, Harry, Jr. "Post-Traumatic Psychosis in *Romeo und Julia auf dem Dorfe.*" *German Life and Letters* 25 (1972): 247–51.

Waldhausen, Agnes. *Die Technik der Rahmenerzählung bei Gottfried Keller.* Berlin: G. Grote, 1911.

Wartofsky, Marx. *Feuerbach.* Cambridge: Cambridge Univeristy Press, 1977.

Wells, G. A. "Kellers Erzählkunst in 'Romeo und Julia auf dem Dorfe.'" *Wirkendes Wort* 31 (1984): 169–81.

Wuthenow, Ralph-Rainer. *Im Buch die Bücher oder Der Held als Leser.* Frankfurt/Main: Europäische Verlagsanstalt, 1980.

# Index

Auerbach, Berthold, 10–12, 14, 83, 92, 119 (n. 31), 125 (n. 20)

Baumgartner, Wilhelm, 34, 35, 40, 126 (n. 6)
Blanckenburg, Christian Friedrich von, 101
Boccaccio, Giovanni
   *Decameron*, 81, 110

Cervantes, Miguel
   *Don Quixote*, 2, 7

Dante
   *Divine Comedy*, 2, 100, 111–12, 117 (n. 4)

Feuerbach, Ludwig, 7–9, 20–21, 28, 33–40, 125 (n. 24)
Flaubert, Gustave
   *Madame Bovary*, 75
Fontane, Theodor, 66–67, 68, 70

Geßner, Salomon, 24, 28, 93
Goethe, Johann Wolfgang von, 13, 23, 25–26, 39, 61, 72, 88, 96, 101, 102, 110, 112, 125 (n. 23), 127 (n. 15)
Gotthelf, Jeremias (Albert Bitzius), 6

Hettner, Hermann, 11, 120 (n. 3), 123 (n. 4)
Heyse, Paul, 10, 67–69, 81, 113

Jean Paul, 24–25, 28

Keller, Elisabeth, 125 (n. 18)
Keller, Gottfried
   *Das Sinngedicht*, 13, 14, 39, 85, 100–115; "Die arme Baronin," 106, 109; "Die Berlocken," 107; "Die Geisterseher," 107–8; "Don Correa," 108, 109; "Regine," 109
   "Der Apotheker von Chamounix," 61
   *Der grüne Heinrich*, 9, 11, 13, 14, 16, 17–40, 42, 47, 48–49, 51, 55, 57, 60, 65, 75, 77, 78, 86, 87, 101–2, 113, 123 (n. 4), 124 (n. 12), 125 (n. 18), 132 (n. 13)
   *Die Leute von Seldwyla*, 11, 14, 15, 49, 60, 85, 126 (n. 3); "Der Schmied seines Glückes," 14, 46; "Die drei gerechten Kammacher," 11, 13, 33–34, 39, 44–45, 49–50, 123 (n. 2); "Die mißbrauchten Liebesbriefe," 14, 121 (n. 10); "Dietegen," 123 (n. 2); "Kleider machen Leute," 13, 44, 45, 64, 68, 106; "Pankraz, der Schmoller," 11, 33, 37, 41–59, 60, 61, 65, 68, 72, 78, 81, 86, 100, 102, 113, 121 (n. 13), 123 (n. 30), 132 (n. 13); "Romeo und Julia auf dem Dorfe," 11, 13, 43–44, 60–84, 102, 113, 122 (n. 20)
   *Martin Salander*, 114, 123 (n. 2)
   *Sieben Legenden*, 85
   *Züricher Novellen*, 14, 85–99, 103; "Das Fähnlein der sieben Aufrechten," 11, 12; "Der Landvogt von Greifensee," 86, 89, 90, 92–93, 99; "Der Narr auf Manegg," 86, 87, 89, 91–92, 99, 119 (n. 30); "Hadlaub," 86, 88–89, 91, 99; "Herr Jacques," 14, 85–99, 102, 103, 113; "Ursula," 89
Keller, Regula, 47, 125 (n. 18)

Lenz, Jakob Michael Reinhold, 3–4, 13, 48, 117 (n. 6)
Lessing, Gotthold Ephraim, 13, 104
Logau, Friedrich von, 13–14, 102, 104–5, 106, 109, 112
Ludwig, Otto, 67

Meyer, Conrad Ferdinand, 10

Richardson, Samuel, 101, 131 (n. 3)
Rousseau, Jean Jacques, 130 (n. 7)

Shakespeare, William, 49, 50–52, 54–56,

57, 65, 72, 81, 82–83, 100
Stendhal (Marie-Henri Beyle)
   *The Red and the Black*, 75
Storm, Theodor, 10, 89

Tendering, Betty, 47, 129 (n. 48)

Vischer, Friedrich Theodor, 47

University of North Carolina
Studies in the Germanic Languages
and Literatures

45 PHILLIP H. RHEIN. *The Urge to Live. A Comparative Study of Franz Kafka's "Der Prozeß" and Albert Camus' "L'Etranger."* 2nd printing. 1966. Pp. xii, 124.

67 SIEGFRIED MEWS, ED. *Studies in German Literature of the Nineteenth and Twentieth Centuries. Festschrift for Frederic E. Coenen.* 1970. 2nd ed. 1972. Pp. xx, 251.

77 J. W. THOMAS. *Tannhäuser: Poet and Legend.* With Texts and Translation of His Works. 1974. Pp. x, 202.

78 OLGA MARX AND ERNST MORWITZ, TRANS. *The Works of Stefan George.* 2nd, rev. and enl. ed. 1974. Pp. xxviii, 431.

80 DONALD G. DAVIAU AND GEORGE J. BUELOW. *The "Ariadne auf Naxos" of Hugo von Hofmannsthal and Richard Strauß.* 1975. Pp. x, 274.

81 ELAINE E. BONEY. *Rainer Maria Rilke: "Duinesian Elegies."* German Text with English Translation and Commentary. 2nd ed. 1977. Pp. xii, 153.

82 JANE K. BROWN. *Goethe's Cyclical Narratives: "Die Unterhaltungen deutscher Ausgewanderten" and "Wilhelm Meisters Wanderjahre."* 1975. Pp. x, 144.

83 FLORA KIMMICH. *Sonnets of Catharina von Greiffenberg: Methods of Composition.* 1975. Pp. x, 132.

84 HERBERT W. REICHERT. *Friedrich Nietzsche's Impact on Modern German Literature.* 1975. Pp. xxii, 129.

85 JAMES C. O'FLAHERTY, TIMOTHY F. SELLNER, ROBERT M. HELM, EDS. *Studies in Nietzsche and the Classical Tradition.* 2nd ed. 1979. Pp. xviii, 278.

87 HUGO BEKKER. *Friedrich von Hausen: Inquiries into His Poetry.* 1977. Pp. x, 159.

88 H. G. HUETTICH. *Theater in the Planned Society: Contemporary Drama in the German Democratic Republic in Its Historical, Political, and Cultural Context.* 1978. Pp. xvi, 174.

89 DONALD G. DAVIAU, ED. *The Letters of Arthur Schnitzler to Hermann Bahr.* 1978. Pp. xii, 183.

*For other volumes in the "Studies" see p. ii.*

**Send orders to:**
**The University of North Carolina Press, P.O. Box 2288**
**Chapel Hill, NC 27515-2288**

The following out-of-print titles are available in limited quantities through the UNCSGLL office:

51 JOHN T. KRUMPELMANN. *Southern Scholars in Goethe's Germany.* 1965. Pp. xii, 200.

53 A. E. ZUCKER. *General de Kalb, Lafayette's Mentor.* 1966. Pp. x, 252.

54 R. M. LONGYEAR. *Schiller and Music.* 1966. Pp. x, 202.

55 CLIFFORD A. BERND. *Theodor Storm's Craft of Fiction. A Torment of a Narrator.* 2nd ed. 1966. Pp. xvi, 141.

57 EDWIN H. ZEYDEL, PERCY MATENKO, AND BERTHA M. MASCHE, EDS. *Letters to and from Ludwig Tieck and his Circle.* 1967. Pp. xx, 395.

58 WALTER W. ARNDT, PAUL W. BROSMAN, FREDERIC E. COENEN, AND WERNER P. FRIEDRICH, EDS. *Studies in Historical Linguistics in Honor of George Sherman Lane.* 1967. Pp. xx, 241.

59 WESLEY THOMAS AND BARBARA GARVEY SEAGRAVE. *The Songs of the Minnesinger, Prince Wizlaw of Rügen.* 1967. Pp. x, 157.

60 J. W. THOMAS. *Medieval German Lyric Verse.* In English Translation. 1968. Pp. x, 252.

61 THOMAS W. BEST. *The Humanist Ulrich von Hutten. A Reappraisal of his Humor.* 1969. Pp. x, 105.

62 LIESELOTTE E. KURTH. *Die zweite Wirklichkeit: Studien zum Roman des achtzehnten Jahrhunderts.* 1969. Pp. xii, 272.

63 J. W. THOMAS, TRANS. *Ulrich von Liechtenstein's "Service of Ladies."* 1969. Pp. x, 229.

64 CHARLOTTE CRAIG. *Christoph Martin Wieland as the Originator of the Modern Travesty in German Literature.* 1970. Pp. xii, 147.

65 WOLFGANG WILFRIED MOELLEKEN, ED. *Liebe und Ehe: Lehrgedichte von dem Stricker.* 1970. Pp. xxxviii, 72.

66 ALAN P. COTTRELL. *Wilhelm Müller's Lyrical Song-Cycles: Interpretation and Texts.* 1970. Pp. x, 172.

68 JOHN NEUBAUER. *Bifocal Vision. Novalis' Philosophy of Nature and Disease.* 1971. Pp. x, 196.

69 VICTOR ANTHONY RUDOWSKI. *Lessing's "Aesthetica in Nuce." An Analysis of the May 26, 1769 Letter to Nicolai.* 1971. Pp. xii, 146.

70 DONALD F. NELSON. *Portrait of the Artist as Hermes. A Study of Myth and Psychology in Thomas Mann's "Felix Krull."* 1971. Pp. xvi, 146.

71 MURRAY A. AND MARIAN L. COWIE. *The Works of Peter Schott (1460–1490).* Vol. 2: Commentary. 1971. Pp. xxix, 534.

72 CHRISTINE OERTEL SJÖGREN. *The Marble Statue as Idea: Collected Essays on Adalbert Stifter's "Der Nachsommer."* 1972. Pp. xiv, 121.

73 DONALD G. DAVIAU AND JORUN B. JOHNS, EDS. *The Correspondence of Arthur Schnitzler and Raoul Auernheimer, with Raoul Auernheimer's Aphorisms.* 1972. Pp. xii, 161.

74 A. MARGARET ARENT MADELUNG. *"The Laxdoela Saga": Its Structural Patterns.* 1972. Pp. xiv, 261.

75 JEFFREY L. SAMMONS. *Six Essays on the Young German Novel.* 2nd ed. 1975. Pp. xiv, 187.

76 DONALD H. CROSBY AND GEORGE C. SCHOOLFIELD, EDS. *Studies in the German Drama. A Festschrift in Honor of Walter Silz.* 1974. Pp. xxvi, 255.

**Orders for these titles only should be sent to Editor, UNCSGLL, CB # 3160 Dey Hall, Chapel Hill, NC 27599-3160.**

Volumes 1–44, 46–50, 52, 60, and 79 of the "Studies" have been reprinted. They may be ordered from AMS Press, Inc., 56 E. 13th Street, New York, NY 10003.

**For a complete list of reprinted titles write to the Editor.**